Stolen Identity

Michael Banister

*To Betty —
a good friend !
Mike*

Andrew Benzie Books
Orinda, California

Published by Andrew Benzie Books
www.andrewbenziebooks.com

Printed in the United States of America

www.stolenidentitynovel.com

First Edition: February 2015

10 9 8 7 6 5 4 3 2 1

ISBN 978-1-941713-16-7

*Excerpt from "Requiem Before the Times of Peace"
by Nancy Hoffman*

Cover photo by Milica Vujicic

Cover and book design by Andrew Benzie

*I dedicate this novel to my wonderful wife, Nora Privitera,
and my two sons, John and Nuri Banister*

I would like to acknowledge the work of my editors:

*Linda Leeb
Barbara Alderson
Nora Privitera
Kathleen Gage
Yofe Johnson*

TABLE OF CONTENTS

CHAPTER ONE:
ESCAPE FROM SARAJEVO, 1992

An automatic reaction can get you killed. Marta turned without thinking toward the explosion across the plaza about 200 yards away instead of away from it as any self-protecting mammal would do to save itself. The flash of the explosion preceded the sound; perhaps that was the cause of Marta's impulse.

The shock wave followed moments later—really, a fraction of a moment later. The wave hit her as she stood looking out a window above the plaza. Staggering backwards, Marta saw the little bakery erupt in smoke, dust and flame. Screaming, crying and shouting came next.

The searing pain of grief burned Marta as the spirits of extinguished lives blew through her, as if on a hot desert wind bound for wherever spirits go once released from their ruined bodies. There must have been 20 or 25 people in line in front of the shop waiting to buy bread. Staggering, Marta fell on the worn sofa inside the open window. Sobs erupted from her chest. She didn't try to stop crying. Instead, she tried to calm her breath and keep her lightheadedness at bay. It didn't work.

The room was spinning. She closed her eyes, rolled off the sofa and lay face-up on the floor, trying to keep from throwing up, sweat covering her face. After several minutes groaning and sobbing, her feelings of horror and panic began to lessen a little. She could almost breathe normally, but she was still not altogether here. Still stunned, she entered a dream-like state, a "lucid" dream where she felt both awake and asleep. The spinning stopped. Her heartbeat slowed to normal.

She knew that if she opened her eyes inside her dream, she would no longer be lying on the floor in the Red Cross building where she worked. Opening her dream eyes, she found herself in an abandoned office building. As she stood up, looking for a way out, an elevator appeared straight ahead. When the elevator doors opened, she saw dozens of people—crying, hurt and wounded people. "No room for the living," a voice said. Try the stairs, she thought. Descending the stairs to the left of the elevator, Marta saw nobody. After two flights the stairs ended and Marta faced a door. She opened it and walked into a vast empty room as long and as wide as the entire building. No exit in sight. Marta re-entered the stairwell and went back up to where she had begun. This time she tried the stairs to the right of the elevator. That set of stairs descended very steeply and made sharp turns like those in a castle tower. Soon, the steps became impossibly narrow, uneven and broken. When the next section of stairs seemed to turn back under itself, Marta stopped at the landing. The landing had a barred, darkened window but no door. She retreated back up the stairs.

She then decided to get into the elevator even if she had to shove her way in. Surprisingly, the elevator doors opened to an empty car. Two men followed her into the elevator. They wore military uniforms and seemed familiar. One had a vaguely sinister demeanor; the other smiled pleasantly at her. No one spoke as the elevator descended. The doors opened onto an empty garden. She walked out of the elevator, leaving the two soldiers behind, and sat down on a bench. A feeling of weariness came over her.

When she closed her eyes, she heard a voice in her head. A little boy seemed to be crying the word "lost." Her lucid but unconscious mind asked, is he lost or am I lost?

Marta opened her eyes, got up from the bench and walked to the shore of a wide river that opened out into a small bay. She felt peaceful and somehow happy despite being lost. Her lucid mind spoke to her again, reminding her that she had to return to consciousness, and then said something that puzzled her—*we'll come back to this place.*

Marta decided to wake up. She opened her eyes, her real eyes, and saw the familiar peeling, cracked ceiling of her building. When she felt she could get up without passing out, Marta rolled slightly to one side and got up on her knees. So far so good. Marta said aloud to nobody in particular, "I really have to leave this place. Not just this place, or this city, but this whole doomed province." She stood up, brushed the dust off her clothes and walked down the hall to the ladies' room, being careful not to look out the window again. It was bad enough to have to listen to the multitude of voices screaming and crying in the plaza, without having to see the carnage.

Before the explosion knocked her backward onto the sofa, she had been taking a break from her nursing duties at the Sarajevo Red Cross clinic. The building housing the clinic was an ancient structure most recently inhabited by a group of law offices. Since the beginning of the most recent troubles in Bosnia—at that time one of the provinces of the former Yugoslavia along with Serbia, Montenegro, Vojvodina, Slovenia, Croatia, Kosovo and Macedonia—the Red Cross had been the only tenant interested in renting space.

The Yugoslavian National Army, known as the JNA, was headquartered in Serbia. The Serbs dominated the Yugoslavian federal government as well as the army. A year earlier the JNA had attacked Slovenia, but the Slovenes forced the army to give up and retreat. Now, in the late spring of 1992, the JNA was attacking Sarajevo, Bosnia's capital, which was not faring so well. Every day it seemed another three or four buildings were destroyed along with numerous vehicles. The number of dead or injured already exceeded several hundred, and the bombardment had hardly begun.

Marta had grown up in Slovenia's capital, Ljubljana. When she graduated from nursing school in 1991, at 26, she took an internship in Sarajevo where she could get more hands-on training than in her hometown. Little did she know she would get that training in a clinic treating hundreds of Sarajevans wounded by relentless Serbian attacks. She decided to leave after this latest attack on the bakery where dozens of people were killed; she could no longer stand to remain there.

Marta wasted no time telling her colleagues. But they knew as well as she that her departure would not be easy or imminent. Deciding to leave and actually leaving were two different things. The snipers and artillery gunners positioned on the surrounding hillsides made it difficult to translate desire into decision. Those gunners formed a tight circle the city's residents dubbed the "Serb necklace." The probability of getting shot or blown up in an escape attempt was very high. And even if she managed to get out of Sarajevo safely, where could she go and how could she find a job?

The press of work, and her fear that escape was impossible, kept Marta working long hours. Later that summer, a few months after the dreadful explosion, Marta's supervisor informed her that a job very likely awaited her at the Red Cross clinic in Serbia's capital, Belgrade. "Of course, getting to Belgrade will be a bit tricky," the supervisor said in a grim tone with a frown on her face. A Croatian woman in late middle age and a native Sarajevan, the supervisor herself could not ever think of leaving the province, let alone take a job in Serbia, where antipathy towards Croats was widespread. More importantly, she could not leave her family or her hometown.

Milan, a young daredevil driver for the Red Cross who had befriended Marta soon after she started her internship at the clinic, overheard this discussion. He offered to take her with him on his next trip to Belgrade to restock the agency's medical supplies. A trip of some 350 kilometers, this would be his third to Belgrade since the Serbian shelling of Sarajevo had begun. Milan, who happened to be Serbian like the gunners surrounding the city, told Marta he thought he could get safe passage through the Serbian necklace. He planned to leave in a week.

Faced with having to make such a sudden decision, Marta now found herself frozen with fear. She wanted to believe Milan knew what he was doing, but yet could not bring herself to commit to joining him. For five days, she vacillated between deciding to risk being his companion on what would no doubt be the most dangerous trip she had ever taken, and choosing to stay behind in one of the most dangerous cities on earth. Finally, the day before Milan's planned departure, Marta made up her mind. "If you still have room for a passenger, I'll go with you. I can't stay here."

Milan explained that the first five kilometers would be the most dangerous, as they attempted to get out of the city itself. Barring getting shot on the outskirts of Sarajevo, the rest of their all-night trip to Belgrade should be uneventful. Milan claimed to know several members of the Yugoslavian army who occasionally took time off to wander into the city for what they called rest and relaxation. With somewhat more bravado than he actually felt, Milan said to Marta, "They told me there are at least two unmanned places in the circle, and one of them is on a secondary road leading north out of the city. This trip we will take that route."

Marta took care of her remaining duties, packed up her meager belongings, and said her last goodbyes to her clinic colleagues. The clinic's head doctor said he didn't blame her for leaving this conflict behind. Marta objected to his use of the word "conflict" to describe what was going on all around and within the city of Sarajevo. "That's not what's happening here," she insisted. "The people of Sarajevo don't have a conflict with anyone; they didn't start these attacks. Milan, a Serb, certainly has no conflict with those Serb gunners who will try to kill him; he just wants to get out of the city alive and to keep his passenger alive as well."

Nor did Marta have a conflict with anyone, except perhaps with herself. Her familiar apologetic complaint replayed itself in her mind: *I've only been here six months and I haven't really been of much use. There's so much more I could do. But I'll get killed before my 27th birthday if I keep pushing my luck.* She had convinced herself that an escape attempt posed no more danger than sticking around in the vain hope the city wouldn't get destroyed—and herself along with it.

As Marta and Milan got into the Red Cross Land Rover the next night, he told her he recently heard the gap in the circle on the north road was not as large as it used to be. Serb gunners were now positioned only about 100 meters from each side. "They are well within earshot of passing vehicles," Milan warned. "The big guns are trained on the city itself, not on the road, but the riflemen can easily pick off travelers attempting to pass through the hole in the circle. Red Cross vehicles have no free pass. If we tried this trip in the daytime, we surely would not make it. But we might make it tonight. There is no moon and lots of clouds."

Very little could be seen in the nearly dark night as their noisy little diesel Land Rover approached the long, straight stretch of road leading into the Serb Necklace. They had no way to know how close or far away the Serb soldiers might be. Well before the Land Rover's entry upon the straightaway, Milan cut his lights and slowed his pace to a crawl, coasting whenever possible to quiet the noise from the engine. Despite having his headlights off, he hoped he would be able to spot familiar outcroppings once they reached the opening. Milan soon recognized the dark outlines of bombed-out buildings sitting some 100 meters on either side of the road that marked the opening he needed to get through.

"Well, here we go," said Milan. He slammed his foot down on the accelerator. As the Land Rover began its passage through the break in the circle, shots rang out, but the shots went wide of the vehicle.

"Hurry!" screamed Marta, as she ducked down onto the floor and tried to cram herself into as small a space as possible. Milan sped faster and swerved the Land Rover from side to side, hoping to present less of a target for the gunners. Marta's screams from the car floor became moans and sobs.

"Don't worry, Marta. They can't see us. We'll make it!"

After a few minutes they heard no more shots. Marta unfolded herself and carefully boosted her body back up onto the passenger seat. Milan released each clenched hand from the steering wheel, one at a time, stretching and flexing them repeatedly. He turned on his parking lights, not daring to turn on his headlights just yet. He rolled his head and shoulders from side to side several times before plucking a half-smoked cigarette from behind his ear and motioning for Marta to light it for him. She took it but shook her head. "Let's get a little farther away."

The two companions let almost another kilometer's worth of Sarajevo's devastated outskirts pass by before they breathed normally and spoke. As they passed by the first of many stands of trees, Milan turned on his headlights and they burst out laughing at almost the same moment, lightheaded at their luck, but also trembling at the thought of what have might been the outcome of their gamble. The forested landscape had a calming effect on them, a reminder that cities and the dangers that lay within them might eventually give way to peace and beauty.

Marta found little else of the nightlong trip to Belgrade memorable. For one thing, the dark moonless night made the countryside almost invisible. The road itself presented little more excitement than an occasional cow deciding to cross the road as their vehicle approached. They also encountered an occasional donkey or dog that had decided to take a nap in the middle of the road.

Marta frequently turned her gaze from the road to check on Milan. She couldn't tell how alert he was, since he mostly stared straight ahead, slouching a bit with his left arm on the wheel and the other on the seat next to Marta's purse.

Conversation slowly returned to the interior of the vehicle. Marta confided she felt a little guilty that her internship work in Sarajevo had been limited to helping the triage nurse interview patients, rather than providing direct treatment to trauma victims of shootings or bombings. She also thought to herself that Milan might think her work less important than the work of many other volunteers. As if reading her mind, Milan turned to her and said, "You know, a lot of people have managed to stay alive with your help."

"I'm not so sure about that. I just keep thinking about all these lovely, innocent people bleeding to death or dying of infection or heart attack. I have some training in infectious diseases and as a surgeon's assistant, but all I am allowed to do is ask questions." Marta cracked the window to get a breath of fresh air.

Getting the hint, Milan refrained from lighting another cigarette, even though his body strongly craved the nicotine. "We all do what we can. I, for my part, am only a driver. I used to drive a taxi here. I have no other skill or profession. But every month I manage to leave and return with this Land Rover full of medical supplies."

"Are you a native Sarajevan? Most of the Serbs I have met here are originally from Serbia itself."

"I am Serb but not from Sarajevo. I grew up in Belgrade. I came here for adventure and to meet some of the exotic women the city is legendary for. How about you? I can't quite place your accent. Maybe Slovenian?"

"Exactly right. I grew up in Ljubljana. But I guess you could say I'm a mongrel: a little Serb, a little Slovene, who knows that else."

Marta kept the conversation going, worried that Milan might be a little bit drowsy driving in the middle of the night. She brushed her hair aside with her right hand. Turning to face Milan, she said, "You know, Milan, I wasn't at all sure I wanted to be a nurse. It wasn't the sight or smell of sick people that I thought I wouldn't be able to tolerate. It was their *hurt* I didn't think I could bear. Their anguish, their fear, their pain." She picked up her purse and several paperback books and tossed them into the back seat to give herself more room to stretch out.

The movement and rustling may have brought Milan back to the present as much as Marta's comment did. He looked over at her as she tried brushing some of the dirt off her jeans. He turned back to the road and straightened up before replying. "But by all accounts you seem to be handling all this stuff better than most. Sarajevo is a whole world of pain and suffering."

"Yes, I'm very well aware of that. And I do handle it well. But there was a time in my life when I never would have imagined I'd be able to do this type of work."

Milan took advantage of a fairly straight and smooth stretch of road to look over at Marta as he drove through the night. "But you must have realized, or at least suspected, your talent even in your late teen years. A career in nursing usually requires some degree of interest and talent, not to mention years of prerequisite courses."

"Yes. By then I wanted to give it a go. Not because I thought I had any sort of talent in the sciences, but because I had discovered I could read people the way we read a book, and I felt drawn to a profession that would allow me to help people." Marta paused to collect her thoughts and to gauge Milan's reaction so far. Nothing more than a glance at her and a return to staring at the road, but she got the impression he wanted her to go on.

She took a breath and continued. "I remember when I was about 14 enjoying my second scouting summer camp in the Julian Alps near Lake Bled. I dearly loved my scouting days—learning crafts, stamp collecting, music, wildlife taxonomy. But that summer at scout camp I encountered a situation that literally changed my life. One of the campers got sick but nobody could figure out what caused the girl's symptoms. She had fever, chills and lapses into unconsciousness. She was a friend of mine so I decided to stay by her side that afternoon. The camp staff had no clue, and my friend was uncommunicative. After about an hour, while I held her hands and tried to soothe her, I received a very clear mental picture of her. I saw her in a way I can only call 'elemental.' There was a glow emanating a little beyond her like an aura. But part of the glow looked murky, muddy, like it wasn't truly part of the aura, it didn't belong there." Marta checked Milan again and sensed he was all ears.

"It occurred to me then—as surely as one can be sure of anything—that my friend had poison inside her. I didn't know if she had eaten something or had been bitten, but I was certain she had been poisoned.

"I immediately ran to the other medical cabin and started screaming that the girl had been poisoned. The resident nurse was skeptical at first, but something in my tone convinced her. She quickly gave the girl this syrup to induce vomiting. That did the trick. After an hour or so my friend was conscious and able to talk. It seemed she had eaten some kind of plant mistaking it for an edible green, when in fact it was highly toxic. She could have died." Marta didn't have to wait long for Milan's response.

"How were you so sure it was poison?"

"I told you, when I saw the discoloration in her aura, it might as well have been a neon sign spelling out 'POISON.'"

Milan smiled and relaxed his shoulders, pulling another cigarette out of his shirt pocket. "So, you're a psychic! That's interesting. We still have another few hours on this long, boring road, so tell me more."

Marta understood Milan's reply was not facetious. "No, not a psychic, not exactly. During the remaining three years of high school I had a number of incidents you might call visions—at least involuntary interpersonal communication. A kind of empathy was growing in me. I sensed when people were in pain or hurt in some emotional or psychological way. But I can't read minds as that idea is commonly understood.

"I decided to get well grounded in medicine and psychology and maybe my new talent would become more defined and focused."

Milan was fully alert now. He lit his cigarette and asked, "You say 'new talent.' Didn't you ever experience that kind of thing before?"

"I suppose I did. You know, I never thought about it like that. When I saw my friend's aura, I didn't make any connection between that and my earlier empathic incidents."

"Give me an example." This stretch of the long, flat road was in pretty decent condition, which allowed Milan to look over at Marta more often as she spoke.

Marta rolled down her window a little more, took a deep breath and continued. "As far back as I can remember—and I can remember pretty far back—I could sort of read people when they spoke. I could tell if they were hiding something, or if they were hurting or afraid. Though I never could tell if someone was sick, physically sick, or just hiding something."

Milan smiled as he stubbed out his cigarette and threw it out the window. "I'm guessing you would have gotten quite a reaction out of people if you had said something about how they were feeling."

Marta nodded and rubbed her eyes. "Yeah, that wouldn't be cool. I figured that out pretty quickly. Folks usually didn't appreciate it when I would blurt out what I was picking up from them. Plus, coming from a three-year-old, that kind of comment would usually provoke laughter or annoyance."

Milan raised his eyebrows and stared at Marta. "A three-year-old! You remember that far back?" He swerved abruptly to avoid a rabbit that ran across the road.

"I told you, my memory is truly phenomenal. I'm not bragging. I remember lots of stuff, and not only isolated events like injuries or dramatic incidents. Almost total recall, you might say."

"How about earlier than three?"

"Before the age of three, I remember mostly emotions, inarticulate pictures of scenes, that kind of thing. After I learned to talk a little before I turned three, I started keeping track of things, in a way. Language, plus the end of the 'terrible twos' as it's called, allowed me to analyze situations and people I encountered. But even at two I wasn't really terrible. Of course my emotions and desires were stronger than my verbal ability, but even at that age I think I kept them under control more than most kids because I could sense the reactions of the adults."

"Wait, wait. Are you saying you remember all this about yourself? Or did your parents tell you about it later, the way we collect and store most of our so-called 'memories'?"

"A little of both. I used to share my thoughts about people with my mom and dad, and they would frequently remind me of those conversations later on. But I do think my memories are more purely memories than is the norm for most of us."

The two of them lapsed into silence for a few minutes as Milan negotiated a stretch of very bad road. Marta watched him, not the road.

"What's on your mind, Marta? Are you 'reading' me?" Milan looked over at her; his look was both curious and apprehensive.

"Not at all. I told you, I'm not psychic or telepathic. It's just a 'knack,' as my grandmother called it. I usually don't go digging around in people's feelings. I can't, anyway, unless someone is directing something at me—conversation, for example. And even then I've got too much respect to pry. I was just going to ask you how you ended up in Sarajevo. I came here almost a year ago when I was 26."

"I came here in 1988 when I was 22, after I finished trade school in Belgrade. I completed a Mercedes-Benz training course in long-haul trucking, got my certificate, and drove a big rig for a couple of years. I gave that up after I basically drove a 16-wheeler into a bomb crater. The company all but accused me of falling asleep at the wheel, and I couldn't prove otherwise. So I quit and took up driving smaller vehicles—panel vans, cabs, etc. I liked Sarajevo so I ended up working as a Red Cross driver after the bombardment began in earnest. I've been here for almost five years."

Marta flashed a smile at Milan. "Stick with it. They need you, God knows, and the job suits you. I get a feeling you're going to be successful for a long time to come."

"Whew, that's good to hear, especially from you. You know, what you just said is essentially what a Rom woman told me not long ago. She was a fortune teller and me and a couple of buddies had her tell our fortunes."

"Huh. Interesting. I'm part Rom myself. Maybe that's where my gift comes from. But as far as I know, my father had no particular knack in that direction, and he was half Rom. But his Rom mother, Shimza, was a pretty intuitive lady. I spent a lot of time with her when I was little. She was my favorite person in the whole world. She was the first to recognize my knack and helped me learn how to use it and when to leave it alone."

"Is your grandmother still alive?"

"Yes, she is. I haven't seen her in over 10 years, but we talk occasionally on the phone. I also talk to her in my dreams occasionally."

"Does Shimza still live in Slovenia?"

"No, she moved away when I was in high school, right after my summer camp incident. She told us she was going to a Rom gathering in Bulgaria and might end up settling there. That's what she ended up doing."

Six hours later, their arrival in Belgrade turned out to be an altogether different experience than she expected—exciting, perhaps not; but a relief, yes. Having just escaped one of the most dangerous cities on Earth—that was exciting. But only when Marta and Milan arrived in Belgrade did they finally feel like they could breathe. As if to help them burn off the adrenalin produced during their road trip, Milan decided to drive Marta around the city and show her the two famous rivers flowing through Belgrade, the Danube and the Sava. She was struck by the immensity and beauty of the Belgrade Fortress, standing atop a majestic 400-foot ridge overlooking the "Great War Island" at the confluence of the Danube and the Sava in the oldest part of the city.

In addition to that beautiful early-morning river tour, Marta would remember the first few weeks in Belgrade very well, especially Milan's friend's apartment where they stayed the first two nights. Milan knew everyone. He knew the city from one end to the other. On their third day in the city, he showed Marta the ornate municipal buildings and introduced her to another friend who owned an apartment building. A few days later she signed a rental agreement and met her future boss in Belgrade's public health department. Her new life in Belgrade had begun.

CHAPTER TWO:
THE RIVERS COME TOGETHER

Fall stretched into winter. Marta began to feel settled. Milan had made two more round trips to Belgrade. He had looked her up to make sure she was okay in her new city. Marta was more than okay—she loved her tiny apartment, mostly for its view of the two rivers' confluence. She also appreciated its nearness to her work, where her supervising doctor put her on the infectious diseases team. The combination of meaningful work and a beautiful city allowed Marta to maintain a certain level of excitement about her future. Having escaped the horrific siege of Sarajevo less than a year earlier, Marta now could focus on her new career, which, despite the long hours at the clinic, was a source of spiritual renewal.

More excitement in her life began the following spring, when she met a son of the Sava River itself. After her shift at the clinic, Marta stopped at a riverside café to have a cappuccino on the outdoor patio. A small group of young fishermen distracted her from the beautiful view. Judging from what she could make out of their conversation, Marta decided they had just finished a day's work on the river. One of them she later learned was Dimitri Sava. He seemed to be the boss of the small crew.

Something about Dimitri reminded her of her beloved grandmother. Dimitri's dark complexion and beautiful, curly black locks triggered memories of long chats with her father about what his Rom mother looked like in her youth. She smiled at the fanciful questions forming in her mind—could this handsome fisherman be, in fact, a Rom prince? Could he be a descendant of one of her grandmother Shimza's siblings? She chuckled softly at her musings.

Dimitri looked over at Marta and saw her staring at him. He was instantly smitten by her otherworldly good looks—a tall strawberry blonde with hazel eyes and Mediterranean features. Something about the intensity of the sudden mutual awareness flowing between them interrupted the attention of the speaker's small audience. Dimitri had a strong urge to go over and introduce himself, but he had to attend to his boat and instruct his crew about tomorrow. He rose from the table and gestured to the others to follow him. As they walked past Marta, Dimitri locked eyes with her briefly, as if to say *meet me here tomorrow.* She understood.

For the next couple of days Marta left nothing to chance. She went to the café each afternoon after her shift. Fortune smiled on her. The handsome young boat captain noticed her visits to the café coincided with the end of his crew's day. On day three, Dimitri remained at his table as his crew returned to the dock. A breeze from the river lifted him out of his chair and propelled him across the terrace to Marta's table.

"I see you and I both like this place and time of day very much," Dimitri said with a smile. "My name is Dimitri Sava. My family owns this river. What's your name?"

Marta chuckled. "Marta Cecelja. My family owns nothing except their memories. May I take a ride on your river some day? It looks nothing like the Sava River I knew as a child growing up in Slovenia." Marta smiled, lifted her cup and drained the last of the foam. Setting the cup down, she waited for Dimitri's reply.

"How about I treat you to a short cruise right now? Not in my smelly old fishing boat, but in that little skiff alongside the pier. There's a wonderful restaurant on the other side of the river that my aunt owns."

Signaling her assent with a smile and a nod, Marta stood and picked up her purse and magazine. Dimitri led Marta to the pier, steadied the little craft, and stepped into it. He reached out and took hold of Marta's outstretched hand as she carefully stepped in. To their delight, their conversation tumbled out with the same alacrity the little boat demonstrated as it zigzagged across this particularly narrow part of the Sava River. Dimitri pointed out a large island some 400 yards distant. "That's the Kalemegdan Park and Fortress. The two rivers coming around the island are the Danube and the Sava. Their origins are in other countries. The Sava begins in Slovenia. What's the river like in your country?"

"It comes down from the Alps. My parents used to take me camping and hiking. We would hike pretty far up into the Julian Alps and set up our camp. Then we would start exploring the river. The

Sava there is a very pretty stretch of water with lots of rapids. When it reaches Ljubljana far below it merges with two other rivers and is a much slower, calmer river. Sort of like this, but smaller."

They reached the opposite shore quickly. They stepped out of the little boat and Dimitri secured it to a piling next to the little dock. They slowly walked two blocks to Dimitri's aunt's restaurant, enjoying the mild breeze coming off the river. Comfortable silences punctuated their conversation.

"Here we are," Dimitri said with a tentative smile. "I hope you have an appetite. The portions here are generous." Dimitri opened the door and followed Marta inside. After the obligatory introductions—"Auntie, this is Marta Cecelja; Marta, this is my Aunt Adrijana Sava"—the couple ordered dinner and watched the sun go down across the river. The little restaurant was really not much more than a storefront café, but Adrijana had made it beautiful—light green paint sponged on the walls, gauzy, net-like curtains on either side of the large picture window, and an assortment of boat lanterns serving as lamps. A couple and a foursome occupied the other tables facing the river. The remaining four tables to the rear sat empty.

Adrijana was a tall, handsome woman in her late 50's, with jet-black hair, angular features, and a pleasant, almost musical voice. Dimitri told Marta his aunt once considered joining the Belgrade symphony chorus, but the press of work kept her from following that dream. She was now the happy owner of this small restaurant, which allowed her to share her other skills—cooking and hospitality. She busied herself tending to diners and overseeing kitchen operations. Western pop music played softly in the background. All manner of boats—fishing, pleasure, sail, and freight—passed by on the river. Raucous gulls trailed the fishing boats.

When they had finished dinner and ordered coffee, Dimitri said, "Marta, you say you were born in Slovenia, but you speak like a native Serb. Though there are not many Serbs in Slovenia, I bet."

"No, not many, maybe five percent of the population. My mom is half Slovene and half Serb. My dad is half Italian and half Rom. I grew up in Ljubljana speaking mostly Serbian and Slovenian, and a little Italian with my dad and his father. I even spoke a little Rom with my dad and his mother Shimza. How about you? You don't look entirely Serb. In fact, you remind me a little of my Rom granny, Shimza. Does the name ring a bell?"

Dimitri tried to suppress a chuckle but failed. "No, I'm afraid I don't recall any Shimza in my family. But I do have a little Rom blood in my veins. One of my great-grandmothers was from the Rom in Bosnia—Sarajevo. But I'd hate to think that my good looks and charm are only due to such a distant ancestor."

Marta smiled at the joke, but then her smile turned into a frown. In a serious tone she added, "I was in Sarajevo less than a year ago. I barely got out alive."

Dimitri put down his cup and waited for Marta to continue. When she didn't, he asked, "What were you doing there? I hear the place is being bombarded constantly."

"Yes. Artillery and snipers surround the city. I had completed my nursing internship there with the Red Cross and stayed on to earn a little money. My colleague Milan, a Red Cross driver, and I left the city in the dead of night. I hope he's okay; he has to make monthly trips out of Sarajevo and back to replenish the clinic's medical supplies. I now work in Belgrade's department of public health. The contrast between these two cities makes it hard to believe they're in the same country."

"Maybe not for long. Maybe Bosnia will do what Slovenia did and manage to separate from Yugoslavia." Dimitri studied Marta's face for her reaction to what he said.

Marta was unsure how to gauge Dimitri's comment, although she did not get the impression he was any kind of nationalist. She played with her food briefly before looking up and asking, "How do you feel about that? As a Serb who presumably grew up in the safety and stability of Belgrade, wouldn't you oppose Yugoslavia's disintegration?"

Dimitri pushed away his plate and leaned back in his chair. "I have no problem with Bosnia or Slovenia leaving the federation, or any other region that wants to. I understand that desire to abandon this fake country called Yugoslavia."

"But why is that? I would have thought everyone in Serbia would want to keep the country intact."

"Not everyone; not even all the Serbs are believers in Yugoslavia. Many are like me. My Sava clan has lived here for two generations but came here from other places. My grandparents came from Zagreb, Croatia. And, like I said earlier, some of my ancestors were Rom, from Sarajevo originally and Zagreb afterwards."

Marta smiled and relaxed. "Interesting. We are both mongrels, it would seem. What did your people do when they came?"

"As far back as I remember the river was our livelihood. Since we Savas settled here, we adopted this Sava River as our own. At a young age, I started working on a fishing boat captained by my uncle, just as he had begun working on his father's fishing boat. Maybe before that, some of my forebears were fishermen on the Slovenian stretch of the Sava. What about your family? It sounds like some of them came to Slovenia from elsewhere."

"Yeah. As I said, my dad is part Italian. He lived in Trieste before it became part of Italy. Like anyone with even a drop of Rom blood, he was a wanderer, always looking for new adventures. His mom is Rom originally from Zagreb; Shimza's folks moved around a lot and ended up in Trieste. Shimza married into a respectable Italian family. Her new Italian husband, my grandfather, took over his father's optician business in the city. But his son, my dad, was more like his Rom mom than his Italian dad. He didn't want to stay in Italy or go into the family's optician business. He took off for Ljubljana where he knew some people. He met my mom there. She was Slovene on her dad's side and Serb on her mother's side, a common pairing in Slovenia, really."

Marta sipped her coffee and looked over at Adrijana as she walked toward them carrying a platter of pastries—baklava, marzipan and croissants. "Enjoy, you two. Someone has to eat these, and it better not be me!" Marta and Dimitri each took a pastry and thanked Adrijana. Marta resumed her story.

"Eventually, my dad talked both his parents into moving to Ljubljana, probably because of the unsettled nationality of Trieste. What an irony, huh? Trieste never became as unsettled as Ljubljana! His dad passed away when I was in high school, and my widowed grandma Shimza moved to Bulgaria.

"As I told you, Shimza was born in Zagreb. My parents first thought of me taking my nursing internship there instead of Sarajevo. But Croatia's decision to declare independence at the same time as Slovenia's declaration made my parents think Zagreb was not as good a choice as Sarajevo. Who would have thought things would turn out bad for both cities? Both are under siege by the Serbs; or, to be fair, the Yugoslav National Army."

It was still light outside when they walked out of the little café.

The place had now filled up with the evening crowd. "I'm glad we had a chance to dine and talk while the place was still relatively empty and quiet," Dimitri said.

"I enjoyed myself. Your aunt is sweet and very gracious."

"I hope we can do this again soon, Marta. May I call on you next week, perhaps?"

"I would like that very much." Marta wrote down her work address and gave it to Dimitri. "In case I can't make it to the little cafe across the river, stop by my office any day but Wednesday. I have a painting class every Wednesday morning and must attend clinical meetings all afternoon; in the evening I catch up on paperwork."

"That's great. What kind of painting?"

"Landscapes and cityscapes, mostly. Watercolor. The city has so many vistas, and not only of the rivers and bridges. Even the narrowest little streets are worthy of my canvas."

"I look forward to seeing your work. Let me ferry you back to the other side, and you can catch a taxi from there."

Dimitri felt drawn to her in a way he'd never experienced with a woman before. He felt a bond with her; they were kindred souls about to embark on a lifelong journey together. That night he had a dream that he recognized—intuitively—as a mixture of scenes from different parts of his life, even parts that hadn't happened yet. He and Marta talked in his dream even when they weren't together, separated by a great distance. They looked for each other, found each other, and lost each other again. A child appeared in the dream, a boy who felt like their boy. And then the boy disappeared for a while. When he reappeared in the dream, he had a brother and was part of a different family. But he still belonged to Dimitri and Marta. When the boy tried to talk to him, Dimitri woke up.

Over the next few weeks, Marta and Dimitri had several more dinner dates. Marta invited him and Adrijana over to her apartment. She was pleased to see that Adrijana loved her paintings. They discovered they had both studied art in college. Marta found Adrijana interesting and friendly. She filled Marta in on Dimitri's background. He was an only child, now 29, a year older than Marta. His parents lived in a small town some distance from Belgrade. Adrijana was a widow whose husband was Dimitri's father's brother. Dimitri's father had two sisters as well. Both were married with several children apiece. Dimitri's contact with his cousins was sporadic but never lost. Those families lived in a slightly larger town not far from where Adrijana and her late husband had lived before she moved to Belgrade.

When they met again, Marta noticed that Adrijana paid close attention when she talked of her passion to do something, to speak out about Serbia's worsening climate of intolerance toward ethnic minorities, especially Croats, Rom and Muslims.

"What I think is absolutely essential," said Marta one evening at dinner, "is more publicity aimed at exposing the government's unofficial campaign against these groups. Not only that, but eyewitness accounts, with photos if possible, of what's going on in places like Sarajevo. Dimitri probably told you, but I was just there and can tell you many horror stories."

Adrijana looked worried when she heard this. "Yes, Dimitri told me a little bit. You have to be careful talking about such things around Belgrade, my dear, not to mention making more public statements like articles or protests. Dimitri probably hasn't told you this," Adrijana paused and looked at him; he gave a brief nod so she continued, "but one of the men on his crew read a letter you wrote to one of our little newspapers. Let's just say he wasn't pleased and told Dimitri so in very strong terms."

Dimitri put down his glass and smiled at Adrijana. "Oh, Auntie, he's harmless. He's just a little excitable, that's all."

"Excitable, certainly, but maybe more than that. My point is that he's fairly typical, even among the civilian populace. You can't believe how rabid many men have become in this climate, especially if they're drafted and indoctrinated and then put in harm's way on our various fronts. Friends are friends no longer. Serbs against Croats, everyone against the Rom and Muslims. It's crazy, and so sad."

Dimitri sighed and commented, "Well, Auntie, I guess we'll find out soon. The gentleman you're referring to just got his draft notice. I'll be sorry to see him put on a uniform, not because I'm worried he'll become a fanatic, but because he's a great crew member."

Marta asked, "Have I met him? I don't think I've met any of your crew who were less than complete gentlemen."

"No," Dimitri replied, "you haven't. You've probably only seen him from time to time at the docks. Goran is a friend from my school days. We've known each other a long time. He's pretty nationalistic and, like my aunt says, speaks his mind to everyone. Nevertheless, he's soon going to leave. I'm very worried about the rest of my crew; none of them have done their military service. If I lose another man, I may be out of business for a while. I'm lucky, I suppose. I finished my 18 months' service two years ago. For now, I'm safe."

Marta didn't say anything more about her ideas, nor comment about Goran. She could picture him when Dimitri described him and recalled how closed he seemed to her the first time she saw him. Thinking about him now gave rise to an uneasy feeling that she was connected to him somehow, and not in a good way.

* * *

Dimitri and Marta began taking day hikes on the outskirts of town and boat rides along both rivers. Marta even joined the crew on Dimitri's fishing boat one day. Fish-wise, the outing was a success, but Marta found the rocking motion of the boat and the smell of the catch unsettled her stomach almost to the point of throwing up. Once back on solid ground, though, she regained her equilibrium and banished her queasiness.

Soon they were scheduling their free time so as not to miss any opportunity to be together. It became obvious to each of them, and to Adrijana, that they were in love. The rest of that summer of 1993 wove the strands of their lives together like a tapestry.

Marta had found considerable satisfaction in her job. She had gained more responsibility as an epidemiology nurse and quickly became a well-respected member of the larger medical community in Belgrade. Dimitri's aunt embraced Marta fully and regarded her as a long-lost daughter. Dimitri's parents took an instant liking to her, as did his cousins and their families. Marta felt she would soon inherit a new family.

But the tapestry Marta and Dimitri had woven contained not only scenes of beauty and hope. Portents of trouble appeared. As Adrijana had warned, Marta had embarked on a perilous course in the social sphere, one that was dangerously close to political. By continuing to advocate for greater protection of the numerous small ethnic communities in Belgrade and other regions where Serbs were in the majority, Marta raised her profile in risky ways, marking her as a troublemaker in the eyes of many. One evening after dinner at Adrijana's home, Marta related a threat she had received by telephone at her office, telling her to cease her outspoken commentary. A deep male voice dripping with malice described in great detail the pleasure he would take in tearing out her throat to make sure she never spoke again. "My supervisor was very worried, and pleaded with me to keep quiet."

Adrijana's reply conveyed a message of caution overlaid with a barely suppressed tone of panic. "And your supervisor is right, my dear. For God's sake, Marta, you are treading a dangerous path. Please, for your safety and our safety, try not to stir things up. You cannot change the situation, you can only expose yourself to danger." Marta considered Adrijana's advice but did not reply.

As Dimitri anticipated, after Goran departed to begin his military service, several other crew members were conscripted. So widespread and numerous were these call-ups that Dimitri saw two complete turnovers among his five-member crew in the span of three months.

These departures were disruptive to Dimitri's fishing operation, but they occupied only a small portion of his attention. Foremost in his mind were his hopes for a future with Marta. They spent almost every evening together, and on most weekends they took excursions around the city and its environs—museums, concerts, the opera, hikes along the river and nearby hills, and parties at the homes of Dimitri's friends and Marta's co-workers. In the fall, with the blessing of Dimitri's parents (in person) and Marta's parents (by telephone), the couple pledged their lives to one another. The wedding was set for the end of February 1994, some four months away. There would be little activity on Belgrade's two frigid, ice-bound rivers in February. For their honeymoon they were to spend a week in Niš, an ancient city in southern Serbia near the Bulgarian border.

Adrijana spent her free time helping the couple plan their nuptials, an outdoor civil ceremony in Topčider Park in suburban Belgrade. Adrijana arranged the catering through her restaurant contacts. By a stroke of luck, Milan would be in Belgrade in February for a well-earned rest from his work in Sarajevo. Although Marta's family in Ljubljana did not attend, due to the still-simmering ill will between Slovenia and Serbia, the number of guests from the Sava clan as well as Marta's colleagues made for a good-sized wedding.

The newlyweds were fortunate in being able to take a full two-week honeymoon due to the lack of work for Dimitri and a very cooperative boss at Marta's clinic. A warmer-than-normal late February to mid-March in Niš made their time there especially enjoyable. Although camping was not an option, hiking was, and they did a lot of that. In addition, they explored the city itself, which was full of cultural and historical treasures.

The most memorable event, however, occurred as they sat in their hotel room after having finished packing for the trip home. There was a knock on the door. Marta experienced a jolt of adrenalin and turned to Dimitri, who said, "Maybe that's the concierge; didn't we pay the bill yet?"

Marta shook her head, "We did; that's not the concierge. I have a feeling I know who it is, but it's impossible." She got up, walked to the door, and opened it. Standing in front of her, smiling, was her grandmother, Shimza. They immediately embraced, laughing. "I had a funny feeling it was you! How could that be? You're the last person I would have expected to see."

Shimza stared straight into Marta's eyes and held her shoulders. "It was time for me to pay you a visit. Aren't you going to invite me in and introduce me to your husband?"

Marta took Shimza by the hand and they walked into the room, as Dimitri got up to meet them halfway. After introductions, Dimitri asked, "Can I get you something to drink? I can make some tea, or we can open the bottle of wine in the fridge. What's your preference?"

"Tea would be great; I don't drink."

While Dimitri was busy in the small kitchenette, Marta and Shimza made small talk. Marta found it difficult to ask why Shimza had shown up; she felt like there was some important reason but was hesitant to ask.

Dimitri came back into the living room with a tray and three cups of tea. "So, Shimza, I get to meet you at last. Marta has told me so much about you, how you were her favorite person when she was growing up. Where have you been all these years?"

"She probably told you that I ran off to Bulgaria to attend a large Rom gathering and conference in Sofia. I didn't really have any roots in Ljubljana and the Rom community in Bulgaria was very inviting.

So I took a job and stayed. Now, though, I'm off to Istanbul to do some work with the Rom community there."

Marta said, "But Istanbul is the other direction from Sofia. What made you come to Niš instead?"

Shimza took a swallow of her tea, looked from Dimitri to Marta, and said with an undecipherable look on her face, "I had a feeling I should talk to you, so I called your father in Ljubljana to find out where you were. He told me you were here and gave me Dimitri's aunt's phone number so I could find out the name of your hotel."

Marta was puzzled by Shimza's expression and asked, "So, is something the matter? I hope nothing bad has happened. Are you okay healthwise? "

"Nothing bad has happened, and I'm the picture of health; healthier than ever for a 65-year-old who can't settle down. First, let me say that I was very happy to hear of your wedding. Adrijana told me it was wonderful." Turning to Dimitri and taking his hands in hers, she said, "And I'm very, very pleased to meet you, Son of the River."

That brought a smile to Dimitri's face. He and Marta waited for Shimza to continue. She released Dimitri's hands and took Marta's hands. "Now, I don't want you to think I'm being nosy, or crazy for that matter. But Marta and Dimitri, you are going to have a wonderful son. He will bring joy into your life, no matter what other events take place to disrupt the calm waters of your world."

This left Marta and Dimitri speechless. Marta spoke first, "I have a feeling you are not just mouthing platitudes. You know something. Please, grandma, tell us more."

"Well, like I said, not long ago I had a feeling I needed to see you. It felt like a dream, but it wasn't a dream. More than a feeling, actually. Remember those times when you and I would talk of such things when you were a child? You probably still have these experiences, these sudden realizations that burst upon your consciousness and won't go away. Anyway, not to be too mysterious, I realized you were pregnant with a son, so I wanted to see you and give you both my blessings."

Marta spoke first, "But grandma, how could you know I'm pregnant; I don't even know that. " Blushing, she continued, "We've only been married two weeks, and I don't feel anything approaching pregnancy." Dimitri leaned back on the sofa and looked from Marta to Shimza.

Shimza smiled and said, "Like I said, it's just something I know. If you think about it, perhaps you'll come to know it, too, before long."

Dimitri asked, "But what did you mean about the calm waters being disrupted? What's that all about?"

"I only know the feeling, the realization, whatever you call it. Into most of our lives, turbulence sometimes comes. I sense your son will be in the midst of that turbulence, but he will put an end to it in a very satisfactory way. That's all I know. That's the picture I get, except it's not really a picture."

"Well," said Marta with a smile, "I'm glad you're not trying to be mysterious! Maybe we should do what the American folksinger says and 'let the mystery be'."

The rest of the evening the three of them talked of family matters, Shimza's time in Bulgaria, her vague plans for the future in Istanbul, and Dimitri's hopes for an uptick in his fishing business. They avoided talk of the political situation in Yugoslavia. When it was a little after midnight, Shimza announced she had to get on the road. Marta and Dimitri accompanied her to her car in the hotel parking lot. After hugs and tears, Shimza drove away and the newlyweds went back to their room. No more was said about Shimza's somewhat disturbing remarks about their son and the turbulence he would see.

*   *   *

When Marta and Dimitri returned to the city they eagerly put together the pieces of their new life. One of those pieces was Marta's pregnancy; she was due to deliver their child in late October or early November. Adrijana, who owned the small apartment building she lived in, offered them a beautiful, spacious, ground-floor apartment. Marta, through her connections in the social services community, hired a young Muslim woman, Amina Sidran, to be their housekeeper and, when the time came, their babysitter. They decided to name the child Dushan if a boy. A suitable girl's name eluded them, and anyway they were strongly influenced by Shimza's prediction.

Like many young newlyweds that auspicious year, their life moved forward like a train approaching a set of parallel railroad tracks. One set of tracks led toward an ever-more joyous life as new parents. The other set of tracks headed into a dark tunnel leading to an uncertain future in a brewing civil war: The possibility of an imminent invasion by NATO forces, or at the very least, imposition of international economic sanctions as punishment for Serbia's genocidal war on its fellow Yugoslav republics.

For Dimitri and Marta, the likelihood of political turmoil stayed in the background as they entered their new chapter as parents. Dushan was born November 1, 1994, a healthy boy whose sunny disposition manifested very early. His parents were besotted with him. He had an unusual ability to charm those around him. It comforted his parents to see how effortlessly Amina took to her new role as a substitute mom when Marta was at work. Indeed, Amina was also smitten with Dushan, and he with her. When Dushan was six months old, Marta returned to work full time.

CHAPTER THREE:
THE RIVERS PART, 1995-1997

The heat wave that had settled on Belgrade in the summer of 1995 caused the air to ripple like a mirage on a desert horizon. "I don't know if I can hold out for another four hours," Marta muttered as she handed baby Dushan to Amina, who had brought the boy to Marta's office for breastfeeding. Marta's lunch hour was over and so was her short visit with her little boy.

Such heat was unseasonable for this spring day. The political temperature likewise was almost as hot as it had been when the Yugoslavian civil war erupted in 1992 more than three years ago. For a few months in early 1995 Marta found encouragement in what looked like the beginning of peace among Belgrade's many ethnic groups. The international community had been brokering lengthy negotiations among the many hostile parties in the country. But the negotiations came to naught and the violence increased.

She had good reason to fear for her own safety as well. Armed militia not only attacked each other but intimidated anyone working for peace. The city's public health department was heavily involved in Serbia's growing refugee problem. Both the department's involvement with refugees and Marta's own personal activism promoting ethnic harmony put her in danger. She had assisted many Bosnian Muslims since her arrival in Belgrade, the latest being Amina. Marta and Dimitri both had received numerous threats.

Amina took the boy to the bathroom next to Marta's office to change Dushan's diaper. Suddenly she heard the front door savagely thrown open. An angry male voice shouted, "You were warned, bitch. Now you pay!" Amina heard Marta scream, "No!" and the sound of a struggle. The screaming got louder, interspersed with kicks and punches. All sounds except heavy breathing stopped suddenly. She heard the noise of someone being dragged along the floor. The male voice said, "pick her up, fool!" and then Amina heard the door open and slam shut.

Amina held Dushan to her chest, her heart pounding. She kept his left ear and face pressed tightly against her blouse, the other ear covered by her hand. She hoped that Dushan had not heard anything; he remained quiet and still, perhaps asleep after his recent breastfeeding. Amina kept her own fear at bay and her breaths shallow and quiet.

After a few minutes of silence, Amina carefully stepped into the office. She kept Dushan's face turned to her bosom to shield his eyes. She feared she would see a horrific sight. Instead, the office was empty. Marta was gone. Clutching her throat and swallowing repeatedly to avoid throwing up, Amina pivoted to her right into the short hallway and walked quickly to the workroom near the back door. She picked up the phone and called the police to report the abduction. Then she quietly let herself out the door and stood for a moment in the alley, still holding Dushan firmly against her chest.

Amina did not wait for the police. For the past three years, ever since her flight from chaotic Sarajevo to the relative calm of Belgrade, Amina continued to see the relentless disintegration of all forms of civil authority and governance. No, she was fairly certain the police would not show up. Even if they did, Amina was a Muslim working for a well-known "Muslim sympathizer" in predominantly Serbian Belgrade. Police assistance was highly unlikely.

She walked briskly down the short alley to the street, speaking soothingly to infant Dushan to keep him calm. After pausing at the alley's intersection with the street to make sure Marta's abductors were not nearby, Amina quickly resumed her brisk walk to Marta and Dimitri's apartment. Dimitri was still on the boat. Amina knew she must keep Dushan quiet until his naptime. They played with his toys in his bedroom. After an hour, Dushan fell asleep without any fuss. Dimitri would return home from the river in a few hours. Amina dreaded having to tell him the news.

Marta awoke in the predawn darkness. She sat up and looked around the small room that had served as her prison cell for the past week. Twice a day she was escorted into a larger room that opened out onto a courtyard to exercise, use the outhouse toilet, and eat a meal of stale bread, hard cheese and a piece of moldy fruit. Otherwise Marta saw nothing save the four walls of the room. She could not tell where she was being held. Today, for the first time, she was able to briefly take her mind off her separation from her little boy and her husband. She repeated her calming words frequently—*Amina and Dushan got home safely, Dimitri is okay*. At other times, she sobbed over her separation from her family. Still, she knew they were alive. Her anxiety and grief came from not knowing what was happening to them. Several times this past week she had dreamt that she saw Dushan and asked him questions. He responded to the questions by smiling at her. She heard the sound of a gentle tide washing a shore. Then she awoke to a darkened room.

What kind of place is this, she wondered. *Maybe a house, maybe an office building*. She sometimes heard the noise of traffic in the distance, and occasionally she heard voices. She couldn't make out what the voices said, or even what language they spoke.

The young guard who escorted her into the enclosed courtyard every day did not speak to or look at her as she stretched and paced around the perimeter. He preferred to sit on his chair and smoke. Marta got no reading from him as she had often done with people she knew. Her sixth sense was blocked; he closed his mind off entirely. *I suppose I should be grateful at his lack of interest in me. Things could be much worse.*

After several weeks of this routine, things changed abruptly. Two men grabbed her by the arms and led her through the courtyard and out a carriage entrance to the street.

"Hey—her hood; you forgot her hood. Put it on her, you idiots!" Marta turned toward this voice. She got a glimpse of the speaker, but someone shoved a cloth sack over her head just as he turned away and walked toward a military vehicle.

I have seen him somewhere. Where? Who is he? In that instant she realized he was keeping her alive instead of killing her like so many other dissidents in Belgrade. Marta was shoved into some sort of delivery van. She found no seats to sit on, only boxes and burlap bags stuffed with something cushiony that smelled like tobacco. She was alone in the cargo area, free to pull off her hood once the van began moving.

It didn't do much good to remove her hood. She couldn't see much; the van had no side windows. Through the front windshield, she could only see telephone poles, row upon row of high-rise tenements, and parked cars. No traffic at this hour—she decided it must be a little before dawn judging from the gradual lightening of the sky.

The van rumbled on for what felt like hours before it stopped. Fear of what might happen to her flooded her mind before she quelled it by letting out her breath and breathing normally. She gagged on the inhaled fumes of gasoline now permeating the stuffy interior of the van. Only a petrol stop. At least two or more hours went by. Signs of habitation disappeared. The asphalt road ended and became very rutted. She was jolted and knocked about the interior continually. The van came to a stop after leaving the graveled road and traversing a dry creek bed. She guessed it was probably noon given the light that was beginning to fill the van's interior.

The side door to the van slid open. An emaciated young man in army fatigues stood in the doorway. He held an unlit cigarette in one hand and a lit one in his mouth. "Don't ask any questions, don't speak to anyone. Just walk over there," he said pointing to a mosque—or former mosque, since the minaret had been toppled and the front door lay on the ground. "Someone will meet you and escort you inside." The man didn't appear concerned that Marta had no hood over her head or that her hands were free.

Marta took in her surroundings. The van sat parked at the entrance to a circular walled compound a good 200 yards across. Inside was the medium-sized mosque that had been badly damaged.

All around the outside of the mosque's compound was a sprawling makeshift army camp in what was formerly an ancient Muslim neighborhood. The Ottoman style houses might easily have been over 100 years old. The streets were gravel and rutted, perhaps by tank treads. Many of the buildings showed heavy damage. The army camp was an improvised affair with the mosque serving as a military headquarters. There were no civilians that she could see, only troops, support staff and medical personnel.

Marta reached the mosque entrance—a gaping hole where the door had been broken off its hinges. She did a double take at the approach from inside of a tall blonde man in fatigues.

He smiled and said, "Yes, you recognize me, don't you?"

She realized she had seen him before dawn as her captors put her into the van. Now she recognized him as Goran, one of Dimitri's former crewmen. She was shocked to realize he had been one of the two soldiers who entered her dream elevator with her back in

Sarajevo. She quickly decided not to show her recognition just yet. "Yes, but I'm not sure where from. I don't think we've ever spoken, have we?"

"No, we haven't. Nor were we ever introduced. I am Captain Bolat, and you are Marta, correct?"

"Yes, but tell me where I've seen you. It was years ago, wasn't it?" Her voice rising, she continued without a pause, "Where am I now, and why? How do you know my name if we've never been introduced? What's happening? Do you realize I have a young child? Your men have taken me away from my baby!" The words tumbled from her mouth like a fast-moving stream.

"Wait, too many questions all at once. Answers will come, perhaps from you yourself; then I won't have to supply them. Answering questions is so tiresome; it's the least favorite part of my job. Come inside, we'll have some tea and biscuits, Turkish style. These Turks left behind quite a good supply of both before they fled at our approach."

Goran led Marta through the beautiful interior of the mosque, undamaged inside save for the obvious defilement by boxes of mortars and rifles, and construction materials lying in haphazard heaps throughout what had been a breathtakingly decorated room. As they entered the mosque office, Goran gestured for Marta to sit down on the divan opposite an imposing desk. Neither of them spoke as they waited for a nervous young man to appear carrying a tray of cookies, glasses of dark tea, and a small dish of lumps of brown crystallized sugar. He wore modern Balkan-Muslim attire—skullcap, collarless white shirt, brightly colored vest and slippers. Marta distracted herself by closely watching the comings and goings of people in the mosque. *Maybe I should just tell him I remember who he is.*

After the young Muslim man departed, Marta reflected on the interaction between him and Goran. Definitely a relationship built on power—and Goran had all the power. The young man seemed to be terrified of him. Others who occasionally came up and spoke to Goran were soldiers in uniform. Goran was obviously their military superior, yet these soldiers were not terrified of him. A striking contrast to the terror of the young Muslim man.

Goran spoke first, interrupting Marta's pensive silence as she perused her situation. "I don't mean to be rude, Marta, but we have to get on with our little meeting and finish our tea.

"What we have here in this region is—to borrow a favorite Western expression—'a failure to communicate. ' It's a failure on the part of these Muslims to understand that this land doesn't belong to them. Their Turkish forebears stole it from us Serbs 500 years ago, and we are simply taking it back."

Marta didn't know what to think as she listened to Goran's words. She feared the implications of his comments. All around her were soldiers and the sounds of distant gunfire and explosions. For some months she had heard stories of the Serbian army's military actions and atrocities committed in non-Serbian enclaves where the inhabitants were suspected of devising plans to secede from Yugoslavia. She now saw those stories were, in fact, true.

She also felt extreme anxiety not knowing what might have happened to her baby and husband. She blurted out, "Captain, before you tell me what I'm doing here, please tell me what has happened to my family. Are they okay?"

"Your question suggests I might know something about your family. A fair assumption. Perhaps you've already guessed, but I do know your husband. I used to work for Dimitri on his fishing crew. Do you remember me now?"

"Ah, yes, of course. Your name is Goran. You were one of the first men to leave the crew for the Army. I see you have risen high in this past year—from draftee to officer."

"Well, as much as I would like to attribute my rank to my competence, I must admit to having some family connections."

"Please, Goran, what can you tell me about Dimitri? Is he okay? Is our baby okay?"

"I have always liked Dimitri. I have no reason to believe he or the baby has been harmed. If you like I will see what I can find out."

"Why not just release me if you're a friend of my husband's? I can find out myself, and you won't have to be distracted from your precious work here."

Goran's eyes widened, and his mouth, which had been frozen in a continuous half-smile, now betrayed the barest frown at Marta's use of the phrase "precious work." "Really, Marta, your impertinent response ill becomes you. You no doubt understand the situation here. You should be able to guess why you are here and why we cannot release you just yet."

"I don't know why you think I know the reason I was abducted. I do not even know where I am. So, what are you going to do with me? Will you at least check on my family?"

"Two answers to two questions. Number one: you are a nurse and we desperately need medical personnel here. You may even be able to treat some of the locals, not just soldiers. After all, an epidemic is an epidemic—it spares no one. Number two: yes, I will see if we can find out about your family. Don't worry—just do your job and everything will be fine. I will see that Dimitri is informed of your situation."

"But how long will my 'situation' last? You surely know that a baby needs his mama."

"Well, I can't say at the moment. And your baby is no doubt being cared for by your lovely nurse maid, that Muslim Turk Amina."

Marta slumped back in her chair. She tried to hide her fear about how much he evidently knew about her family and home life. Was he protecting them as well as monitoring them? She felt a sudden inspiration to approach Goran with a new attitude.

"Goran, you don't know how happy I am at what you say. I appreciate your offer. And I will gladly work here after your assurances that my family is all right. Just not too long, okay?"

"As I said, I cannot promise anything. We need you here, and you'll stay as long as we need you."

"I will help in any way I can. You say there's an epidemic here? Where is 'here', exactly?"

"Have you heard of Novi Pazar? That's where we are. And where we'll stay until our work is done. Troublesome people, these locals. Most have fled the town proper; many are now living in a vast tent city you passed through on your way here. At first, even though they impeded our progress through the area, we left them alone because they seemed no longer a threat. But now they're coming down with dangerous diseases, diseases which of course are a threat to our troops. Now do you see how we can use you? Helping both sides in this struggle, much as you used to do back in Belgrade."

*　　　　*　　　　*

Goran wasted no time in putting Marta to work. She worked 12-hour shifts six days a week, and eight hours on Sundays. The army had constructed a temporary hospital in the camp made out of former shipping containers, now sterilized and hooked together in a huge square with an open courtyard area in the middle. Two doctors and two other nurses besides Marta worked in this makeshift medical center. Her astonishing workload treating troops and locals suffering from both physical and epidemic-related wounds caused the remainder of that summer of 1995 and most of the fall to pass quickly. Marta lived in an abandoned "Turk" house not far from the Mosque. The other medical personnel resided there as well, guarded by a soldier. They worked as a team, despite any supposed but suppressed political differences. There was a small outbuilding in the back of the compound where two Muslim servants lived. One of them was the young man who served Marta and Goran tea on her first day in the camp. Speaking surprisingly good Serbian, he told Marta his name was Séifulláh. "That's a lovely name," Marta told him.

"Thank you," Séifulláh replied, bowing slightly. Some days later, as she greeted him, he responded, " Call me Séif."

"Séif? Is that a nickname?"

"That is what my friends and family call me; that and Séifu." Marta smiled. "Séif… Séifu… Séifulláh. I like them all. I assume you're not a local, since there are very few locals still alive, at least not around here. How did you end up in Novi Pazar?"

"I'm originally from Zupanya, Croatia, near Serbia's northern border. When Croatia became almost as dangerous as Bosnia, and my parents were killed, I decided to leave for a safe Serbian city. I knew Novi Pazar had a large Muslim population and, even though it was in Serbia, I thought I would be safe here. I was wrong, as you see. It turns out the Yugoslav army had Novi Pazar on its list of places to "pacify" in Serbia. I was captured—which I realize is a whole lot better than the alternative. So, here I am, a tea boy. I am sure they keep me alive because I speak their language better than any local and I have some skill as an interpreter."

It didn't bother Marta that her new friend was a Muslim. Before Marta gave birth to baby Dushan, neither she nor Dimitri had the slightest concern over hiring Amina, a Muslim from Bosnia, as their maid and babysitter. They knew their decision might raise the eyebrows of their colleagues and friends in Belgrade, but they stuck to their choice. They were impressed with Amina's integrity and fortitude despite (or perhaps because of) what she had endured in her short life growing up in Sarajevo. Because of her job, Marta had access to Amina's intake file. She had learned quite a lot about Amina's experiences in Sarajevo. Amina and her family lived in the Muslim neighborhood—the middle of the target zone. When Amina's apartment building was destroyed in a particularly devastating artillery attack, Amina lost her entire family and almost lost her own life. She escaped from the city by hitching a ride on a Pepsi truck headed to Belgrade, not long after Marta had also left as a passenger in Milan's Red Cross van.

While Marta worked as a nurse in that field hospital in Novi Pazar, as a prisoner of the Yugoslav army unit, Séif shared information about recent events in the ongoing conflict. Both were careful not to spend too much time together in open view of the soldiers in the camp. In the very early morning they found time to talk together away from prying eyes.

Apart from those rare occasions when Marta could have an unguarded conversation with Séif, she worked most of her waking hours, from early morning to late in the evening.

Time continued to pass quickly. The end of Marta's second year at the camp was approaching. Her training and experience in epidemiology and infectious diseases were invaluable. The prevalence of disease had diminished significantly. The army's "field operations" also seemed to be drawing to a close.

But Marta's hopes of release from her servitude were dashed one morning when Goran informed her she would be accompanying the troops to the next location.

"But, Goran, I understood once you were done here, I would be released. Is that not what you told me?"

"No, I told you I could not make any promises."

"But you did make one promise. You promised to get information about Dimitri and the baby and to let Dimitri know I was safe."

"I only promised to try. And I did try, several times. Finally I have something to report. Dimitri has apparently left the country with the boy. One family friend said Dimitri fled after being threatened. His aunt also has disappeared. The apartment you lived in now houses an army office."

This bit of bad news left Marta speechless and unable to work. She refused to leave her room. Neither threats from Goran nor sympathy from Séifulláh were effective in getting Marta out of her depression. Finally, realizing that tears and lying in bed were only making her feel worse, Marta rose and resumed her duties. Marta jumped back into her routine with added determination to improve or save the lives of her patients. *If I can't help my own family maybe I can help these unfortunates all around me.* She welcomed Séifulláh's companionship; even Goran's apparent sympathy helped lift Marta's spirits. Her dreams of being with Dushan, while less frequent and harder to "read," buoyed her spirits even more. She felt sure he and Dimitri were alive.

CHAPTER FOUR:
A PROMISE KEPT, 1997-1998

Milan had little hope that this trip to Belgrade would be any more fruitful than past trips had been. It had been over two years since he learned from Marta's husband of her abduction and disappearance. On Milan's last trip to Belgrade a month ago, their apartment was now being used as some sort of military office. Milan could not find out what happened to Dimitri and Dushan.

Milan parked his Red Cross van across the broad avenue from Marta's apartment building. He watched people entering and exiting the building. They appeared to be military personnel. He wondered if he should go inside and inquire about the former residents. *Probably just get myself in trouble; my name is probably up to be drafted, and I definitely don't want that.*

After about half an hour he saw someone he recognized leave the building dressed in army fatigues. The soldier was Jovan, one of Milan's high school classmates. In those days, Jovan wore his black, straight hair long, and looked a lot like the Beatle George Harrison. Now Jovan looked impressive as a soldier—clipped military haircut, over six feet tall, slim, muscular, with an assured way of walking. When Jovan's motorcycle pulled away from the curb, Milan followed at a discrete distance.

Milan saw the motorcycle pull into a petrol station, so Milan did the same. As he got out of his van and approached the pump, he pretended to see his former acquaintance for the first time. He and Jovan registered simultaneous looks of surprise as they walked toward each other and shook hands.

"Milan, is it really you? How long has it been?" Looking at Milan's Red Cross van, he said, "So, you work for the Red Cross?"

"Jovan, this is amazing! I haven't seen you since your sister dumped me for the university. Yes, I'm a driver for the Red Cross.

What about you? How long have you been in the army?"

"Not long. I was drafted six months ago. They haven't deployed me yet; I'm an office go-fer, basically. I'm not looking forward to being sent to one of the army camps. I think you know as well as I what is going on at the fringes of our Serbian empire."

"I hope you can stay in Belgrade. I can tell you, it's not pretty in the other regions. I work in Sarajevo, believe it or not, and every month I drive this van out of the city and back to replenish our medical supplies. Have you heard what is going on in Sarajevo? Almost daily bombardments, assassinations, kidnappings."

"Oh, yes. I've heard, although it's not exactly a front page story, obviously."

Milan paused while Jovan reached for the petrol pump and began filling his tank. "I have a favor to ask, Jovan, and I have a confession as well. I saw you leave an apartment building a few minutes ago. I recognized you and followed you here. I apologize for pretending to just see you here for the first time."

Jovan laughed and clapped Milan on the shoulder. "I guess I can understand the reason for your caution. We soldiers are not exactly known for our hospitality."

Milan exhaled and smiled. "I didn't know how enthusiastic you were about being a soldier. I can see that you're not a fanatic, so I would like to ask if you can find out something for me. The people who used to live in the apartment where the army offices are now were friends of mine. Can you find out where they moved to? I would owe you a big favor, seriously."

"Sure. I'll see what I can do. I don't think it would be too difficult: it's certainly not a matter of violating state security. What are their names, your friends?"

"The husband is Dimitri Sava. He is, or was, owner of a river fishing boat. The wife is Marta Cecelja; maybe she took her husband's name. I actually only knew Marta; she married Dimitri after she moved here from Sarajevo several years ago. She's a nurse and was working for the Belgrade public health department. I'm worried about her. She was something of a thorn in the side of the city's right-wing establishment. I'm afraid she opened her mouth one too many times and got into trouble. Now that I see they're no longer in their apartment, I'm very worried."

"I'll do what I can. Where can I get in touch with you? When do you return to Sarajevo?"

"I still have to load up my van. I'll be here for another few days. I'll be staying at the Red Cross office near the Fortress. Can you stop by, or shall I stop by the army office?"

"Don't even think about coming to our office. They would certainly snatch you up and draft you, assuming you haven't served your military service yet. Even if you have, they might still take you in. I'll come by tomorrow evening. See you then."

"I really appreciate it, Jovan. I'm forever in your debt."

Jovan wondered how he would deal with the situation if he were deployed to one of the army's several fronts and ordered into combat. Now, a day after his encounter with Milan, the time had come to make a decision. He'd heard a rumor from two different sources that several hundred recruits were to be ordered to report for infantry training. *It's now or never*, he thought.

On a clear night after hearing that troubling rumor, Jovan met Milan in a quiet neighborhood near the Fortress. "I have some bad news and some good news, Milan. The bad news is irregulars within the army abducted Marta a couple of years ago. Dimitri abandoned the apartment with the baby several months ago. The good news is that Marta's abductors, under orders from Captain Goran Bolat, have put her to work as a nurse at a military base in Novi Pazar, up north."

Milan sat on the low wall running along the river. "I don't know what to say. I wish I had some way to get to her, to help her."

"Well, I have a plan. I just heard that my unit is going to be sent for infantry training and then deployed somewhere. I have no intention of taking part in that plan." Jovan pulled an official-looking piece of paper out of a thin file folder. "This is an order from the commanding officer here, under whose command is Captain Goran Bolat, Marta's abductor." Jovan scanned the order and looked at Milan with a mock-serious expression before continuing. "This order directs Captain Bolat to release Marta to me, Corporal Jovan Durkovic, pursuant to her transfer to the army base in Zupanya, Croatia. She will be working there as a nurse under the auspices of the Red Cross, and my Red Cross driver, Milan Vukadin, will transport us." Jovan handed the paper to Milan and smiled.

"How did you manage that?" Milan asked, examining the paper. "This is official letterhead."

"Let's just say we office monkeys can get into a lot of stuff when we want to. Plus, security's pretty lax in the army, and especially so in that office. They're still in the process of setting up the layout of the office. Nothing is secure. I had plenty of examples of orders and correspondence from the C.O. to model this on."

"Are you sure you want to do this, Jovan? I don't know what the punishment is for desertion, but I wouldn't be surprised if it was death by firing squad."

"Right you are. Yes, I'm aware of that. But death could be my fate anyway in this insane war. Let's get out of here."

"Before we leave the city, let me stop by the Red Cross office and let them know I've been ordered by the army to transport a soldier and a nurse to Zupanya. The Red Cross has other drivers and vehicles who can do the Sarajevo run."

Marta had just walked out of the camp mess hall when she saw a Red Cross van park nearby. Milan and a soldier got out of the van. Her first thought was to run over to Milan and greet him, but a powerful sensation told her to stay calm. Willing herself to breathe and appear uninterested, she watched as the soldier entered the officer's mess while Milan remained next to the vehicle. He looked over at Marta and quickly shook his head and placed his index finger to his lips. An unmistakable sign—*you don't know me.*

Trying hard not to reveal her interest, Marta watched as Goran and the solder approached Milan and the Red Cross van. Goran inspected Milan's vehicle and some documents he produced. Goran handed a different document to the soldier and then turned to look at Marta. He motioned for her to join the group.

"Marta, I have been given orders to transfer you to our camp in Zupanya. You'll be working under the auspices of the Red Cross, and this driver here will transport you and Corporal Durkovic."

Looking at Goran and the soldier standing side by side, Marta immediately recognized this man as the other soldier in her Sarajevo "elevator" dream. Marta had a sudden inspiration. "Captain Bolat," she asked (using Goran's military title in front of the soldier and the Red Cross driver), "would you consider allowing me to take an assistant with me? Séifullah Hamid has been invaluable in my work here. He is a native of Zupanya and could provide even more valuable assistance there. He speaks several languages and has shown considerable skill as an interpreter."

Goran, who had just turned away to return to his office, stopped and faced Marta. The distracted look on his face turned into a frown. Before he spoke, however, Marta awakened her knack from her inmost self and gave Goran a mental push.

The frown on Goran's face faded and he sighed. "Fine. I don't need him here, and since our unit is probably moving to the eastern border, he would be of no use to us there." He turned away and walked back into the building. Marta, Jovan and Milan stood still until Goran was gone. Jovan and Milan sat in the Red Cross Jeep while Marta walked to her quarters to collect her meager possessions and inform Séif of his new duty assignment.

The foursome had put several miles behind them before they were calm enough to speak. Milan, driving, broke the silence by addressing Marta, who sat in the back seat next to Séif. "You are a quick thinker, Marta. My second-biggest worry was that you'd blow our cover by greeting me."

She answered, "And I'd guess your biggest worry was that Captain Bolat would suspect something?"

"Right. But Corporal Durkovic here pulled off a miracle."

Jovan smiled and looked back at Marta. "No, not a miracle. It was just very fortunate that the commanding officer had so much correspondence lying around, and that my job allowed me access to the files."

Keeping his eyes on the road, Milan said to Marta, "You know, that bit about needing Séif as your assistant seemed incredibly risky. I never would have thought Bolat would agree to something like that, especially on the request of a prisoner. I definitely felt something in the air when you looked at him after he stopped and frowned."

Marta stared out the window and replied, "Like I told you back when you and I were leaving Sarajevo, I have a knack for persuasion when the need arises. Let's just say, I felt the need arise."

Séif looked as if he couldn't decide whether to cry or laugh. When his face settled down, he looked from Milan to Jovan, two Serbs, one in a JNA uniform, and then addressed Marta. "I'm guessing, Marta, that you are perhaps not in the dark as much as I. Do you have any idea where we're going? I mean, other than to another JNA camp?"

"Well, the only thing I know is that my good friend Milan

Vukadin has once again delivered me from evil. However, I'm afraid I am not acquainted with his friend. Nor did I have any advance knowledge of what just occurred. And most importantly, I have no idea where we're going except that it is most certainly not to another JNA camp."

Jovan again turned around to look at the two passengers in the back. "Allow me to introduce myself: Corporal Jovan Durkovic, at your service; a former school mate of Milan's, and a most unwilling JNA draftee. We ran into each other last week and learned that we had compatible short-term goals. Milan wanted to find out why a JNA office was inhabiting your apartment, Marta, and I wanted an excuse to desert, not to mention a vehicle so perfect as this Red Cross Land Rover."

Séif, still uneasy at Captain Bolat's mention of Zupanya, asked, "And where exactly are you planning to desert to?"

Milan looked away from the pockmarked road briefly and addressed him and Marta in the rear view mirror. "We thought we'd leave that choice to Marta. What will it be—Sarajevo, Zagreb, or... perhaps Ljubljana?"

At the name of her hometown, Marta's face lit up. "Why, Ljubljana, of course! My parents live there. Once we're there we'll be out of danger, and I'll be able to investigate where my family has gone to. What about you, Séif? Are you okay with Ljubljana?"

"Of course; I don't care much for the other alternatives, nor do I wish to go back 'home' to Zupanya."

When the Land Rover reached the Slovenia-Serbia border, both the Serbian and Slovenian outposts were deserted. Jovan had hoped that would be the case since the cessation of hostilities between Serbia and its former Slovenian province. In any event, he had changed out of his military uniform, burned it and buried the ashes some miles back. The Land Rover breezed through Slovenian villages and towns without incident and the foursome felt totally relaxed for the first time.

Milan delivered his passenger cargo to Marta's parents' Ljubljana home and departed for Italy, where the Red Cross office desperately needed drivers to transport refugees from Croatia to hospitals in Italy. Jovan found civilian work with the Slovenian army interviewing Croatian refugees and providing intelligence he gleaned about the

JNA's movements and plans. Séif decided to remain in Ljubljana and was offered work at the local Muslim community's mosque.

Marta herself found work as a nurse in the capital's main hospital. At the same time, she tried very hard to get information on the whereabouts of her husband and child. She was unable to locate Dimitri's Aunt Adrijana, who Marta suspected might be living on a relative's farm outside Belgrade. She continued to believe Dimitri and Dushan were still alive, thanks to little Dushan's questioning probes into her dreams. She hoped her dream-state responses were enough to reassure Dushan and that he could reassure Dimitri that she was alive and safe. Dushan's whereabouts were revealed in a vivid dream she had not long after arriving in Ljubljana. Though vague, the dream showed a vista of a bay or river, overcast sky, and fishing boats anchored offshore. She recognized the scene; it was the same scene she dreamt after witnessing the bakery explosion in Sarajevo. An echo of that earlier dream child's voice floated over the water. She saw an English name painted on one of the fishing boats: "Celtic Warrior."

During the first few months, as Marta's informal investigation continued unsuccessfully, she kept herself emotionally and physically occupied by working in the hospital. Marta's parents worked in town. Her maternal grandparents were elderly and increasingly needed tending. Even though Marta had a heavy workload, she gladly took on the burden of their care to relieve her parents, who were themselves getting on in years and beginning to experience health issues. Her father told her that his mom—her widowed grandmother Shimza—had left Bulgaria for Istanbul. That was more than three years ago and Marta hadn't heard anything from her beyond the occasional dream "conversations" with her. *She has to be pushing 70 by now; I hope she's doing okay.*

She was grateful for that responsibility because it made time pass more quickly. Marta had little time to nurse her heartache over the absence of her husband and baby. But she knew they were alive. Her dream visits with Dushan *told her* as much. *I only wish he could speak to me, maybe he could tell me where they are. Soon, maybe, I'll be able to show him how to give me pictures.*

CHAPTER FIVE:
A TEMPORARY REFUGE, ISLE OF MAN

On a June afternoon in 1999, in a country far away from what was now called "the former Yugoslavia," Dimitri sat on the edge of an old dilapidated bench, scraping mud off his boots. He watched Dushan play at the shoreline where the River Sulby entered the harbor in the small town of Ramsey at the north end of the Isle of Man. They always walked along the shoreline on their way home—Dimitri from work at the local fishing company, and Dushan from daycare.

Four years ago Dimitri's wife had disappeared, but each morning as he awoke, for a brief moment or two he lived in the happy past, oblivious of that tragedy. Then he remembered. The memory slammed into him like a freight train every morning without fail. Sometimes young Dushan—if he was sleeping in Dimitri's bed as he often was—awoke to his papa's quiet sobs. "Are you sad again about Mum?" he asked in his near-perfect English he learned at daycare.

"Yes, my champion. I miss her terribly. And I know you do too, don't you?"

"Yes, papa. In my dreams I see her smiling at me. Does she have brown hair? She does in my dreams. And green eyes?"

"Green eyes, yes, but her hair is a little blond and a little red, and straight. Strawberry blonde, the English call it. Her eyes green and golden like color of the ocean." Dimitri worried that his descriptions and stories of Marta were the basis for Dushan's "memories" of her. *He cannot remember her without me to help him; I must never let him forget her.* But often Dimitri felt a sense of relief talking to Dushan about Marta. *It's almost as if the boy really does visit with her in his dreams, to hear him talk about her.* Somehow, Dushan managed to keep up Dimitri's hopes that Marta was not dead.

When Dimitri fled to the Isle of Man a little over two years ago, he carried with him his two-year-old boy, his memories of his missing wife, and the unceasing nightmares of the Yugoslavian civil war. He arrived as a refugee, a designation bestowed upon him by the British government. This badge of honor earned him a fair amount of respect and sympathy from the residents of this little "crown dependency" where he was placed. He was lucky enough to have been sponsored by a small religious congregation in Ramsey that found Dimitri a job with the local fishing fleet.

In the time he and Dushan had been on this small island they learned that its inhabitants were good people. Not many of his friendly neighbors could appreciate what he had experienced. Most at least had a cursory knowledge of recent events in the former Yugoslavia, now fractured into Slovenia, Serbia, Croatia, Herzegovina and Bosnia.

The Manx, as the locals called themselves, were mostly a mix of Celtic and Norse stock. Although almost no Slavs lived on the island, the fishermen Dimitri worked and associated with were a generous and gregarious lot and welcomed Dimitri as a colleague. Being a single dad earned him sympathy as well, especially when he explained his wife's abduction. That horror story might have been too incredible for some folks' sheltered minds to fully comprehend, but they certainly understood grief and loss.

Since Dimitri and Dushan's flight from Yugoslavia, young Dushan had shown little of the trauma that Dimitri felt. *He remembers the stories I tell of his mama. He is strong and those stories will make him stronger.* Dimitri often found himself in awe of Dushan's capacity for healing himself and his papa. Dimitri learned from Dushan the extent to which one affected by tragedy can grow and develop emotional strength. The boy often woke up at night asking for his mother, but was quickly soothed by Dimitri's stories of her—her strength, compassion and fearlessness. Dushan adored his papa, and his papa thanked God for this priceless treasure in his life.

On this particularly sunny afternoon, Dimitri mused about the remarkable stories Dushan's teacher recounted of how he helped her manage her other little charges in the daycare center. "He really is a remarkable little boy, Mr. Sava. He seems to have an innate sense of compassion for other children's struggles. One little boy in particular is very needy, but Dushan makes a point of cheering him up and playing with him. We're lucky to have him here."

Dushan's cheerfulness never failed to push back Dimitri's

memories of civil war. He wouldn't have thought it possible that such a young child who had lost his mother and his home could maintain such a sunny outlook on life, let alone lift his papa's spirits out of the horrors of that recent nightmare.

Dimitri recalled their first days on the island. Soon after they had been flown from Belgrade to London, they traveled by train to Liverpool and by ferry to the Isle of Man. Dushan had loved those adventures in transportation, but the ferry ride thrilled him most of all. *So many simple things bring him joy*, Dimitri reflected.

When they arrived in Ramsey they met with their sponsors, a group of humanitarian souls who had found them a place to live, daycare for Dushan, and job and crash course in English for Dimitri, who had only studied it years ago in high school. Even though there were some half dozen churches of different denominations on the island, and Dimitri was nominally a Christian, it was ironically a non-Christian group, the local Baha'i community, that stepped up with an offer of no-strings-attached support.

Dimitri recalled that day as if it were yesterday. Twenty-four hours after their arrival, Dimitri and Dushan sat in the sunny courtyard of the Manx Bahá'í Centre, waiting to meet a representative of the group that would be their sponsor. The secretary of the Centre, who had greeted them and ushered them into the courtyard, made a strong impression on Dushan. "Does that lady look like my mama? I think she does." Dushan had a look of wonderment on his face, his golden brown eyes sparkling as they opened wide.

Reminding himself to try to speak his slowly improving English with Dushan as much as possible, Dimitri replied, "You have very good memory, my little champion. What do you see when you remember mama?" Dimitri had long since stopped worrying that talking about Marta would trouble the boy beyond his strength.

"I remember her smile and her hands." As he said that, he played with the little finger puppets the secretary had given him a few minutes ago. Dimitri smiled, warmed by Dushan's memory of Marta. Dimitri of course recalled her appearance painfully well, but mostly he remembered Marta's laugh and the way she used her hands when talking excitedly. Dimitri used to tease her about "showing your Italian side" when she got carried away telling a story about her latest triumph at work.

The Centre representative introduced herself as Jaleh Kilpatrick.

She had light brown hair, long and straight, olive skin and an aquiline nose. Dimitri rose to greet her. "Good morning, Miss Kilpatrick. Or are you Mrs.?"

"It's Mrs. My husband is Thomas Kilpatrick. He is an attorney and helps the Centre sometimes."

"Mrs. Kilpatrick, this is my big boy, Dushan Sava. I call him my champion. He is so fearless." Dushan beamed as he removed his finger puppets and extended his hand to Jaleh.

"Well, little champion. Would you like to play in our playroom over there while your papa and I have a little talk?" Dushan nodded and ran over to the little light-filled room just off the courtyard. He quickly involved himself in the construction of a castle with a large pile of cardboard bricks stacked against a back corner.

Jaleh turned to Dimitri and smiled. "So, Mr. Sava, tell me a little about yourself. You're our first refugee family from Yugoslavia."

"No more Yugoslavia, only 'former Yugoslavia,'" Dimitri replied, holding back the choking sensation rising up from his chest. "I am Serb. I born in Belgrade and was fishing boat crewman on Danube and Sava Rivers for 15 years. I am 35 years now. When I was 29, I married my beautiful Marta Cecelja. She was Slovenia girl but was nurse in Belgrade when we met. The troubles started short time after." Dimitri paused to get calm again before continuing.

"Marta and me, we were so sad by the troubles, sad and afraid. We work very hard to calm people down. We try make them remember good times before bad politicians and soldiers destroy Yugoslavia. But I see now foolishness of our hope. Even then I see foolishness, and danger most of all. I had great fear of those many gangs, that they would shoot us to make us keep quiet. Many times I tell Marta don't speak about these things, just we have to think how escape madness."

Dimitri shifted in his chair and paused again, blinking back tears, before he could continue. "But I am sad to say, Mrs. Kilpatrick, that Marta not listen. She always believed all people same as her, they must live together in peace. But she different than most people. Her papa is half Italian half Rom. Her mama is half Slovene half Serb. Marta had blindness to other people's hatred. It was blindness that maybe killed her." Dimitri lowered his head and wiped his eyes with his sleeve. Jaleh got up to retrieve a box of tissues from a nearby table for Dimitri.

Dimitri took a deep breath and continued. "One day some crazy people come to her office. They fight with her and drag her away, maybe later shoot her, I don't know. Our maid Amina hears whole thing; she was in bathroom changing baby diaper. When evil men leave, Amina steps into office and nobody is there. My beautiful Marta, mother of my boy, was taken away and maybe never coming back. I am impossible to work after that. Even I could work, other people tell me not to come back to my fishing boat because I am husband of 'agitator.' Then someone burn my boat. After they put note under my door to leave Belgrade or me and boy be killed. I tell Amina to leave and escape crazy place Belgrade; it is not for her, good Muslim girl from Sarajevo. I hope Amina escape like me. I pray Marta escape too. I don't know. Maybe she did. Dushan tell me many times his mama talk to him in his dreams."

Jaleh took Dimitri's hands in hers and held them as he composed himself. "I know how difficult this must be for you, especially having a little son to raise after such a tragedy and having to flee your homeland. Many of us here in our little Bahá'í community on the island and in Liverpool have experienced such things. I myself, and many of the Bahá'ís here, are refugees from Iran. We know what it is like to have to flee one's homeland in the face of murderous oppression."

Jaleh opened a manila folder and perused it for a few seconds. Setting it down on the desk, she smiled and said, "If it's okay with you, we have arranged an introduction with the owner of a fishing boat here in Ramsey. With your experience on those two rivers, you should have no problem getting on a crew. We also have a list of boarding houses here in Ramsey. The government will provide you with two months rent to give you time to receive your first paycheck. Also, my husband Thomas will make an appointment with you soon to go over your legal status."

In the two years since that interview, Dimitri and Dushan had settled into a peaceful life. Dimitri earned enough to be able to move into a small apartment, a modest improvement over the boarding house. Mr. Kilpatrick helped Dimitri understand his new legal status on the island. Dimitri's only worry now was that the fishing crew was due to head out to the Outer Hebrides in a week, and would spend a month on the water before returning to Ramsey. It was the first time in two years that he had been invited to join such a long expedition.

Dimitri needed a babysitter.

CHAPTER SIX:
A DARING PROPOSAL

Carolyn Markos's dream frightened her more than her other generic anxiety dreams with absurd events and people acting as stand-ins for real-life events and people. This dream featured a menacing person, the very man she transacted business with about six months earlier in Liverpool. He was a Bosnian, once a wealthy merchant from Sarajevo. Forced to flee by the advancing Serbian army, Mr. Aksoy chose Liverpool as his new home, a home that was very accommodating to him and his millions.

In her dream, Carolyn found herself cornered in an alley with Aksoy's Mercedes blocking the only way out. Aksoy and his driver got out of the car and began walking into the alley.

"You're late, Ms. Markos. Too late, I'm sorry to say. Time is money, and you're out of time if you're out of money."

Carolyn's first reaction was alarm—Aksoy used her maiden name instead of her married name, Owens, the name she had used since she and her ex moved here from Liverpool over 12 years ago. Nobody knew her maiden name.

When Carolyn saw Aksoy's driver reach into his jacket pocket her heart began beating faster. Then the driver pulled a ringing phone, cord and all, out of his jacket and offered it to Carolyn. She woke up to the sound of her own phone ringing. Her tee shirt was soaked and she could hardly breathe. When the phone rang a third time she raised herself up on her elbow and started to reach for it almost in a fugue state. Before picking up she groaned aloud, "I've got to move, there's no way I can stay ahead of him as long as I'm anywhere in the British Isles."

Carolyn owed Aksoy a tidy sum--3,000 pounds—the balance of the 5,000 pounds she borrowed to use in her little side job. When she borrowed the money, she was working as a placement specialist for an adoption agency in Douglas, capital of the Isle of Man. Most of the agency's clients these days were refugees from war-torn Yugoslavia. Her co-worker Derrick Nelson had just returned from holiday in Liverpool and told her about meeting Aksoy at a casino there. Aksoy had told Derrick that if he and Carolyn ever wanted to break out of the rut they were in working for a government agency, they would need some seed money to "get serious about the refugee problem in the UK."

Carolyn recalled how before Derrick's meeting with Aksoy she and Derrick had talked about ways to get around the red tape impeding locals from adopting refugee children, not to mention making a lot more money than they earned at the agency. Several weeks after those conversations, Derrick told her about Aksoy.

"I met someone who says he can help us move some of these refugees into homes a lot quicker than the 'proper' way to do it. It will take some money to pay off the right people, but he knows a man who might help us with the money. I don't know if we should get involved with him. He seems a bit slimy. What do you think?"

"I say we go for it. Don't be so paranoid. You know as well as I that we can do plenty of under-the-table adoptions with enough seed money. Let's meet with the guy."

Mr. Aksoy impressed Carolyn as pretty sophisticated and easy going. They borrowed money from him and started their new career as adoption expediters. A rented office in Liverpool would be their home base. Aksoy would use his contacts in the Balkan refugee community, and Carolyn and Derrick would procure couples who wanted to adopt and could pay top dollar for an "expedited" adoptions. Carolyn and Derrick completed quite a few adoptions under their new system before someone turned them in. Carolyn told herself it probably was a family who turned out not to want a war-traumatized child after all, or a birth parent who belatedly and unexpectedly showed up looking for his or her child. Carolyn tried very hard to believe, unsuccessfully, that she and Derrick were merely providing a service by arranging adoptions for families who were either ineligible for the agency's services, or did not want to go through the long bureaucratic process. But that was only part of the story. Carolyn and Derrick charged exorbitant fees for what they did, always off the books and in advance. And the children were not, as Carolyn tried to convince herself, unloved or homeless or destined to be a public burden. Often she and Derrick, and Mr. Aksoy before them, lied to birth parents to convince them of the advantages, or lied to them about how much money they would receive for giving up their child for adoption.

It was the latter practice that got them in trouble and led to their legal troubles. Several birth parents referred to them by Aksoy complained to the Liverpool police that they had not received their fee. The police told the agency in the Isle of Man about the irregularities. The agency questioned Carolyn and Derrick, who denied involvement. But their denials were unpersuasive and Carolyn and Derrick were terminated. The Isle of Man social services oversight board issued subpoenas in anticipation of a possible criminal prosecution. The investigation turned up numerous bank deposits of cash—often thousands of pounds at a time, much more than a civil servant could earn. Shortly afterward, one of the adopting families attempted to contact the Liverpool office to inquire about returning the child, who they claimed was autistic and unmanageable. The family naturally wanted their fee back. When they learned that the office phone was disconnected, they called the police. This confluence of events made their prosecution for child abduction a virtual certainty.

What finally put the nail in the coffin for Carolyn was Derrick's decision to cooperate in the investigation in exchange for no charges being filed against him. With a likely criminal prosecution facing Carolyn, and the impounding of her bank account, Carolyn became terrified and desperate.

During the legal process, unable to access the money in her bank account, Carolyn asked Aksoy for an extension of the loan's due date. Aksoy was not sympathetic.

"I didn't escape from the hell of Bosnia just to give away my hard-earned money. You will come up with it, and I don't think I need to spell out what will happen to you if you don't." Carolyn didn't doubt that Aksoy was capable of doing her harm should he feel it necessary.

When the phone rang, Carolyn was not in the mood to talk to anyone, let alone the man she feared was on the other end of the line. Before she could pick up, the phone's fourth ring activated her message machine. She listened as her obnoxious cousin Burt Sandor, calling from San Francisco, left a message. She was nursing a hangover from her binge last night, a binge brought on by her legal troubles and not having found a real job in the two months since being fired. She had so far avoided starvation and eviction by taking the odd babysitting or typing job.

Even if it hadn't been 4:00 a.m. when Burt called, she probably wouldn't have picked up the phone when she heard his voice on the answering machine. "The stupid bastard has lived in the States since 1994 and he still can't remember the time difference," she grumbled as she turned over in the bed and pulled the covers over her head.

Carolyn recalled her mixed emotions five years earlier when Burt and his wife Irene left Liverpool to attend graduate school in a place called Palo Alto. *At least I won't have to talk to the conceited ass at family get-togethers,* she thought. She was also bitterly envious of Burt's undeserved good fortune. Carolyn always felt that Burt owed his well-to-do upbringing to his mother's choice of husband. Burt's mother, Margaret, had married Bruce Sandor, who along with his brother Dennis claimed to be heirs to what Margaret proudly referred to as "the Sandor family fortune." Carolyn often wondered what the source of that family fortune was, but Margaret never explained.

Dennis, unlike Bruce, squandered most of his inheritance as a single young man. He fell prey to foolish investments, although to his credit he restored a beautiful home in Liverpool to its former magnificence and turned it into a Bed and Breakfast inn. When Dennis finally married Carolyn's aunt Helena Markos, they were not blessed with wealth or children. At least they had their B&B to live in, until they lost it when they could not keep up the payments on the mortgage. After that Dennis went back to work for a coal mining company. He was killed in a mine accident a year later.

Nor was Helena's brother David Markos, Carolyn's father, blessed with wealth, and he did not improve his financial portfolio by marrying Carolyn's mother, Lisa Boudros. Lisa was a waitress who abandoned her job once she became pregnant with Carolyn. Carolyn often brooded on the unfairness of her situation in the Sandor-Markos family trees.

Burt's undeserved good fortune only got better, or worse from Carolyn's point of view, with the birth of Burt and Irene's two sons. Danilo was born six months before their departure for the States, and Markos was born almost exactly a year later in Palo Alto, California. Burt named Markos after Burt's grandmother's family name, which in Carolyn's view was purely to curry favor with Burt's mother, Margaret. Carolyn often recalled that when Markos was born, the old moneybags Margaret couldn't stop talking about the honor Burt did to the Markos line. Nor did Carolyn believe for moment Burt's reminder that Carolyn herself should feel honored by that name because it was her name as well, through her father. She remembered how annoyed she felt several years ago when Burt called her from California to tell her he had decided to honor her Markos family name by naming his second boy Markos. "And I'm sure your ma and grandma were pleased as well," she replied, trying to let just enough scoff into her voice without being offensive.

What really got Carolyn's goat was the way Burt managed to sweet talk his mother into setting up a trust for the boys. "Not a farthing for anyone else in the Markos-Sandor clans, you can bet," Carolyn muttered. Carolyn and Burt were second cousins—or first cousins "once removed," Carolyn could never get it straight—and grew up in Liverpool. Irene Argyris was also a cousin of some sort, and lived in Liverpool as well. Carolyn was six years older than Burt and eight years older than Irene. Up until Carolyn went off to college, the three of them saw each other at least every other month at family gatherings. An only child of working-class parents, when Carolyn graduated high school she considered herself lucky to have been admitted to a local college on a full scholarship, where she got a degree in social work. Not long after graduation she married Trevor Owens and got a job in her field in the Isle of Man's capital city of Douglas, in the Irish Sea near Liverpool.

Burt was admitted to Cambridge University, as was Irene two years later. Those two were excited to be attending the same school. They had been dating, and some time in Irene's second year—Burt's final year—she accepted his marriage proposal. Burt received a very generous offer of a scholarship in the MBA program at Stanford University in the United States. The scholarship would easily support them both and, as it turned out, their expected child.

Irene believed she had always loved Burt. But as their marriage matured she recognized something in Burt that he had been hiding, or at least unconsciously suppressing. What she had always attributed to his assertive personality was much more than that. Burt always had a knack for getting his way. One story Irene heard from one of Burt's elementary school friends, who recounted an incident in third grade. The teacher, Miss Kerry, was about to discipline Burt for some misbehavior, and told him to spend the rest of the geography lesson in the coatroom. Burt's response electrified everyone in the room. When he complained of unfairness his complaint conveyed a strong refusal to obey. To the astonishment of everyone, Miss Kerry abruptly backed off. "I think you've learned your lesson, Burt, so stay in your seat and we'll continue the lesson." Burt's facial expression was part smile, part bewilderment, but something else was communicated—a sense of relief mixed with vindication at winning the right to go unpunished. The rest of the class was anything but relieved. Most were annoyed that Burt had escaped what he so richly deserved. Others were simply dumbfounded that Miss Kerry didn't follow through—she had a well-deserved reputation as a disciplinarian.

When Burt and Irene were kids, it would often annoy Irene when Burt got pushy, as she called it. But as they grew into their late adolescence her feelings toward him became warmer. She assumed that Burt had matured into a less self-centered person. Later, several years into their marriage, Irene came to believe that Burt hadn't changed at all. Perhaps she had been unconsciously deflecting his pushiness. Or maybe he had perfected the subtlety of his assertiveness to the point that others, including Irene, were unaware of it.

At first, she wanted to believe in her own skill in dealing with self-centered people. As she passed through puberty, she got better and better at it, a skill that became a necessity during her years in secondary school. She attended a ritzy private girls' school, and those girls could be mercilessly cruel. Irene learned how to cultivate the goodwill of those classmates who were not really her friends but might otherwise have become her enemies. She learned to use her knack without drawing attention to herself. With a degree of subtlety she became quite proud of, Irene fostered the impression that she was a friend to, or at least an ally of, everyone. That was not to say she had no deep friendships. There were a few girls with whom she became close and hoped to remain so. But those friendships fell away once Irene became infatuated with Burt.

Her first realization that what she once called Burt's assertiveness had never gone away, and in fact was much more than assertiveness, occurred about three years into their marriage. It was January 1996. They were living in Palo Alto and Burt was about to finish his MBA. Burt announced that they should take a vacation in Vancouver,

British Columbia with their two boys to celebrate his impending graduation from Stanford. Danilo was then a little over two and Markos was a year younger. Burt told Irene he wanted them to go as Americans, not Brits on student visas.

"But, Burt, we've talked about this before. Remember what the foreign student advisor, Mr. Zeigler, told us? We're not eligible. Plain and simple."

"It doesn't matter what Zeigler thinks. I think otherwise. I've made an appointment for us at the immigration office in San Francisco. Let's just find out what the truth is."

Looking back at that time, Irene recalled her shock at what happened at the immigration office. Burt finessed the immigration official, despite their clear ineligibility, into granting them their green cards. Irene now understood it for what it was—a talent for persuasion that was extraordinary in the fullest sense of the word. That experience helped Irene understand not only how Burt's talent worked, but also helped her appreciate her own strength in dealing with Burt.

After their US citizenship was granted, Burt's career took off like a rocket. Irene's career aspirations, which had been put aside with Markos's birth in November 1994, were further derailed when he was diagnosed four years later with a terminal form of leukemia. Adding shock to Irene's depression over Markos's sickness was Burt's announcement, six months after that, of his plan to adopt a third son to "replace" Markos. This scheme of Burt's was the reason for his phone call to his cousin Carolyn.

A few minutes after listening to Burt's message, Carolyn's hangover seemed to be a little more manageable, so she decided to get up and call Burt back. She threw back the covers, sat up in bed, and hit the call back button on her phone. When Burt answered on the first ring, she croaked into the phone, "Burt, you sot, were you drunk when you called? Do you know what time it is here?"

"So sorry, Carolyn. I've been rather overwhelmed of late. I have some bad news."

"Bad news? I'll give you bad news. I've been let go. Do you hear? Let go after 12 years of stellar performance reviews. And for what, you may well ask? For a violation of the rules. Seems the powers that be got their knickers in a twist over my brilliant little solution to the boom in all these immigrant orphans arriving in Douglas and

Liverpool seemingly by the boatload. I merely cut through the red tape and found good homes for lots of them. Helped me pay my bills too, I might add. Now, guess what I do to make ends meet. I'm a babysitter, Burt, a babysitter of all things!" Carolyn didn't feel like mentioning the pending criminal case or her predicament with Aksoy.

There was a momentary silence on Burt's end. Then, having gathered his wits and figured out something sympathetic to say, he responded, "Oh, damn, Carolyn, I'm so sorry! How terrible. That's awful about your firing! Especially since that's sort of what I was calling about. I wanted to avail myself of your services. My mom told me what you'd been doing. And she was quite proud—you know how upset she was becoming about the influx of refugees: 'a bloody horde of the great unwashed, and they can't even speak proper English.' She approved of your little under-the-table adoption scheme."

"That's not bloody likely to happen now, is it? And thanks for your sympathy for my plight. Do you realize it's been almost three months since I was let go? Did you ever respond to my letter telling you the bad news? No, I'm afraid you didn't. I'm getting desperate, Burt. Anyway, what's the bad news you're so obviously dying to tell me?"

"It's terrible news, in fact, Carolyn. My little Markos was diagnosed with leukemia and doesn't have long to live."

All dislike of Burt aside, Carolyn's response was warm and sincere. "Oh, Burt, I'm so sorry to hear that. That's awful! I apologize for being short with you and crying about my own troubles. I feel terrible. Is there no hope for the lad?"

"I'm afraid not. He's not expected to live more than six months, probably less. Part of why I called was to ask a huge favor of you."

"You name it. I'll help out in any way I can."

"Well, this may seem a little callous of me, Carolyn, but I had been hoping to hire you to facilitate one of your expedited adoptions. I would like to adopt a boy Markos's age, and as soon as possible."

"Isn't it a little premature, Burt? I mean, most parents would want to wait a fair amount of time before adopting another child. And, anyway, why adopt? Why don't you and Irene just have another child? You're not even 29 yet."

"Let me explain, but what I'm about to tell you, Carolyn, is in the strictest confidence. I trust that our conversation will not be repeated or disclosed to anyone, especially not to anyone in our family."

"Of course not, it goes without saying."

"The reason we need to adopt is really two-fold. I'm primarily worried about Irene. She's been incredibly fragile about this. If I could convince her that we have the golden opportunity of an emergency adoption of another four-and-a-half-year-old boy, I really think it would pull Irene out of her maternal depression. It might also help Markos and Dani by distracting them from Markos's illness."

Carolyn found this primary reason less than convincing. "What's the other reason?"

"The other reason has to do with my mom's trust. You probably didn't know that she set it up so that each boy will inherit half of the money in the trust at age 21, but if they die before that their share reverts to my mom's favorite charity. Besides the pot of money in the trust, there's also a lot of 'maintenance' money in the trust for their upbringing, which is paid to me on a monthly basis. She still controls the trust, you know. The pot of money in the trust is quite generous, as she never tires of telling me."

"But how does adopting another child help you keep the trust intact?" Carolyn began to get a picture of the real reason behind Burt's call.

"Not just a child; a boy Markos's age, and before he dies. I want to, for want of a better word, replace him."

Carolyn was rendered momentarily speechless. "You mean to tell me you want to deceive your mom into thinking the adopted son is actually Markos? Just so you could keep receiving your monthly checks? Doesn't your mom know what Markos looks like? Hasn't she visited you there in California?"

"No, she has never made it over here; she's afraid of flying with her bad heart. And the only pictures I've sent her have been baby pictures. I really think if I could adopt a boy the same age, and with at least some degree of family resemblance, I could pull this off. You know, Carolyn, my request is not as bad as it might seem at first. If mother were to hear that her little Markos died, I worry that it may devastate her. She's not in the greatest health, you know."

Carolyn paused while she collected her thoughts. What Burt seemed to be suggesting made her very uncomfortable.

"Burt, I think you're about to ask me to buy, or steal, a child for you. Is that basically it?"

"Not at all. I want to adopt a four-and-a-half-year-old boy. I want to complete the adoption as soon as possible. I don't want to have to go through all the bureaucratic formalities; nor do I have time to do that. I am hoping that with your knowledge and expertise, and as a merciful gesture to your cousin, you would help me accomplish this. As you know, I have money. I realize adoptions are not cheap, and I'm willing to pay a premium to expedite the matter."

"And just how would this boy, assuming one could be found, travel to the USA without what you call the bureaucratic niceties being taken care of? I've handled several unofficial adoptions, but never one involving international travel."

"Not to worry. I've got it covered. When Markos was an infant, barely a year old, Irene and I took him and Dani to Vancouver, a city in western Canada, for some R&R. Irene, Dani and I had gotten our first American passports, and I was able to put Markos on my passport because he was so young. What I'm hoping to do now, if it all works out, is to fly to London with that same passport, which still has Markos's name and baby picture in it. I'll proceed to the Isle of Man, or Liverpool, or wherever you hopefully will be awaiting me with my brand-new adopted four-and-a-half-year-old boy. We will all—you included—fly back to San Francisco pretending that the 'new' Markos is now a few years older. Since the photo in my passport is that of an infant, it won't matter that the older child doesn't look like his baby picture."

Carolyn was again rendered speechless, not just by the audacity of Burt's proposal, but by the excitement of it as well. Especially the idea that she would be paid and would accompany them to the States.

"Burt, this is going to be a very risky operation. Assuming I can find an orphan, how do we make sure the boy doesn't say something suspicious, or worse, at the airport?"

"I'm not worried about that. In all likelihood, the boy will be either too sleepy to say anything, or he'll be too overwhelmed by the sights and sounds of Heathrow airport and the anticipation of flying. We can play it by ear. And don't forget, I am an airport executive at the San Francisco International Airport and as such will have a certain privileged status when it comes to moving through customs."

"I don't know, Burt. This really sounds terribly risky. I'll have to think about it. Can you call me back later today? And don't forget the time difference."

"Fine, I understand your nervousness. I also want to say that Irene and I are completely on the same page on this. We are desperately hoping this can happen. We're willing to offer you $20,000 if you'll help us, and of course pay for your airfare and all expenses."

"Well, I can tell you right off I hardly think your offer is generous. I'll assume that that's the going rate for foreign adoptions in the States. But in this particular situation, I would have to ask for double that. This looks to be a very complicated and risky request."

"I had a feeling you would try to bargain with me. I would hate to think you're trying to take advantage of me. I'm not a millionaire, you know. Other than this trust, and the monthly maintenance stipend I get from my mother, I'm really not as well off as you appear to think. I'm a simply a low-level bureaucrat at the San Francisco airport. I make a good salary by British standards, but a pittance by San Francisco standards. It's definitely not a salary that puts me into your imaginary category. But, look, let's cut to the chase. I can raise my offer to $30,000 but no more. Will you at least give it some consideration?"

"Your story touches my heart, Burt, it really does. Sure, your offer sounds fair enough, even if not as generous as you pretend. But, OK, let me see what I can find out from my sources. I'll call you back later today or tomorrow. But I have to say that even if it looks like I can swing it, I'll need you to wire me the money immediately; I'm in a very, very serious bind."

Breathing a sigh of relief, Burt said, "Sure, I can do that. When you're ready to go forward with the adoption, call me with your bank's name and account number."

"I'd just as soon not use my regular bank. Long ago, before I married Trevor Owens, I had a bank account in Liverpool under my maiden name. I never closed that account and have always kept a little 'mad money' in it. I'll have you wire the funds there when the time comes."

Carolyn put down the phone and went outside to the little balcony of her second-floor apartment. Looking out at Ramsey Harbour, she had a moment of deep sadness at the idea of leaving this pleasant place, possibly for good. On the other hand, the thought of prison reappeared in her mind. After a few minutes in the chill early morning air, she walked back inside, sat on the edge of the couch, and asked herself some hard questions. *Really, Carolyn, what has your life here amounted to when you honestly think about it? Or your life in Liverpool, for that matter? Don't you think you deserve a change?*

She lost track of the time as she sat on the couch reviewing all the failures in her life. Gradually she came to a realization that was deeply unsettling, frightening even: there was absolutely no way she could find another orphan so quickly or without the customary adoption fee she and Derrick normally paid out to Aksoy. She would have to do something different, something bold, something that flooded her mind with thoughts of immorality and danger. What Burt was proposing, while it offered a way out of her financial dilemma, nevertheless paralyzed her with fear.

That fear, however, was quickly replaced with a greater fear when she remembered her nightmarish encounter with Aksoy and his threats. But then a curious thing happened. Her fear of committing the crime of child abduction merged into the fear of being killed by Aksoy and transformed that fear into hatred—hatred that escalated first from hatred of Aksoy, then to hatred of Turks, hatred of Yugoslavians, hatred of immigrants in general. Her hatred was reawakening her long-suppressed emotional reaction to having to deal with refugees for the past few years. She realized she even hated her own ethnic background. *Being Greek never did me a bit of good, now did it! I'm still a foreigner here, and will always be a foreigner.* She could feel herself warming up from all the angry feelings welling up inside her. At that moment, she made her decision.

Carolyn got up from the couch and picked up the phone. She dialed the home number of her former colleague in Douglas. "Elaine? This is Carolyn Owens, your old partner in crime."

"Jesus, Carolyn, do you realize it's not even 6:00 a.m.? And I don't appreciate being called your partner in crime. I had no part in your little under-the-table adoption operation. "

"Now, now, you know I was only joking. And you also know that Derrick and I made some very sad couples a lot happier, not to mention helping out with the growing national problem of orphans and broken, dysfunctional, and possibly criminal families being dumped on England from all over Eastern Europe."

"Whatever you say, Carolyn my dear. What's on your mind? I hope you have a good reason for waking me up at such an ungodly hour on a Saturday."

"Well, this is a little embarrassing. You know it's been almost three months since I was fired. I am almost completely destitute and haven't been able to find a regular job. I've been doing some temp work and even some babysitting. I was wondering if I could get on with that hoity-toity babysitting network you once told me about. I just need a little cash to pay a few bills before I find a real job. Could you give me their number?"

"I guess so, maybe. But you know they only use experienced adults with stellar references."

Elaine's hesitant response was what Carolyn dreaded, but she took a breath and plunged ahead with all deliberate boldness. "Could I give your name as a reference? They would certainly think highly of me with a recommendation from you." Carolyn listened to her heart beat for what seemed like forever before she heard Elaine's quiet reply.

"I guess I could do that. But you can't seriously hope to support yourself doing babysitting. It's only occasional work at best. And the babysitting clients are mostly well-to-do young wives bored with shopping and talking on the phone."

"I don't care. I just need a few days work in the short term to meet my rent and pay a few bills. I feel certain I'm going to be working at a real job very soon—I've had a couple of positive interviews in the past week or so. And what's more, I have some babysitting clients right now, and I'm sure they could provide me with recommendations."

"Fine. I'll give them a call later this morning. Are you still using your married name? You know, as long as I've known you, I've only known you as Owens."

"Yeah, all my papers and stuff are still under the jerk's name. For now, I'm not going to complicate matters and change my name."

When Elaine had given her the phone number of Elaine's friend's babysitting network, Carolyn decided to make a call after lunch.

CHAPTER SEVEN:
CAROLYN GETS A JOB

The sun shone bright late in the afternoon as Dimitri hung up the pay phone outside his favorite café. He had just gotten off work and had only another 15 minutes before he had to walk over to Dushan's daycare center and take Dushan home. Dimitri was starting to get nervous. His fishing crew was scheduled to leave for the North Sea in a week, but he had not yet found a babysitter who could stay with Dushan for more than a couple of nights, let alone live in his apartment for a month. Each of the half dozen names he was given by the Ramsey agency were either unable to commit to a whole month, or they couldn't move in to the apartment and live there with Dushan, or they charged too much, or they were too young and inexperienced.

Dimitri decided to expand his search. He pulled out a couple of names he had been given of babysitters in Douglas. He mumbled, "I doubt anyone in Douglas wants to come all the way up here in Ramsey for babysitting job. But maybe someone likes to take vacation."

After half an hour on the phone with four or five babysitters, he was not optimistic about his chances. He was even less optimistic as he pondered whether to bother calling this last number. It was, he was told, a high-end referral agency that catered to a different class of client than Dimitri, and he doubted he could afford anyone listed in their directory. "What do I got to lose? Here goes nothing."

Instead of a live person, he got an answering machine listing a series of phone numbers but no names. The recording specified the areas of the island where the owner of each phone number would take babysitting jobs. Dimitri called the first number in the Ramsey portion of the list, and someone answered. He was encouraged when he spoke with a woman who identified herself as Carolyn Owens.

"Miss Owens, hello. I am Dimitri Sava. I have four-year-old boy, and I need babysitter. My job is fisherman. My crew will soon leave for month fishing job in North Sea. I am single father with nobody to take care of boy while I gone. So I need good person to live in apartment and take care of him."

"Thank you for calling me, Mr. Sava. Yes, I might be able to help you. But we should meet and discuss it."

"Yes, that is good. And excuse me, but do you have reference? Someone you worked for before?"

"Of course. In fact, my previous job was also for a fisherman, Mr. Carson Leary. You may know him."

"Yes, I do know him. He is fisherman on another boat. Is nice guy. I will speak to him."

"If you are satisfied with what he says about me, shall we meet in a couple of days? How about Monday?"

"That is good. I will call you after I speak to Carson."

Carson Leary confirmed that Carolyn had been a good, diligent and pleasant babysitter. Dimitri decided to meet Carolyn and check her out.

Dimitri was relieved yet again when he met Carolyn. She looked to be in her thirties. She seemed pleasant, attractive even. Dark hair and an almost Mediterranean complexion, darker than many people Dimitri had met on this island.

"You have a nice apartment," Carolyn said as she took off her coat and handed it to Dimitri. She stepped into the living room and smiled at how neat everything was. "Oh, I see you have an aquarium. I love tropical fish."

"Actually, Miss Owens, they are fresh water. Please, will you have some tea? I just made a pot."

"Thank you, yes." Carolyn sat at one end of the sofa. Hearing a young voice humming wordless in another room, Carolyn said, "That must be the little lad, no?"

"Yes. Dushan, come in and meet Miss Owens."

Dushan stepped into the room, smiled, and then ran back out, giggling.

Carolyn and Dimitri chuckled and turned to the matter at hand. Dimitri spoke first. "Miss Owens, like I said on phone, my fishing crew and I will be at sea for almost one month and I need good person to stay with Dushan. But I am not very rich. Maybe a little rich when I return, if fishing is good. Will you accept 100 pounds?"

Carolyn forced a brief frown to cross her brow but then said after a pause, "That will be fine. In all likelihood this will be my last babysitting job. I am taking an office secretary job in six weeks, so this job with little Dushan will almost bring me up to then."

Dimitri smiled and said, "That's wonderful. I am happy for you. And happy for me and Dushan also. He is good boy and I think everything will be fine."

Over the next two cups of tea, Carolyn and Dimitri finalized the arrangement. As Carolyn stood and put on her coat, she said, "This will give me a chance to wind things up here in Ramsey and look for an apartment in Liverpool. And speaking of Liverpool, is it okay with you if I take little Dushan with me for a ferry ride to Liverpool one day to just stroll about the neighborhood I have in mind?"

"Sure. I think ferry ride he will enjoy. He loved very much the ferry we took when we came to the Isle of Man."

Carolyn looked at Dimitri with a hint of worry on her face. "And you're sure you won't be out at sea for more than a month? I don't want to over extend myself here; I have to be able to begin my new job on the date agreed."

"Right. I understand. They are telling us boats will catch all salmon they can hold probably less than month, for sure not longer, and then we return immediately."

"Why don't I continue taking the lad to his daycare at least half days two or three days a week so he doesn't feel bored?"

"That is good idea. I hoping he could continue in his daycare at least some days. He likes the teacher and she likes him. And he has couple little buddies there."

As Carolyn began to walk to the door, Dushan trotted into the room holding a little Star Wars action figure and proudly held it up for Carolyn to admire. She smiled and said, "Now, let me see. I think that must be Luke Skywalker. Am I right?"

"No, no, no. It's Bobafett. Luke is on my bed. Do you want to see my room?"

They walked hand in hand and Dushan proudly pointed out his most prized possessions. Carolyn gushed in amazement at his collection of stuffed bears, rabbits and dogs. Dushan showed her his parakeet, took it out of the cage, and let it hop onto her finger. Putting the little bird back into the cage, Dushan led Carolyn out of the bedroom and into the kitchen. He then showed her his proudest accomplishment—how he could entice his parakeet to chirp in rapid staccato by opening the tap at the kitchen sink.

After his new babysitter left, Dimitri breathed a sigh of relief and collapsed on the sofa. When Dushan came into the living room, Dimitri said to him, "Come, my little hero. Let's go eat pizza. I have something exciting to tell you." At the pizza place, he called his boss to confirm he would join the crew when their ship departed in a week.

Carolyn's reaction, on the other hand, was anything but relief. She felt like throwing up as she drove back to her apartment. When she walked in the door, she decided she couldn't go through with it. She picked up the phone and dialed Burt's number.

"Burt," she cried into the phone, "I can't do it. I don't have it in me." Her voice cracked and she only just managed to contain the sobs that were threatening to erupt.

"Carolyn, I'm glad you called, even though it's 6:00 a.m. for Christ's sake. Listen, don't do anything yet; just let me get dressed and pour myself a cup of coffee and I'll call you right back."

Half an hour later, Carolyn felt no closer to making a decision when the phone rang. She picked it up and when she heard Burt's voice she said, "Look, Burt, this is killing me. I feel like shit. I don't know which of my emotions is worse: my dread at the thought of going through with this, or my anger at you for even suggesting it. You dangled a bag of money at me and wore me down with your sob story about little Markos. Well, what about this little boy over here, not to mention his daddy? Any thoughts about the impact on them?"

"Why don't you give me a picture of the situation? What's the dad do for a living? Where's the mom? What kind of vibe did you get from their relationship?"

As Burt asked these questions, Carolyn felt a calming sensation arise in her chest. She walked over to the couch and sat down. She took a few breaths before answering. "He's a refugee from Yugoslavia. They live in a tiny apartment in an old part of town, one of those low-income developments built after the war. He's a fisherman. Single. Widower, I assume; he suspects his wife was killed in the war."

"And the boy? How does the dad treat the boy?"

Again Carolyn felt herself becoming calmer. "I don't know, Burt. I didn't really see them interact. The dad seemed distracted, worried.

Didn't talk to the boy, really. Nor did the boy talk to the dad." Carolyn stood up, walked to the sliding glass balcony door and opened it. The breeze from the sea calmed her even more.

After a long pause, almost as if he were waiting for Carolyn's mood to change, Burt's voice came back over the phone. "Well, how do you feel about the boy having to grow up in poverty in an economically depressed area like the Isle of Man? Realistically, what chance do you think he has to succeed in life?"

This question felt like more than a question. And of course, it was. Carolyn felt the question blossom into a conclusion, a reality, a certitude. Minutes passed as she stood in silence, allowing the feeling of certitude suffuse her with well-being. She could feel herself agreeing with Burt's implied judgment as to the boy's chances in life with such odds stacked against him. She felt her sense of self-contempt begin to dissipate as she saw the boy living his life as an American living and growing up in San Francisco, instead of remaining in this immigrant limbo as a foreigner with no chance of obtaining citizenship or material success. A thought formed itself in her mind: *This change will no doubt save him from the exploitation by the criminal element all too common in the immigrant community.* The other, certainly more dominant, emotion she felt was the combined excitement of earning $30,000, the relief at the prospect of avoiding criminal prosecution, and the idea of traveling to San Francisco, probably even staying there for good.

When Burt was silent for a moment, Carolyn made her mind up and said, "I hope I'm doing the right thing, Burt. Buy our plane tickets. We're in business. When you get here we'll be returning in the company of a four-and-a-half-year-old boy named Dushan Sava."

"That's great. His name almost sounds Greek. What's he look like?"

"Olive complexion, hazel eyes, brown hair. Listen, I'm supposed to be moving into their apartment in less than a week. His dad will be on a month-long fishing trip off the Outer Hebrides islands. Like I said, the boy's mom is no longer in the picture. You should meet us in Liverpool in about a week. You remember that Bed and Breakfast our uncle Dennis used to run near the River Mersey? It's no longer in the family, but still quite nice, from all accounts. The boy and I will be staying there waiting for you. Make sure you have the money and tickets all taken care of. Including my one-way ticket to SF. I don't want to be locked into a return date just yet. My UK passport is practically brand new. I got it under my maiden name right after I divorced that pig Trevor. One of my bank accounts, the one in Liverpool, is where you should wire my fee. I'll call you back with the branch and account number."

The next order of business for Carolyn was to inform her landlord that she was moving out in a week. She decided to donate her meager assortment of furniture to the local thrift store, along with her kitchen stuff and many of her clothes. *I'm going to have to do a bit of shopping in San Francisco. I'm sure Burt will be only too eager to help me out in that endeavor!* Carolyn planned on staying in San Francisco and taking advantage of Burt's hospitality as long as possible.

Over the next few days, Carolyn sold her car and wrapped things up in Ramsey. She called the B&B in Liverpool and reserved a room for herself under her maiden name, Carolyn Markos, but didn't say anything about the boy. Using her married name, Carolyn Owens, she called the babysitting agency and had them remove her phone number from the answering machine. She told the owner, "I only used the service once before I was hired by a temp agency in Douglas to do clerical work. Thanks for including me on the listing, though. It no doubt would have come in very handy had this regular job not come through."

After concluding her business with the agency Carolyn called Dimitri's work and left a message for him to call her. He called her late that afternoon and they confirmed the date she would show up at his apartment. She then called Burt again to make sure that he had taken care of air tickets and gave him her Liverpool bank's info. He told her everything was set and he would meet her at the B&B in four days.

CHAPTER EIGHT:
THE FIRST JOURNEY, 1999

Dimitri agreed with Carolyn's suggestion that she and Dushan accompany him to the docks to see him off. The boy seemed to be very excited to see the ship, a huge, high-speed craft that would transport Dimitri and 14 other fishermen from Ramsey to the Outer Hebrides. There, the crew would embark on a fishing trawler much larger than the modest boats they used in the Irish Sea. As they stood on the dock in the glorious morning sun, Dimitri felt things couldn't be better. He would earn a lot of money from this fishing expedition, perhaps enough to use as a down payment on his own boat, or even move into a bigger apartment. And Dushan appeared to be taking the prospect of his papa's imminent absence pretty well. Of course, being so young, Dushan couldn't really imagine how long a month would feel.

"My little champion, what do you think I bring you back the biggest salmon in the whole Atlantic?"

"And bring me a shark, too, papa; I want to see a shark!"

Carolyn asked Dushan, "Do you really want a shark? Maybe a small shark that won't be so dangerous?"

"Yes, a small shark and a small salmon that I can put in my fish tank at home. They can be friends."

Dimitri smiled at Carolyn, who didn't return the smile but seemed preoccupied at something. "You are okay, Miss Owens? Maybe you are tired at being up so early in the morning?"

"Yes, but I will have to get used to getting up this early for the next few weeks with this little early bird of ours, won't I? Does he ever let you sleep in?"

"On Saturdays and Sundays are his sleepy mornings. The other days he jumps out of bed happy to see his daycare pals."

Their conversation was interrupted by the horn announcing the commencement of boarding. Dimitri gave Dushan a long hug, trying to keep a dry eye while Dushan was distracted by the hum of the ship's motors. "You see, Mr. Sava, Dushan will be just fine while you're gone. And, Dushan, your papa will be back soon, won't he?" Dushan nodded his head vigorously, still not taking his eyes off the gorgeous ship, which in his mind was as big as a battleship.

Dushan and Carolyn waved to Dimitri as he boarded the ship. When it pulled away from the dock, Carolyn and Dushan took a taxi back to Dimitri's apartment. She gathered up Dushan's clothes and a few toys and packed them into his backpack. They then walked the few blocks to Carolyn's apartment. After retrieving her already-packed suitcase they walked back to the harbor and waited for the next departure of the "Isle of Man Steam Packet" to Liverpool, a three-hour ferry ride.

"Are we going to catch up with Papa's boat, Carolyn?"

"No, remember when we talked about visiting a place called Liverpool? We're going to do that now on this really cool boat. You'll love it."

Once on the boat, Dushan explored the magnificent old ferry from stem to stern, and laughed at the sea birds diving for fish in the wake of the boat. Carolyn prepared Dushan for meeting his "Uncle Burt." "Do you know who we're going to see in Liverpool? Did your papa tell you? You have an Uncle Burt who lives in America, and he's coming to Liverpool to take us on an adventure with him to America."

"Wow! No, my papa doesn't talk about Uncle Burt. He doesn't talk about his family, except he talks about my mama."

"You're going to really like Burt. And what's more, you get to fly on an airplane, a real jet that flies so high and so fast. Have you ever flown before?"

Dushan looked up momentarily from the tremendous, broadening wake of the ferry and said, "My papa says we flew here from where we used to live. But I don't remember. I was only two."

"Well, you're gonna love this plane. You can walk around, eat lots of good food, and even watch movies!"

"I didn't know we were going to fly anywhere. My papa only talked about a boat ride across the water."

"First we have our boat ride, and then after we have our big airplane adventure to America, we'll bring you back to Liverpool. Your papa will come get you and bring you back home then."

Dushan's return to staring at the seabirds diving at the boat's wake signaled the end of the discussion for now.

Carolyn added, "I forgot to mention one thing. Uncle Burt wants me to ask you if you remember your whole name—all three names. Do you?"

"I only know my first name is Dushan and my last name is Sava. I don't think I have a middle name."

"You have three beautiful names: Markos Dushan Sava. Your papa always calls you by your middle name, Dushan, because he likes it the best. And guess what? Uncle Burt and Aunt Irene have two wonderful sons, Dani and Markos, your cousins. Markos has the same name as you and he is the same age as you. Isn't that cool? You are going to be such good friends."

"I have a friend at daycare named Danny. I like his name. Does Markos look like me?"

"A little bit; mostly he's just your age and he has a fish tank like you do. "

After disembarking at the Liverpool ferry terminal, Carolyn looked for a taxi. She and Dushan put her suitcase and his backpack into the boot and took a pleasant hour-long tour of Liverpool that Carolyn hoped would take Dushan's mind off of his separation from his papa and being away from his home. Dushan pointed to a double-decker bus and exclaimed, "Look, there's no driver on the top!" Carolyn smiled but was too distracted to say anything.

When they entered the B&B, Carolyn was startled to see Burt sitting in the living room. "Burt, I thought you wouldn't show up until tomorrow."

"I got a great deal on our airfare and jumped on it. Plus, it's a red eye, which should make things go a little more smoothly for all of us, especially Dushan. Speaking of Dushan, this must be the little man himself. How are you?"

Dushan smiled timidly and then said, "Are you Uncle Burt? You don't look like my papa." Dushan looked around the opulent living room. "Is this your house? Can I go upstairs?" Before Burt could reply, the proprietress entered the room, smiled at Dushan, and replied to his question, "Sure you can, if that's okay with you, Mr. Sandor. We have no other guests at the moment." She was a pleasant middle-aged woman with a vaguely Irish accent. Turning back to Dushan, she said, "My name's Mrs. Williams. With whom do I have the pleasure of speaking, young man?"

"My name's Dushan. My papa's gone on a fishing trip and I'm going on an adventure with Carolyn."

Burt rubbed Dushan's head affectionately, "Yes, Dushan, I'm your Uncle Burt. We've never met. And this beautiful house is not my house, but it used to belong to my Uncle Dennis, who was also your papa's uncle. You can explore the house if you like." Dushan wasted no time in scampering up the grand staircase.

At Burt's mention of Uncle Dennis, Mrs. Williams said, "I do remember Dennis, Mr. Sandor. Quite a character; some would say eccentric. But he was quite wealthy by all accounts. As you can see, this Bed and Breakfast has been quite lavishly restored to its 19th century glory. My late husband Shay and I bought the place and did some additional work ourselves. We're quite happy with the way it has turned out." Mrs. Williams smiled at Carolyn before turning back to Burt and asking, "Do you know what your Uncle Dennis has been doing since he sold the place?"

"Actually, he passed away not long after he and my Aunt Helena sold the place. A pity, that."

Carolyn was puzzled. "Burt, what's going on? I wasn't expecting you until the day after tomorrow. I reserved two nights here. But I didn't book a room for you."

Mrs. Williams looked at Carolyn and said, "We do have another room available, Mrs. Markos. But it doesn't appear to be necessary. Your cousin has made a change in plans for the three of you."

The barest hint of a frown passed Burt's face before he turned it into a smile and looked at Carolyn. "That's right, Carolyn. Our flight leaves tonight a little before 11 p.m. It's about 2 p.m. now, and our train to Heathrow leaves in about an hour. We should probably get moving. I went ahead and paid for the first night of your reservation and cancelled the second."

At first, Carolyn didn't know whether to feel annoyed that Burt had upended her plans for a little holiday in Liverpool, or relieved that she could leave the UK sooner than expected and wing her way to San Francisco. The latter emotion won the day. She turned to Mrs. Williams, smiled, and said, "I'm genuinely sorry we won't be able to enjoy your beautiful B & B; maybe another time."

"It's quite understandable. Mr. Sandor tells me unforeseen circumstances got in the way. Best laid plans, as they say." Mrs.

Williams picked up an antique-looking ledger book from the entry hall desk and said, "I'll be in my office when you get ready to settle up the bill, Mr. Sandor."

When Mrs. Williams left the room Carolyn turned to Burt and said, "Well, I'm packed and so's the boy."

Burt raised his eyebrows at that and asked, "You mean that rolling bag is all you have?"

"That and Dushan's little backpack. I didn't have much I wanted to keep, or any way to take more than one suitcase. Besides, I'm very much looking forward to shopping in San Francisco."

"I'm sure you won't be disappointed. I'll show you around after we get you both settled in at my house."

*   *   *

Burt turned out to be right when he said a red eye flight would make things go more smoothly, especially for the boy. Dushan was sound asleep when they checked in, although he awoke as they boarded the plane. The airport security personnel didn't question Burt's passport showing a photo of his infant son Markos listed on it. Since Carolyn's passport was in her maiden name, there was no risk of Carolyn Owens being detained. After takeoff, Dushan spent much of the long flight walking up and down the aisles, playing games, talking to other kids, and watching in-flight movies. He was once again fast asleep upon arrival at San Francisco customs, where Burt was recognized as an employee.

CHAPTER NINE:
A NEW BEGINNING, SAN FRANCISCO 1999

Dushan awoke in a strange bed. He could see it was still dark outside. He didn't know where he was or how he got here. He recalled riding a train to an airport. He must have fallen asleep before they arrived, because he remembered watching a huge silver airplane through a massive airport window as it rolled up to a large enclosed ramp that looked like a tunnel. Then he, Carolyn and Uncle Burt entered the tunnel. He recalled running through the tunnel laughing, and then clapping his hands when the tunnel entered the airplane. After that, there was a jumble of memories involving sitting in a funny seat and pressing buttons to make the seat tilt backwards and forwards. He must have fallen asleep for a while because he remembered waking up on the plane. He played games with other children on the plane and watched some strange movie with cartoon people. He remembered waking up when Burt carried him into another airplane. Then the next thing was waking up to Carolyn rubbing his head and unbuckling the belt that held him in his seat. With eyes closed, he heard, "We're in San Francisco now. This is going to be fun." He must have fallen asleep again after that.

Dushan threw off the blue covers as he sat up. In the dim orange glow of a small nightlight near the bed he saw a fish tank across the room next to a door. A boy lay sleeping on a bed up high on top of another bed that was empty. Dushan quietly tiptoed over to the fish tank. He counted six beautiful fish of dazzling colors. Three of them stuck together, another was half-buried in the gravel, and two others hid in a little toy castle sitting on the gravel. Dushan laughed at a snail shell that moved across the gravel floor with little crab legs sticking out.

A boy's voice brought him out of his investigation of the fish tank. "Hi, I'm Dani. Are you Dushan?" Dushan looked up at the boy in the top bed. "Yes, I'm Dushan. Uncle Burt told me about you. Is

Uncle Burt your papa?"

"Yeah, and my mom is Irene. I think she's still asleep."

"Is this San Francisco? Carolyn said we were going to visit you guys in San Francisco. How old are you?"

"Almost six. I just finished kindergarten and I'm gonna go into first grade at the end of summer."

"What's kindergarten? I go to daycare in Ramsey."

"Kindergarten is school, you know, kindergarten, first grade, second grade. Where is Ramsey?"

"It's on a big island. You have to take a ferryboat to get to it. Carolyn took me on the ferryboat to Liverpool. Then we met Uncle Burt and flew in two airplanes."

"Hey, I was born in Liverpool."

"You were? Really? Do you know my papa? Burt said he and my papa are brothers, but my papa never told me he has a brother." Dushan's expression changed slightly when he said that. He walked over to the bottom bed and rubbed his hand over the glossy planets and stars that glowed from the bedspread. "Who sleeps here? Doesn't anyone sleep here?"

"That's Markos's bed, my little brother's bed. He can't sleep in his own bed cuz he's too sick. He sleeps with my mom and dad. Markos is only four and a half. How old are you?"

"I'm four and three-quarters, and on my birthday I'll be five. Is that your fish tank? I have a fish tank at home but it's not this big."

"That belongs to me and Markos. Some fishes are his and some are mine. Those three orange fishes are called clown loaches; they're mine."

"You mean those striped ones that are swimming together?"

"Yeah. They're really funny. Sometimes they chase Markos's fishes out of the castle and take it over. Me and Markos pretend they're pirates fighting a battle. See that little fish hiding in the gravel? He's really a little eel, my dad says. He just peeks at us from the rocks and stays there."

Dushan walked around the bedroom and examined more things. He stood in front of a large, closed trunk. "Can I open this up?"

"It's Markos's, but he won't care. He doesn't play with his toys anymore. He's sick, really sick. We're all really worried about him. I hope he doesn't die." Dushan closed the half-opened trunk and stared at Dani. A look of genuine concern and sympathy showed on his face as he turned away from the trunk and walked closer to Dani.

"What is he sick from? Once when I was sick my tummy hurt and I was throwing up a lot. I hate throwing up."

"Mom says it's leukemia, which means something is wrong with his blood. You can meet him later; he sleeps a lot. Hey, wanna go outside and see my backyard? We have a really cool tree that's easy to climb. My dad built a floor inside the tree branches that we can stand on."

"Cool, but it's too dark outside, isn't it?"

"Nah. Our yard has a magic lamp that lights up when you step out the back door. Come on, let's go."

Dushan looked around for his clothes and found them folded on a chair. His backpack was opened up, empty, and sitting next to the chair. Dani saw him looking around and said, "Maybe your mom unpacked your stuff and put it into the closet."

"Carolyn's not my mum. My mum's lost."

Dani's face fell. "What do you mean lost? You mean she couldn't find her way home?"

"No... but... " Dani's question triggered Dushan's longing for his parents and his home, and deep sadness for Dani and his brother. "I want to go outside and see your yard."

Dani led the way downstairs to the kitchen. They walked outside onto a small wooden porch. When they stepped onto the grass of the backyard, Dushan looked up and said, "Wow, is that the tree house Uncle Burt made?"

"Yeah, you wanna go up into it? I know the best way how to do it. Follow me."

Dushan carefully followed Dani as they climbed up the wooden rungs attached the trunk of the massive tree. About 10 feet up there was a wooden platform nestled inside the larger branches.

Dushan squinted through the dim light of early morning. "What is that over there? It looks like a castle or church."

"It's the Palace of Fine Arts. It has a really cool museum inside called the Exploratorium. My dad says he'll take us so you can see it. And that pond over there? It's sort of like a castle moat; it goes in between those columns. Lots of ducks and swans live there. And hawks—do you have hawks where you live? Sometimes they dive down to grab a duck if they're hungry. I've never seen it, though."

"I saw pictures of a palace in London. I've never seen a real one.

Is that the ocean way over there? What is that? Does this pond go to it?"

"Nah. That's the bay. It's connected to the Pacific Ocean. See that?" Dani pointed over Dushan's shoulder. "That's the Golden Gate Bridge. My dad says we can walk all the way across it someday. Some kids in my class told me it's really windy on the bridge but you can't get blown off. See, there's a wall that holds you but you can still see the water."

The boys stood motionless on the platform, the wispy early summer San Francisco fog gently blowing past them. The noise of the kitchen door opening drew their attention from the bridge. A boy's voice called out, "Dani, what are you doing? Is that our cousin?" Markos was standing on the kitchen porch in his flannel pajamas.

"Hi, Markos. Yeah, this is Dushan. He came all the way from Liverpool. You shouldn't be outside; it's cold here. Mom says you need to be careful of the cold."

Dushan followed Dani down the ladder rungs on the tree trunk onto the kitchen porch. Dushan stared at Markos. "Hi Markos. I like your tree house."

Dani put his hand on his little brother's shoulder and said, "Hey, let's go in before mom gets mad at us for being out in the cold with Markos."

Dushan and Dani followed Markos into the kitchen, Dushan closely watching Markos tottering on his feet. His thin arms had several bandages on them, and he appeared to be bald underneath a blue stocking cap.

"What happened to your hair, Markos?" Dushan asked as they sat down at the kitchen table.

"It all fell out because of my leukemia. I go into the hospital every two weeks and they put chemo into my arms. Then they put bandages on. It hurts and makes me sleep more."

Dushan asked, "Will it make you feel better?"

"Yep. My mom and dad say I'll be sick for a while and then I'm supposed to be okay."

Dani, playing the responsible older brother, said, "Hey, let's go back to our room so Markos can lie down if he feels like it. I can show Dushan my comic book collection. Can you read yet?"

"Yes, I can read, mostly picture books. What's a comic book?"

"You'll see; let's go."

Quietly, the boys tiptoed up the stairs. Just before they got to the bedroom door, the door beyond it opened and a woman stepped out. "Hi, you three. I heard you talking. Markos, do you feel okay?" She took a step toward Markos and started to reach for his hand, but Markos stepped back and put his hands behind him. "I'm fine, mom."

Irene understood Markos's need to maintain a certain degree of independence, especially in front of the other two boys. She turned to Dushan and said, "Hi, Dushan, I'm Irene, Markos and Dani's mom. How did you sleep?"

Dushan smiled and replied, "I don't remember going to bed. I don't remember how I got off the airplane. I guess I was sleeping a long time."

"Well, good. I'm going back to bed so Burt won't wake up. Oh, Carolyn's asleep in the downstairs bedroom. Try not to wake her. You can play for a while in the bedroom. When Burt wakes up, I'll make us some breakfast." Irene gave Markos one more look to gauge his feelings. He smiled weakly in return. Irene returned to her bedroom.

The younger boys followed Dani to the bedroom. As he showed Dushan their prized Star Wars action figures, Dushan couldn't get his mind off Markos.

"Markos, my middle name is Markos. And your papa is my papa's brother. Did you know that?"

"No, my dad doesn't talk much about his family. I think they live in Liverpool. Where are you from?"

"I flew in an airplane from Liverpool with Carolyn and Uncle Burt. But I never been there before. Our house is in Ramsey and my preschool is there and my friends are there. But me and my papa aren't from there. We're not English, either. We came from Serbia, where I was born. But I don't remember it much, except sometimes in dreams."

"What about your mom? Is she still back at your house?"

Dushan put down the X-Wing Fighter he was holding and looked away. Then he turned back to Markos. Dani looked at Dushan and said, "You don't have to talk about it if you don't want to."

"That's okay. My papa talks about my mum a lot. He tells me stories about her. But I don't remember much about her, only the stories he tells me. Sometimes I dream about her and then she talks to me."

Markos sat up straight and stared at Dushan from the big easy chair. "Is your mom gone or something?"

"She's missing. My papa says some bad men took her and won't let her go."

Markos's eyes widened and he said, "Whoa, took her? Why? Why did they take her?"

"Papa says she was too brave and made the bad men angry at her because she was brave. So they took her away to make her be quiet."

Markos and Dani sat very still, watching Dushan fidget on the floor. Then Dushan asked Markos, "Can you open this trunk?"

Uncrossing his legs, Markos replied, "Sure. And you don't have to talk about your mom if you don't want to."

"It's okay. I don't really remember her much. I was only a baby when they took her. I have nice dreams of her. And Papa tells me stories of how he met her before when Serbia was a good place to live."

Markos re-buttoned his pajama top and took off his little cloth cap. Dushan pointed to Markos's bald head. "Will your hair grow back?"

"I guess, once my leukemia goes away. I don't care about my hair. I just want to stop feeling sick."

"Are you feeling sick now?"

"Not now, no. Only after they give me the shots. Then I feel sick for a couple of days and I just want to sleep."

The three boys lapsed into silence again. After a minute or so, Dani got up from the floor and walked to the bookcase. "I have some new comic books we can read. Markos, would you like to see the new Incredible Hulk comic dad brought from the airport?"

"Sure. Are you done with it?"

"I haven't started it, but I can read another one. Dushan, here's another Hulk I got last month."

"I've never read comics. I'm not really a good reader yet. I'm just learning my letters and I can write my name. My papa speaks Serb to me at home. But at daycare we only speak English; my teacher shows us stuff and helps us to learn to read. I speak English better than my papa does. But I still can't read very good."

"That's okay. Why don't I read this one out loud. Markos can't really read very well yet either."

After 10 minutes or so, Markos lay back in the huge chair and closed his eyes. Dani stopped reading and looked at him. "Markos, me and Dushan are going back outside for a while so you can rest. We'll see you at breakfast." Markos mumbled "OK," and the two others left the bedroom.

CHAPTER TEN:
IRENE'S INVESTIGATION, 1999

Irene lay on top of the covers in her bed in the dark room. Burt lay snoring in the next bed. Twin beds became a necessity early in their marriage because of Burt's persistent snoring. Probably because of her conversation with the boys just now, rather than Burt's snoring, Irene knew sleep would be impossible and decided to have a talk with Burt's cousin Carolyn. *I need to get something straight. She might be jet lagged, but this is important.* She slipped quietly out of bed, exited the bedroom, and closed the door. Avoiding the half dozen squeaky stair steps, she slowly walked downstairs. Crossing the living room of the elegant 19th-century Marina District house, Irene opened the door to the bedroom on the right.

Carolyn was sitting up on the edge of the bed fully dressed and pulling on a sweater. "Hi, Irene. I was just getting dressed to go sit outside in the back, but I heard the boys go outside and didn't want to interrupt their getting-to-know-you ritual."

"The boys are what I want to talk to you about, Carolyn, Dushan in particular. Can you tell me more about him? What his family is like? Why did they give him up for adoption?"

"I'm not surprised Burt didn't fill you in on the details. As you know, he can be pretty closed and self-centered. Well, here's the deal in a nutshell. A month ago, when Burt called me and told me the bad news about Markos, he told me you and he wanted to adopt a boy about the same age as Markos. In effect, as Burt said, you two wanted to 'replace'—his word—Markos with another son. You didn't want to 'start from scratch.' Again, those are his words, not mine. So, in my last few months working in my office before my resignation, I scouted around for such a child."

"You say you scouted around? How exactly did that work? Isn't there a lot of paperwork and bureaucracy?"

"When you've been doing this as long as I have, and when you're presented with such an influx of immigrants from all over as the world's social order breaks down, it's not hard to do such an adoption expeditiously. I found a single father in desperate straits with a four-and-a-half-year-old boy. The father was a refugee from the former Yugoslavia; his wife had been assassinated for her political activities. The father was a mess emotionally, and destitute. No job, living in a homeless shelter with a little boy. He suffered from post-traumatic stress. He was quite frankly unable to properly care for the boy, and he knew it. Since the boy was so young, the father believed he would adjust to a new home and family without much trouble. It really was not that difficult, Irene." When Carolyn finished saying this she was amazed at how fluent and natural her story sounded. She almost believed it herself. Almost.

"But I thought Burt said something about telling the boy he was on some sort of vacation?"

"Yes, well, we didn't really tell him it was a vacation. We told him he would live here for a bit and his papa would come over after a month or so to visit and bring him home. Burt figures he can make up something soon to tell the boy so he will understand he is being adopted. But still with his papa being able to come visit once in a while. The boy doesn't know what happened to his ma; he thinks she was taken away by some bad people and is being kept prisoner. Nobody really knows what happened to her."

"I don't like this. It looks to me like you're just putting off the inevitable sad, traumatic climax to a bad situation."

"Well, don't worry. It'll all work out, you'll see. Just relax and try to make the boy feel at home. I have a good feeling about the lad; he seems to have more than a full measure of empathy and wisdom. I wouldn't be at all surprised if he and your boys hit it off right away. You wait, it'll be fine. And let me assure you, the alternative would be far, far worse. His situation with his destitute, traumatized father was just impossible. And sooner or later he would have learned the truth about his possibly murdered mother. I don't see how there could be a good outcome for the boy if he were still living there. Besides, his pa hopefully will be visiting him here from time to time." Again, Carolyn felt a little in awe at how effortlessly she delivered this story.

Irene was not at all confident as she got up to leave Carolyn's room. She was not sure she believed Carolyn's story, at least not all of it. It seemed to her that if it were a legitimate adoption Carolyn would still be working at the agency. After all, she was only 35 and had worked there barely more than 12 years. Without a doubt, Irene felt herself in a bit of a bind. It would be difficult to get the truth out of Burt without causing a scene and possibly making the whole thing blow up.

In the kitchen, Irene put on the coffee, cracked half a dozen eggs in a bowl, shredded some cheese, and began cutting up a bunch of green onions.

Probably in response to the smell of coffee and sautéing onions, Burt came walking downstairs moments later. "Good morning, my sweet. Are you making breakfast for all three of us? How about the boys?"

Irene turned from the stove and looked at Burt. "I'm not sure what I'm doing just yet, Burt. And I'm not sure what you're doing, either. I'm very concerned about what's going on here. I think you and Carolyn have cooked up something and you're not being completely forthcoming with me." She turned back to finish whipping up the eggs.

"Calm down. I haven't cooked up anything. I have simply adopted a boy whose father in the refugee-infested British Isles was about to go off the deep end and was eager to give his son a better life." Burt sat down at the little kitchen table and poured himself a cup of coffee from the carafe.

He took a long slurp from the cup and continued, "My personal motivation, as I'm sure you're wondering, is the same as yours. Or the same as yours should be. Have you given a thought to what will happen to Dani once Markos's tragic death descends upon us? I thought, and still think now more than ever, that little Dushan—who by the way, is exactly Markos's age—will provide the kind of sibling sustenance that Dani desperately needs once our beloved Markos is gone."

Irene listened to Burt's explanation without turning around. She didn't need, and for sure didn't want, to see the expression on his face as he constructed his story. Despite Burt's argument's superficial rationality and appeal to Irene—and Irene couldn't deny that Dani would certainly benefit from having a new stepbrother to fill the void of Markos's death—Irene understood that Burt was not as concerned about Dani's emotional health as he purported to be. Burt was more concerned about his own financial health. Irene remembered only too well how elated they were shortly after Markos was born. The registered letter from Burt's mother, telling them that she had set up a trust for the boys' benefit, simply stunned Burt and Irene. The generosity of the gesture—an initial corpus of $200,000 and a $1,000 per month support allowance for each boy—was conditioned, however, by the provision that should either son not live to age 21, that son's portion of the trust would revert back to Burt's mother. At the time, neither Irene nor Burt paid much attention to that provision, and certainly didn't see it as a cause of worry.

Now, however, Irene saw the reality of that provision through the prism of Burt's materialism. It seemed crystal-clear to Irene that Burt's little scheme to adopt a boy Markos's age was motivated by a plan to *actually*, not just figuratively, 'replace' Markos. Burt's mother had never visited them in California, and had stated on several occasions that she probably never would. Margaret's oft-repeated rationale, "I can't bear to leave my wonderful British world," still rang in Irene's ears. As far as Irene knew, Margaret had never been informed of Markos's illness. And it certainly seemed likely that Burt never intended to inform her.

Irene poured the eggs into the skillet over the sautéed onions and watched as the mixture slowly congealed into a breakfast omelet. The boys marched in looking like they were dressed for a hunting expedition. All except for Markos, who was still in pajamas. Dani asked, "Hey, mom, can we have some breakfast? We're hungry."

Irene turned away from the stove, set the spatula on the counter, wiped her hands on her apron, and smiled at the little troop. "Sure thing, guys. Dushan, do you like omelets? I put green onions and melted cheese in it; is that okay?"

"Yeah; I like all that stuff. My papa says I'm a gourmet. What's a gourmet?"

"A gourmet is somebody who likes all kind of delicious food. This omelet's going to be delicious." Irene took three plates out of the cupboard and set them on the counter. "Why don't you boys have a seat at the table on the back deck; I'll bring your food out to you. Markos, are you going to eat anything or do you not feel like it?"

"I'll have a little bite, maybe. Don't give me too much."

Irene turned back to the stove, picked up the skillet, and began spooning small portions of omelet onto the boys' plates. She and Burt carried the plates out to the deck and set them down in front of the boys. Burt looked at them and asked, "Dani, you and Dushan look like explorers. Are you going somewhere?"

Dani looked up from his plate. "Can you walk us over to the pond at the Palace. I wanna show Dushan all the different kinds of birds."

Burt turned to Markos. "Markos, I see you're not dressed; I guess that means you're not feeling up to a walk?"

"Not really; I'm still pretty tired. My tummy doesn't feel very good. I think I'll play with my Legos."

"Well, that's okay. But I can't go for a walk now; I have to get ready for work. But your mom can take you, can't you Irene? It'll give you all a chance to get to know one another."

Irene welcomed the excuse to get away from the house, not to mention Burt and Carolyn, and keep company with Dushan and Dani. She knew Markos could entertain himself with his toys and would in all likelihood take a nap. "Absolutely; I'd love to go exploring with these two. And we'll bring back something for Markos from the Exploratorium gift shop."

Markos put down his fork and looked at Dani and Dushan, who were all excited and dressed for a safari. "Actually, mom, I do feel a little better. Maybe I'll get dressed and go too. Is that okay?"

"Sure thing, little man. You have a couple more bites of the omelet and I'm sure you'll feel better. We won't go too far so we won't get tired out."

CHAPTER ELEVEN:
GETTING TO KNOW YOU, 1999

Irene and the boys ambled along the sidewalk and crossed to the lawn at the edge of the pond at the Palace of Fine Arts. They were walking slowly, both because there was so much to see on the edges of the pond, but also to allow Markos to keep up without getting tired. Irene was concerned that this little walk might be too much for him, but he was adamant that he wanted to come along. It broke her heart to see him gamely keep a smile on his face, while at the same time try to keep his little cap from blowing off in the chill late-June breeze in that San Francisco neighborhood. The knowledge that he very likely would not live out the remainder of the summer was something that Irene tried to stuff away in the back of her mind. She had enough to worry about with this latest scheme of Burt's. *But who knows, Dushan and Dani do seem to be hitting it off, and might very well become fast friends as well as stepbrothers.*

Irene walked over to where the boys had veered off the path and were standing almost at the edge of the water itself. They were crouching down examining the remains of a duck that appeared to be half-eaten, perhaps by a hawk that was interrupted by something.

Dushan looked up and said to Irene. "I think it's a duck, Aunt Irene." Addressing no one in particular, he asked, "What happened to it?"

Irene noticed that Dani waited for Markos to answer. "Probably a hawk got it; or maybe an eagle." She felt a wave of warmth emanate from Dushan and Dani and wash over Markos.

Irene waited for the boys to finish turning the duck's body over with sticks before she suggested they walk over to the Palace columns. But they didn't get very far when Markos looked up at her with a pained look on his face. "Mom, I don't feel very good. I have a headache again, and my legs really hurt."

"That's okay, Markos. We'll go back inside and rest. Then after awhile maybe we'll have lunch. You didn't eat much breakfast anyway."

As they started their walk back to the house, it seemed to Irene that Dushan was making a point of walking next to Markos; he was even holding his hand while they chatted. Markos's smile and body language showed he welcomed the camaraderie. Dani moved up to Markos's other side and the three boys traipsed back to the sidewalk holding hands.

Irene followed behind as the three boys went inside the house, still standing as close to one another as possible. Irene became aware that Dani's whole response to Markos's condition had changed with the arrival of Dushan. Even though Dani was not yet six years old, it almost seemed to Irene that he was consciously processing Markos's worsening illness, and was relieved to have another boy's help. Irene and Burt hadn't told Dani and Markos the whole truth about Markos's leukemia, that it was probably going to be fatal and possibly very soon. But during the past several weeks Dani seemed to have been weighed down by his own fears about that possibility. Irene could feel Dani perk up in the presence of Dushan. And Markos, too. Now that she thought about it, Irene realized that Dushan's arrival was working its magic on her as well.

Carolyn was in the living room when the four of them came inside. She had a Bay Area street map spread out in front of her on the coffee table, and was poring over the Marin County section. Irene greeted Carolyn, who seemed engrossed in the map and simply responded with a "hello." Irene watched the boys walk into the kitchen, arm in arm. It was a very touching sight to see Dushan and Dani giving Markos a hand. Irene entered the kitchen, warmed up some leftover omelet and offered it to Markos.

"I don't think so, mom. I just want a glass of milk."

"You want to drink it here, or would you like to have it on the back deck?"

"The deck. Can Dani and Dushan stay with me?"

Dani immediately responded, "Yeah, mom, we'll stay with Markos." Dushan took the milk carton out of the fridge and asked, "Where are the glasses, Markos?"

Markos looked up and said, "In that cupboard there. It's too high; you have to stand on a chair."

"Here, let me get the glass," Irene said as she opened the

cupboard. "I'll leave you boys alone for a little while. I'm gonna talk to Carolyn in the living room."

When Irene walked into the living room, Carolyn had closed the map and was gazing out a window. She turned to Irene. "I'm very sorry about Markos, Irene. I had no idea. But the boy is still surprisingly strong. He certainly shows a lot of will to do things."

Irene let out her breath in a sigh. "Yeah, but especially this morning, even though he is tired out now. It looks like little Dushan has triggered something in Markos. In Dani, too."

"Burt said Markos's diagnosis was leukemia. Do you know what type? Some are more benign than others."

"His is Acute Lymphoblastic Leukemia, ALS they call it. It's really, really bad; one of the worst."

Carolyn sagged into the sofa, letting her head roll forward as if in prayer. "Has the doc given you a prognosis?"

"Yes, well, a ballpark figure, as they say here in the States. We can expect to see his condition deteriorate quickly, even suddenly. He'll probably leave us in a couple of months at most."

Irene stopped talking and wiped her eyes. She stifled a catch in her throat that could become a sob. She sat down opposite Carolyn. "Carolyn, what are your plans?"

"I don't rightly know. I was hoping to stay away for quite some time and investigate the employment picture here in California. To tell you the truth, I don't fancy going back to the miserable UK."

"You're welcome to stay here for a month or so if you decide to try to get work in San Francisco; or even longer. We have plenty of room, and I could certainly use some help with the boys, especially Markos."

"That's very kind of you. A month would be about right, I think."

Irene got up and walked back to the kitchen. "I'm going to see how the boys are getting along."

Carolyn put on a windbreaker and her shoes and walked out through the front door. With no destination in mind, she turned left, toward Chestnut Street. She was preoccupied with how she and Burt were going to finesse Dushan's transition from adoptee to stepson. *Poor Dushan, he thinks he's only here for a month's vacation. So do Dani and Markos, apparently. And Irene, she thinks Dushan believes he's been adopted with his pa having visiting rights. What a screwed-up mess! I just hope Burt can come up with something brilliant before Irene decides to talk to Dushan about his adoption.*

She was even more anxious with the knowledge that what she did was no adoption at all. It was a child abduction, plain and simple. Burt never asked for details and she never gave any. "I don't think he really wanted to know," she murmured to herself. She didn't really think Burt would care even if he knew the truth. No, her real concern was the possibility, however unlikely, that the criminal investigation into this abduction might turn up some information linking the crime to her. Carolyn had been mulling over that possibility since she and Burt and the boy flew out of London. But she felt fairly confident that using her maiden name was a good way to cover her tracks, since her loutish ex-husband took off to Aussie-land almost immediately after their divorce. *There's no way they'll ever find that idiot now.*

It occurred to Carolyn that, in a strange sort of way, her apprehension about staying out of reach of the long arm of the law was helping her suppress her self-loathing at her betrayal of the boy and his father. But the fact remained that no matter how much rationalizing she engaged in to try to put a positive spin on the situation, she had done something terrible. Over the past week or so, Carolyn frequently resorted to telling herself that maybe it was not so terrible after all. *The boy will no doubt have a much better life here in the USA than in the immigrant-infested UK.* Carolyn had always been good at justifying her many moral failings. Her barely suppressed racism and xenophobia helped her ignore the reality of what she had done. In addition, her fear of getting caught provided her with the adrenalin necessary to keep going. There was also the excitement of starting a new life in America with her huge adoption fee. Her new motto could well be something she read in the new San Francisco-based murder mystery she brought with her on the flight from Heathrow: "Shit happens, life goes on."

In that spirit, Carolyn quickened her pace up to Chestnut Street. She needed to find a bank. There was a large check in her purse drawn on Burt's account. Turning right on Chestnut, she walked until she came to the first bank, whose marquee said "Hibernia Bank of San Francisco." "How fitting," she muttered, before walking into the lobby.

Using her recently obtained UK passport, Carolyn opened a bank account under her maiden name, Carolyn Markos, and felt a sense of elation to see the initial balance of $30,000. *That little nest egg will keep me comfortable for quite a while, especially with no rent and Burt's generous offer to pay for my expenses while I'm getting on my feet.*

The days passed slowly for Dani as he struggled with his fears over Markos and his curiosity over Dushan. There was so much Dani wanted to know about Dushan, mostly just how he felt about him and Markos. Dani noticed that his mom also seemed to want to get to know Dushan. She liked to hang out with "the boys" as she called Dani, Markos and Dushan. But the way she acted around Carolyn was different. She didn't smile when talking to her like she did when talking to the boys.

Dushan, at least at first, stayed close to Carolyn when she was around and usually talked to her about his dad. When that happened, Dani noticed that his mom stopped what she was doing and watched Carolyn as she answered Dushan's questions. Dani got the impression that Carolyn didn't know much about Dushan's dad at all. Dani wondered if Carolyn was making stuff up. But he didn't say anything right away.

Maybe Dushan felt the same way about Carolyn, because after a few days, he stopped asking her questions. Mostly, Dushan liked to stick close to Dani and Markos. He said he wished he had some brothers and sisters at home, because he liked big families. Dushan talked about his daycare a lot. He said he liked to pretend those kids were his brothers and sisters.

One time Markos asked Dushan to speak Serbian so they could hear how it sounded. When Dushan complied, Markos cracked up. "It sounds like you have some marbles in your mouth when you talk!" That made Dushan laugh, so he spoke some more, even sang a song he said his dad sang at home. The boys tried to sing it with Dushan, which only made Markos laugh even harder. Then Dushan tried very hard to teach the song to them, and Markos was much better at sounding like Dushan than Dani was. Dani was very happy to see Markos enjoy himself so much.

Markos had good days and bad days. More and more bad days. The morning after Dushan taught him the Serbian song, Markos threw up his breakfast and didn't want to go outside afterward. Dushan suggested he and Dani cancel their plan to walk to the playground and instead stay home and play with Markos. Dani was happy about that. After they'd been playing all morning and it seemed like Markos felt much better. Markos said he wanted dad to take them all to a movie tomorrow, which was a Saturday and dad didn't have to work. Dushan said he'd never seen a movie and wanted to go very badly. But the expression on mom's face said *let's see how it goes*, and Dani understood her point: Markos might not feel up to it when the time came. That was okay. Anything that would help Markos feel better was okay with Dani. He was pretty sure Dushan would agree with whatever everyone decided to do.

CHAPTER TWELVE:
BURT'S NIGHTMARE, 1999

The dream began like many of Burt's other dreams in the past month. The two airport executives who were his immediate superiors stood at the door to Burt's office with a burly police officer at their side. One executive was yelling at him, "You're fired." The other told the cop to arrest him. Burt protested, "What's going on? Haven't I been a fast-rising star in this organization? Innovation, numbers, safety record, hasn't everything improved around here since I arrived?"

"Innovation? I'll give you innovation! You stopped loving your kid when you found out he was defective. You stole another kid to take his place. Don't deny it; we heard all about it from Interpol."

At this point in the dream, there was a new element that wasn't in the earlier dreams. Carolyn walked into the office escorted by a London bobby. She was crying and pleading with everyone, "I didn't steal anyone; he was just an immigrant. He had no life. His father sold him to me. Burt made me do it."

Burt started to walk around his desk when his son Markos appeared, being wheeled into the office in a wheelchair. Chemo tubes stuck out from his arms. He was crying. At that point, Burt broke down crying and collapsed. The dream impact with the floor woke him up, but he was still crying.

The nightmare left Burt exhausted and overwrought. He quickly suppressed the sobs so as not to wake Irene. The image of his little boy sitting accusingly in his wheelchair wouldn't go away. Burt was tempted to stay home from work today, but realized that the situation at home was likely to be worse than at work. He dressed quickly and left the house while it was still dark outside. A half hour later, Burt was sitting in the San Francisco International Airport (SFO) executive cafeteria trying to work up an appetite.

By noon, Burt wished he had stayed home. He was not having a great day at work. He hadn't slept much since he returned with Dushan and Carolyn. Irene was mad at him; more than mad—suspicious. He could tell she didn't believe his story about Dushan. And it didn't feel too good to know that Carolyn knew more about the so-called adoption than he did. He had no idea, or control over, how she pulled off this child abduction that they're calling an adoption. For all Burt knew, Interpol or the FBI could be hot on her trail—and his—at this very moment.

Burt had never been one to worry much about how his actions affected others—unless they had power. But this time he could not put out of his mind some serious unease about the hurt he was about to cause little Dushan and his father. Clouding that guilt was the anxiety about what might happen once the father found out what happened. Burt figured that Dushan's father would find out what happened about mid-July. Assuming Carolyn had covered her tracks adequately, and the authorities had no leads as to where Dushan was, Burt would be able to put into play the second part of this adoption. In late July or perhaps August, he would announce to the family that Dushan's dad's fishing expedition failed to return to port. He was unsure whether he should make a much more definitive scenario, that the dad had been killed in a fishing accident, or that the boat capsized off Scotland. He knew it would be difficult to get Irene to go along with this explanation; difficult was an understatement—she would be furious at him for lying to her. But he had to convince her, and he knew she would see there was no other way.

As if those things didn't create enough anxiety, there was the continuing tragedy of Markos's terminal leukemia. Burt was beside himself with anxiety over how Markos might react if he lived long enough to hear about Dushan's father's disappearance. That bogus news was going to be bad enough for Dushan; how could it help Markos's condition to have to hear that?

But on a very deep level—in a place Burt was scarcely aware of—was the emotional effect of Markos's impending death. The tragedy itself was something that, even though kept at arm's length and not discussed, was made even more corrosive by the not-quite-hidden guilt that haunted virtually every dark corner of Burt's unconscious mind, guilt over the trauma to Markos's innocent replacement. Burt's selfish attempt to retain Markos's share of the "Sandor Children Trust" threatened to undermine his mental stability, not to mention the love of the woman who once adored him unconditionally. Burt's life-long ability to manipulate others through sheer force of his amoral will was being worn down by what felt increasingly like a slow-motion tsunami of self-hatred forming at the deepest part of his being. The more he denied, ignored, suppressed and fought back at this tsunami, the more haunted he became, not only in his dreams but in his waking life as well.

Compared to all this, Burt's difficulties with his new managers at SFO should have paled into insignificance. But those difficulties wouldn't go away. Every day, those bozos came up with some new procedure and/or criticism they laid on Burt. He suspected they were up to something, maybe planning to lay him off or transfer him so they could replace him with one of their own former colleagues from Kennedy Airport in New York.

Burt had a plan he hoped would protect him from those machinations at work. Ever since he heard about the new program planned for the Southern California Logistics Airport (SCLA) in Victorville, he'd been actively seeking a position there. He would be second in charge of a department dealing with the SCLA's hoped-for status as a foreign trade zone. The department's mission would be to make it easier for the Victor Valley Economic Development Authority to convince international carriers to use the airport as a base for shipping foreign products to Southern California.

The second round of interviews at SCLA had gone well. Burt was fairly positive he'd get the job. But "when" was the tricky question. It might be soon, it might be next spring. In the meantime, to ready himself for sooner rather than later, he'd been scouting around the Victorville area looking into housing and school possibilities. Talk about bargains! For what he and Irene had been paying in rent in SF's Marina District, he could buy two houses in Victorville. The schools were mediocre, but that didn't really bother Burt. Irene was a good teacher and, before Markos's diagnosis, had been looking forward to resuming her teaching career. *Hell, maybe we'll even home school the boys.*

For now the main task was to work with Irene and the boys to ease Dushan's transition into the family, even though he didn't know he was to become a family member. The other thing that had to be dealt with was Carolyn. Burt hadn't had much of a chance to talk to her about her plans. He needed to make it clear to her that if she planned on staying in the States for the foreseeable future, she had to get cracking on the job and apartment hunt. Burt didn't really fancy having her around forever.

CHAPTER THIRTEEN:
MARKOS'S LAST SUMMER

Irene was beside herself. She and Burt sat in the living room facing each other. Burt sat on his hands and fixed his gaze on the floor lamp in front of the picture window as Irene berated him. She tried to keep her voice down so as not to alert the boys, who were in the backyard. Her lips pursed, she hissed at Burt loud enough to make him face her. "Burt, you can't be serious! Lost at sea? How do you know that? How do I know that you and Carolyn haven't been lying to me from the outset! This will devastate the boy. Hasn't he had enough sadness—haven't we all had enough sadness this summer with what's happening to Markos?"

Burt pulled his hands out from under his legs and spread them out on his legs. "Look, Irene, it's true. I heard about the storm on the BBC last night. A large fishing trawler in the North Sea sank in a huge storm. The crew, all of whom came from the Isle of Man and Liverpool, were lost, no survivors. I'm just as torn as you are. I wish I had never come up with this plan. I wish I had never adopted the boy. But we're in it to the end, is the way I see it. We have to take the next step. We have to tell him sooner or later."

Irene's throat tightened and she began salivating the way she usually did when she was nauseated and about to throw up. But she forced herself to open her mouth and take several deep breaths. She could feel Burt's mental push, but her defenses were too strong to let it dominate her. She realized, though, that the situation was completely in Burt's hands, and she had no power at all to change it. Certainly not in a positive way, that was for sure. Barely able to speak without choking up, she gave Burt the kind of answer that wouldn't provoke him. "Well, don't tell him now, for God's sake, what with Markos's situation. Just say that his dad's ship failed to return to port as scheduled. It might be stranded somewhere temporarily. The search is ongoing. How about that? That way, Dushan won't be hit with such bad news. In fact, he would never have to be told that the ship eventually turned up sunken. Hope springs eternal, kind of thing. But, Burt, I want to remind you that I have always thought, and still think, that this adoption was a terrible idea from the get-go. Not that what I think matters; you never consult with me about anything important, do you Burt?"

Irene stood and walked into the kitchen without another word. Burt walked upstairs to his study. As she began putting dirty dishes in the sink she looked out the window and watched the boys playing in and around the tree house. Dani was on the ground trying to climb up the tree as Markos and Dushan, playing some variant of "king of the mountain," blocked his ascent. All three were laughing heartily.

Even though Dushan's expression was joyous and he seemed to be firmly entrenched in the moment, Irene knew from her conversations with him over the past few weeks that he was getting anxious to return home. Irene had almost run out of excuses when she replied to his frequent questions. But she got the feeling that on some level Dushan created a reason for why he was here. He seemed to intuitively grasp that he could help the family, especially Dani and Markos, deal with Markos's sickness. Dushan genuinely loved Markos and Dani. The little threesome had become fast friends, so much so that Irene could *almost* believe that this terrible news might actually work out for the best. Dushan and Dani did everything they could to keep Markos's spirits up. They told jokes and ghost stories, read their favorite comics to him, played imagination games with him, and acted out their Star Wars battles for his amusement. It seemed to Irene that all three of them knew, despite what they were originally told, that Markos would not recover from his illness. But Markos thrived on their attention and, while with them, was developing a sense of calm acceptance of his approaching death.

When Dani and Dushan were alone, unaware of being discretely observed by Irene, they allowed each other to cry and express their hurt over the unfairness of the world. Irene wondered how much of Dushan's hurt was grounded in his fear of never seeing his father again. She didn't let herself dwell over-much on that possibility, and in fact got the impression that Dushan had no such fear. She could sense his anxiety and longing, but not fear. *Time will tell how all this will turn out.*

It was Markos himself who chose the time of his passing. Chose and announced. He had just been brought home from his last stay in the California Pacific Medical Center in the Pacific Heights neighborhood of San Francisco. He'd been there for three days, in and out of consciousness. At home again, when lucid and in not too much pain, he talked to his parents, his brothers, Carolyn and the hospice nurse who visited him daily. Often, when the family could not tell whether he was fully "here" or elsewhere, Markos spoke of visits from people no one recognized. "A man on a fishing boat. It passes by a giant fortress. It's not on the ocean, the boat is on a river on an island. That's funny, dad and mom: the island has a long river running through it and the river has a smaller island in the middle of it. And that island has a little mountain. But, sometimes the mountain is a fortress, sometimes just a mountain."

The family members asked him questions, kept him alert and enthusiastic about what he saw, the stories he told. Dani and Dushan, especially Dushan, listened most closely to Markos's stories. Of course, Dani and Dushan recognized the resemblance of some of those stories to Dushan's descriptions of his home on the Isle of Man. But the stuff about the fortress and the island in the river on the bigger island, that was new to Dani. Although Dushan had a dim recollection of his father's fishing stories and a giant fortress in between two rivers, he had never related those stories to Dani and Markos. Dushan also suspected Markos was so close to dying he could talk to spirits, but was relieved that Markos said nothing about meeting anyone in that spirit world who might remotely resemble Dushan's mother or father. He didn't want to believe they were gone. More than that, he *knew* they were not gone. They were waiting for him to return home.

One afternoon as heavy fog was just beginning to lift outside the house, Markos closed his eyes and hummed the Serbian tune Dushan taught them a couple of weeks ago, his oxygen tube vibrating. He tried to lift his arms as if to conduct an orchestra, but didn't get very far. He let his arms drop. He stopped humming before reaching the end. He would finish the tune in his next life.

Irene placed her head across Markos's chest. She was not listening for a heartbeat; she knew there was none. She cried softly. Burt looked at the boys; they looked at Carolyn. She looked at her shoes as she sobbed and reached for a tissue. Dushan put one hand on

Markos's hand and the other on Dani's shoulder. "I'll never forget you, Markos." Dani placed his head next to his mom's, on top of Markos's belly.

After a few minutes, the group's tears stopped one by one. Irene in the lead, they walked slowly out of the room. "Life goes on," said Burt to no one in particular as he walked out last.

CHAPTER FOURTEEN:
ROUGH SEAS, 1999

The end of the fishing expedition couldn't have come at a better time. Dimitri was weary of being out on the storm-tossed Atlantic. He was grateful that the ship had caught its fill a week earlier than anticipated. The crew would still get its full month's contracted salary, plus a share of the profits from the catch.

Another reason for Dimitri's rising sense of relief was the knowledge that he'd soon be home and with his "little champion" again. He was lucky to have found such a great babysitting arrangement with Carolyn. Now it was time to relieve her of her charge and resume his normal life.

When the ship docked at Ramsey Harbour, Dimitri decided to splurge on a taxi rather than wear himself out on the long walk to his apartment. He felt rather well off and it would be worth it to see his boy a little sooner.

Even though it was well after sunset, Dimitri didn't see any light coming from his apartment window as he walked away from the cab. There was no answer when he knocked on the front door and rang the doorbell. *Ah, they're probably enjoying a movie. I'll surprise them when they return.*

He let himself in and put his suitcase in the bedroom. Then he noticed the fish tank. The four little fish floated dead on the surface, and the tank was barely half full. Apparently nobody bothered to feed the fish. And the little oxygenator was turned off. Walking into the dining room, Dimitri saw that their little parakeet lay dead on the floor of the birdcage. In English Dimitri spoke to the empty apartment, "This is terrible. How could Carolyn forget to take care of fish and bird? Dushan would not forget to remind her." Dushan's little bed appeared to be made just like Dimitri left it three weeks ago. Likewise, Dimitri's own bed was in practically the same state of disarray it was in when he left that morning. More troubling was the rollaway bed he borrowed for Carolyn: it was still folded up and the sheets and blankets were still folded up and sitting on top. "This is very strange."

Dimitri went to the kitchen to see if Carolyn had made any meals. The fridge was almost empty and smelled of rotten vegetables, sour milk and moldy cheese. The dirty dishes in the sink appeared to be the very ones Dimitri left for Carolyn to take care of. Turning to the living room, he saw a pile of unopened mail lying on the floor just under the mail slot next to the front door. More and more frantically, he searched through the apartment, but it was horrifyingly clear that no one had been here since he left.

"Shit! What did that bitch do to me? Where is my little Dushan?" His rising sense of fear flooded Dimitri's mind. He collapsed on the sofa and breathed in quick, shallow breaths. Covering his eyes with his right hand, he began to sob—at first quietly but then more loudly.

Dimitri ran out of his apartment and up the staircase to the second-floor apartment. Mr. Conley, the neighbor, answered the doorbell on the second ring. "No, I sure haven't," he replied when Dimitri asked if he had seen Dushan or Carolyn lately. "In fact, I haven't seen hide nor hair of the boy for over three weeks. I saw the three of you leave for your boat that morning, but didn't see them return to the apartment at all."

"Please, can I telephone police with your phone? I am so sorry it is late. I just got back from fishing trip and now my boy is gone and so is babysitter."

Dimitri called the police and reported what had happened, struggling to stay calm. Breathing was difficult as was coming up with intelligible English as he struggled to make his report over the phone. A police car arrived in less than 15 minutes. After the police officers left around midnight, Dimitri began cleaning up the apartment— throwing out the rotten food in the fridge, emptying the fish tank and birdcage, and taking the garbage out. He went through the unopened mail on the floor and threw most of it in the trash.

He picked up his copy of the police report and turned to the statement he made describing Dushan and the arrangement he had with the babysitter: Dushan's age and where he was born; Dimitri's nationality and the circumstances of his wife's disappearance; the babysitter's name, Carolyn Owens; how he found her—through a babysitting agency and a recommendation from his colleague Carson

Leary; the agency's phone number; what Carolyn said about taking Dushan with her to visit Liverpool because she hoped to find work there.

Then came a part of the statement that caught him up short. Dimitri recalled one of the police officers, Inspector Angus Ailshie, asking, "Now Mr. Sava, can you give us a phone number for the babysitter?"

Dimitri remembered thinking a minute and then answering. "No, Inspector, I don't have number. Maybe I write it down somewhere, but I do not remember I asked her for it. I was fool to let her take my little boy with knowing so little about her."

Dimitri remembered the inspector trying to be helpful when he replied, "Well, why don't you look around some more. Hopefully it'll turn up, otherwise I guess we'll have to hope we can track her down through her employer." Ailshie left Dimitri's apartment soon after taking his statement, but Dimitri could not get up from his chair for almost half an hour. At that point, after wracking his brain trying to recall whether or not he had gotten Owens's phone number, he realized he hadn't. He climbed into bed and cried himself to sleep. But his sleep was far from restful. Nightmares frequently woke him up.

The next day he went to work, and it was a good thing he did. He knew he shouldn't sit around the apartment and obsess over the situation. At the end of his shift, Dimitri went to the police station to see what he could find out. Inspector Ailshie didn't seem entirely comfortable to see Dimitri walk through the door. Speaking in a distracted, hesitant manner, the inspector began describing the status of the investigation. "Mr. Sava, we contacted the babysitting agency and left a message asking them to search their personnel files for a Carolyn Owens being listed. You say you called the agency about a month ago?"

"Yes, that is right. There was only recording listing different phone numbers for different cities. I called number for Ramsey, and the person who answered said she was Carolyn Owens. I spoke with her and checked out her reference. She babysat three times for man I knew here on docks. She came to my apartment, met my son, and agreed to take job."

"Well, did you happen to write down the Ramsey number?"

"No, I'm so sorry. I did not think to do that." Dimitri squirmed in his seat but couldn't get comfortable. He uncrossed his legs, folded his arms across his chest and said, "She was coming over so I thought I would just talk to her."

"That's too bad, Mr. Sava. But we'll try another approach. Let's hope the agency's records will show all phone numbers listed on a given date or during a given period. I'll call you if I find out anything."

As he watched Dimitri leave the office, Ailshie felt conflicted at not having told him everything about Owens. When the inspector left Sava's apartment last night, he had a strong suspicion that Owens was the same Carolyn Owens who was being charged up in Douglas with crimes relating to the recent bogus immigrant adoption scandal. This morning, as soon as Ailshie got to the office, he confirmed his suspicion by calling the Douglas police department. He made up his mind quickly to keep Sava in the dark for a while yet. *It wouldn't help to just spring this on Sava right away. It's going to hurt bad enough soon, but let's not make it any harder on the chap.*

Before he left work that day, Ailshie got a call back from the person in charge of the babysitting agency. "Inspector, your message said you needed the list of the referral numbers that were in place on or about the first week of June, is that right?"

"Yes, I've been told a potential client of yours called a Ramsey number around that time period and spoke with a woman who identified herself as Carolyn Owens."

"Well, I've combed through our records and we had a Ramsey referral for a Carolyn Owens. My file indicates, however, that Ms. Owens had her number removed less than a week after the date you gave us. I can give you her number if you wish."

"Thanks. Also, do you have any registration information on her? What I mean is, did she have to fill out any type of form or application to have her name listed with your service?"

"Yes, she filled out what we call a 'short form' registration, which is available only to applicants who have, shall we say, stellar references. In her case, she verbally provided a reference from a colleague at the Douglas Social Services Agency, a woman named Elaine Burton, and we simply noted Burton's name and phone number on the short form along with Ms. Owens's phone number. She also gave us the name of a local, meaning Ramsey, client of hers, a Mr. Carson Leary."

"Thanks. That will be a big help."

As he feared, the number for Carolyn Owens had been disconnected. It was too late in the day to do a trace on her with the phone company, or to phone Carson Leary or Elaine Burton, so Inspector Ailshie decided to go home. Not that he was going to put this case out of his mind even when he arrived home. No, this one had strong appeal. Theft of a child. More than that, theft of a single dad's child. And even more than that, a refugee's child. A refugee, at least in this little corner of Europe, was often judged harshly, as if losing one's country were some sort of sin.

Angus had seen a bit of that prejudice in his own life. Like many citizens of the Isle of Man, Angus came from elsewhere, which might as well be nowhere in the eyes of some of the locals. Some "nowhere Manx" came from Ireland, some from Scotland, England, Wales, and others from the continent and Scandinavia. Lately, at least since the breakup of the former Yugoslavia, many immigrants had come from Eastern Europe. These days, probably fewer than half of the Manx were native born, or if they were natives they were only first generation.

Angus's people came from Liverpool most recently. But immigrants from Liverpool were often suspected—by the native Manx, at least—of being less than English. After all, Liverpool was full of Irishmen, as everyone knew. Not to mention all manner of immigrants and "foreigners" from God knows where. Angus couldn't recall how many times he had to respond to polite questions as to his ethnic heritage, even when the questioner knew he came from Liverpool. Indeed, that had been true even though Angus was born on the Isle of Man.

Even without the constant, if amusing, discussions of his ethnic heritage, Angus had seen enough prejudice against "minorities" and immigrants to put him firmly in the "one-world" camp, to use a term he'd heard used by his friend Jaleh at the Bahá'í Centre. So Angus was committed to finding out what happened to little Dushan Sava.

Angus decided to get to know Dimitri a little better while he pursued the criminal investigation. Dimitri had a story, and Angus wanted to hear it. Besides, it might help Dimitri's mental state to share some of his grief.

CHAPTER FIFTEEN:
THE TRAIL GETS COLD

"**D**ouglas Social Services, Elaine Burton speaking. How may I help you?"

Ailshie decided to pretend ignorance. "This is Inspector Ailshie of the Ramsey Police Department. Is my understanding correct that a Ms. Carolyn Owens used to work in your office?

"Indeed she did, Inspector. In fact, I worked with her a good part of the 12 years she worked here, 10 years at least. Unfortunately, due to some unprofessional conduct on her part, she was terminated about three months ago."

"What kind of unprofessional conduct?"

"I'm surprised you don't know. Illegal adoptions. I would have thought your police department and our police department might share this kind of information. Well, as you know, the Isle of Man, like the UK proper, is practically flooded with refugees and illegal immigrants. Many are in dire straits, especially those widower men with young children. I suppose Carolyn was moved by the plight of the children and decided to see what she could do to have them adopted by families here and in Britain itself. She and a co-worker, Derrick Nelson, set up an unofficial adoption office in Liverpool. That, of course, was highly illegal, and they were both found out and fired. Possible criminal charges pending, too, I heard. I understand she has been doing a little babysitting recently to make ends meet, most recently for a man named Carson Leary, who had called us for a reference. Are you calling about that case?"

"Not about Leary, no. I'm investigating a child abduction, and right now Owens is the prime suspect. It looks like one of her other babysitting jobs turned into an abduction, much to the surprise and horror of her client, the child's father. We don't know what became of either the child or Ms. Owens."

"Oh, my God! That's sickening! That's definitely not what she and Derrick were doing before, at least not according to the termination file on them. What they did was to arrange true adoptions, albeit illegal ones; the parents or parent, as the case may be, actually gave the child up for adoption. There were no abductions alleged."

"What can you tell me about them, Ms. Owens and Mr. Nelson? Is it Miss Owens or is she married?"

"She's married, or I should say was married; she recently divorced. She and her ex split up last November. She was married when I came to work here about 10 years ago. I never did know her maiden name, though. But Derrick Nelson, now there's a mystery, at least as far as I'm concerned. Very private fellow. Single, maybe; I don't really know. I just suspect single 'cause he was quite a carouser. He and Carolyn's ex were drinking mates, I'm told. But I expect you already know Carolyn's ex—Trevor Owens is his name—has already split for Australia or some such."

"No, I didn't know that. I didn't even know his name or anything about him. Do you happen to have any further information on Nelson, like an address or phone number?"

"I'll have to pull up his file from storage; let me put you on hold for a moment."

Angus took advantage of the pause to look up Derrick Nelson's name in the department's Rolodex of local criminals. Nothing. When Burton came back on the line she provided Ailshie with Nelson's address and phone number.

"Thanks for that, Ms. Burton. I may have to contact you again for more information. Will you be taking any vacation out of the area in the next few weeks?"

"Vacation? Hah. The work around here is never ending, and the pay is hardly adequate for me to take a vacation. Maybe to Liverpool; does that count?"

"That's fine. Just ring me up with the particulars on where you'll be and how to reach you."

"Speaking of Liverpool, I recall that Carolyn sometimes took short vacations there. I suspect she had family there, but I'm not sure. She never talked about her family."

"That is helpful. I'll look into it. Thanks again."

Ailshie decided to drive the 18 miles to Douglas the next morning. According to Burton, Nelson lived in the Douglas city center.

Tooling along in his 1959 Peugeot 403, Ailshie liked to imagine himself as the great American detective Lieutenant Frank Columbo, played by Peter Falk. "Hell, I've got the paunch; I just need the cigar, the glass eye, and the rumpled raincoat," Ailshie said to his rearview mirror. He sighed and addressed his mirror again, "Hell, who am I kidding? I'm more 'Rumpole of the Bailey' than 'Columbo.'"

Nelson proved to be a cagey character, at least at first, suspicious about Ailshie's motives. A short, stout man, he reminded Ailshie of the actor Peter Lorre, not just because of his appearance but also because of his suspicious demeanor. Ailshie was not surprised at Nelson's reaction to him, but it got tiresome being viewed this way. *I don't get it, I'm only asking about the whereabouts of his friend. For all he knows, his friend might need help, or maybe he's been named in his rich uncle's will.*

After the first five minutes of the interview, the entirety of which Nelson dominated by asking most of the questions and skillfully dodging Ailshie's questions, Ailshie managed to steer the conversation around to Trevor Owens. Nelson seemed relieved that the question had nothing to do with him. "Well, Inspector. I can't say as I've seen much of Trevor these past few months. Or at all, as a matter of fact. I'm told he packed up and moved away to Australia or New Zealand. I've not heard a peep from him since last December, if you want to know."

"Were you two good friends, colleagues, what?"

"Mostly we shared a pint or two at the pub after work. I didn't work with him; he was a luggage handler at the Douglas airport. We used to know each other from our school days and we ran into each other a few months before he got divorced last fall from a coworker of mine, Carolyn Owens."

"What do you know about Carolyn."

"Very little other than knowing her casually in the office. I thought she was an okay sort; bright but not too talkative. Most of what came out of Trevor's mouth, though, were complaints about Carolyn: you know, the usual stuff, she was a whiner, she was frigid, she was secretive, he couldn't do nothing right, blah, blah, blah. After awhile, I guess he got the hint I wasn't interested in his problems with Carolyn and he stopped talking about her."

"Did Trevor or Carolyn ever talk about her relatives? Did you know her maiden name?"

"No to both questions, Inspector. Me and her only talked in the office about work stuff. Me and Trevor mostly talked about football, although he, like Carolyn, liked to rant about the problems all the immigrants were causing on the Isle and the rest of Britain and Europe."

"I understand those immigrant problems you mention had something to do with your dismissal from the agency, is that right?"

Even though this question touched on a sore subject, Nelson was no longer nervous or wary. "Yep; I don't mind telling you I made a big mistake listening to Carolyn's scheme. It was a quick and dirty solution to what was becoming a huge caseload logjam at the office. We thought—she thought, and I guess I accepted her logic without thinking about the legal aspects—it made a lot of sense. Apparently, one of the families we helped in adopting a kid didn't think much of the kid after all and contacted the Douglas office to give him back. That's when the shit hit the fan. The Douglas office—which hadn't known anything about our "satellite" office in Liverpool—fired us immediately. They were going to charge me with a crime unless I came clean with the whole scheme. I decided to cooperate, but I guess Carolyn is still in hot water, right?"

"Well, let's just say my office is interested in finding out more about Carolyn. If you hear anything let me know. Perhaps Mr. Owens will write you and if so, please save his address and write him back. See if you can get more information about Carolyn, especially her family, where she came from, etc. Sounds like from what you say about their relationship, Trevor wouldn't be shy about answering your questions. Please keep in touch."

"I'll do what I can, but like I say, I've no information on him at all; just that he moved to Australia or someplace for a job."

After getting nowhere with Derrick Nelson and Carolyn's ex-boss, the next item on Angus's agenda was to have another talk with Dimitri, mostly to reassure him that steps were being taken, progress being made, new avenues explored.

As Angus turned onto the river road leading to Dimitri's neighborhood, he spied him sitting alone on a park bench on the bank of the Selby. *I'll bet he used to bring the lad down here to feed the ducks.* Angus parked his Peugeot and waved.

Dimitri looked up and smiled at Angus's approach. "So, what news, Inspector? You have heard nothing I see on your face. I heard nothing also. I am just working and sitting in front of TV and eating and crying. Yesterday I decide to move out of apartment because memory of what happened doesn't let me sleep. Now I living in my old boarding house on Waterloo Street. I thinking I will move to nicer apartment maybe, but money is still problem."

Angus sat next to Dimitri and put a hand on his shoulder. "We'll get to the bottom of this. Have faith, my friend. Actually, I want to take a new tack that might prove helpful. What can you tell me about your wife: where she's from, how her abduction took place, how you met, whatever you can tell me. You never know, there might be some clues hidden in those details."

"Sure. She was not Belgrade girl originally. She Slovenian girl, from Ljubljana, worked as public health nurse in Sarajevo and Belgrade. In Belgrade was where she really shine. Brilliant nurse, all medical people in hospital like her. Sarajevo before that, only work as intern. She escape Sarajevo with Red Cross guy, Milan Vukadin, while Serb army is trying to destroy city. After that, she speak and write newspaper letters about justice and all people equal and deserve protection. As I think, she was killed because of her activities for protecting rights of people like Muslims, Roma, Croats.

"We meet at café on river few times, then eventually get married. Her name Marta Cecelja; she keep her last name; says my name, Sava, is name of river, not woman!"

"What have you done to try to find out what happened to her?"

"I pretty sure what happened to her; she murdered. Amina, our maid and babysitter, see whole thing. Men drag her out of office saying she will pay. Pay! What that mean? Only mean they kill her."

"But still, you must have done some checking for her, right?"

"Yeah, sure. I look all over Belgrade. I ask million questions. But then fascists start threatening me, tell me to take baby and leave Belgrade, leave Serbia, leave Yugoslavia! Someone burn my fishing boat. My crew already leave before that; they get threats too, or get drafted into army. My family get threats. My Aunt Adrijana move out of city; stay on farm of my cousin. Army take her apartment, use it for office space. Army take her brother's auto repair shop. Amina is threatened and goes with Adrijana when I tell her to leave. Then, finally, someone try to run me off road while I driving in car with Dushan. When I get home, I see windows broken and my apartment wrecked. My stuff all over floor. A note says I will die tomorrow if I no leave. I find refugee agency and leave with baby. We stay in Liverpool for few weeks. They bring me here, and the rest you know."

"But did you ever try to contact Marta's family in Slovenia?"

"I only know her father last name, Cecelja. I never meet her parents or family because of bad relations after war with Slovenia. I cannot call anyone there. In 1997 and 1998, no Internet. Even today, almost no Internet here. I have no computer and no money to buy one. Besides, I believe she killed. If not killed, if she escape, why nobody contact my family?"

"If you don't mind, I think I might be able to contact people in Slovenia and see if there's any record of her there. What did you say the name of the city was where she used to live?"

"Capital city, Ljubljana. She had parents and grandparents there. No brothers or sisters. But she never work there, only student, then she go to Sarajevo and work as nurse."

"You say you were able to leave Belgrade with the help of a refugee agency. Did you tell anyone in your family that? What about your Aunt Adrijana?"

"I could not call her, so I sent letter. I don't know if she receive letter. But anyway not much to tell in the letter. I did not know where agency would send us. I did not even know name of agency. Just that we were on list to go."

"Dimitri, you're a prince. I have a good feeling about this. I think we will get to the bottom of your wife's disappearance one way or another. For now, let me take you out for a bite to eat. You're done working for the day, correct?"

"Yes, finished working. That very nice of you, Inspector. I just have to go home and change. How 'bout I meet you at Café Neptune, on other side of harbor in hour or so? It is good place, not too expensive for fisherman and policeman."

"Fine. I'll meet you there. Maybe I'll have some news for you by then."

CHAPTER SIXTEEN:
FIRST REUNION

In the two years since Milan and Jovan delivered Marta and Séifullah to Ljubljana, Marta never ceased searching for her husband and child. She was grateful that the volume of work at the municipal hospital helped her put her longing out of mind.

As she was completing some mid-morning paperwork, the phone rang at her desk. It was Séif. "Marta, you won't believe who's shown up here looking for you!" Séif was practically shouting from excitement into the pay phone to be heard over the street noise of a busy Ljubljana intersection.

"I give up, who? I'm too busy to play games."

"Well, I can't tell you now; the news will get in your way. Why don't I meet you at lunch time with your mystery guests?"

"That'll have to do, I guess. I can wait an hour."

Marta sat in the cafeteria nibbling at her salad as she nervously awaited Séif and whoever it was that wanted to meet her. She practically choked on her artichoke when she saw Amina and Adrijana enter with Séif.

"Oh my God!" Marta exclaimed as she jumped up from the table and ran to the group with arms outstretched. "How did this happen? How did you find me? I can't believe you're here and safe! You look just the same."

The women hugged as Séif beamed in the background. Adrijana wiped her eyes, took a deep breath, and said, "Séif told us your story. I can't believe we found you. We can thank Amina's brilliant idea of posting a notice in the local mosque newsletter. You look fantastic, Marta, just as beautiful as ever."

Amina's smile stretched from ear to ear. "Marta, I am so glad to see you! You can't believe how devastated we all were when you were abducted. I heard the whole thing from the bathroom of your office after I had finished diapering little Dushan. I took him home and told

Dimitri what happened. We were so afraid you would be killed."

Marta's eyes opened wide. "Dimitri and Dushan, what about them? Where are they?"

Adrijana answered with a frown, "Nobody knows. Dimitri, Amina and our whole family were harassed after that. Dimitri received numerous threats of death if he didn't leave. He eventually closed his business after his fishing boat was burned. He left the country with Dushan. He sent me a letter saying some agency was taking them out of the country, but he wasn't sure where and didn't say which agency. I and most of the rest of the family have lost most of our property in Belgrade and are living on a distant cousin's farm outside of the city. I guess we Savas are not pure enough for the Serbian Army. Amina has been staying with us. She's a member of the family now."

Marta motioned them to sit down with her at an empty cafeteria table. "How did you even suspect I might still be alive, let alone be here in Ljubljana?"

"We had no choice but to hope for your survival. And if somehow you were able to survive, we guessed you might try to find your way to Slovenia rather than return to Belgrade. Speaking of your home, how is your family?"

"They're all fine, my mom is still working for the city. My father is about to retire from his travel agency business. My mom's parents live here but are in poor health. For now, they're taking it easy in their little apartments in the city. Shimza, my dad's widowed mom, may still be living in Istanbul, although she might have returned to Bulgaria. I'm sure you remember her, Adrijana, she called you to find out where Dimitri and I had gone on our honeymoon. But tell me, have you any idea where Dimitri and Dushan fled to? I miss them terribly. Somehow, I just know they're okay, I just don't know where."

Adrijana frowned. "The Red Cross doesn't know anything. There are various NATO agencies and national agencies that might have some record, but we haven't been able to get in contact with them except for the Americans. No luck there."

Marta sighed. "Yeah, I've tried some of the refugee agencies without luck. I don't know where else to turn."

Séif jumped into the conversation at that point. "I think for the time being we need to get to work finding a place for Amina and Adrijana to stay, and maybe jobs. They probably shouldn't try to return to Serbia. Their names might be on some kind of list. You remember Jovan, Marta? The former JNA soldier who helped you, me and Milan escape? I got in touch with him this morning just before I called you. He was overjoyed to hear about these ladies' adventure getting here, but he warned them not to try to return. He's pretty sure their flight out of the country was discovered, their names recorded and they would be arrested upon their return."

Marta turned to Amina and Adrijana. "No problem in the housing department. My mom's parents live in a small duplex they own in the old part of town, right near the Dragon Bridge, and the other unit in the duplex is vacant at the moment. You can live there rent-free until you find work. You can stay indefinitely, for all I know. I'll check into it."

CHAPTER SEVENTEEN:
A COLD CASE, 1999-2000

When Angus began looking for Marta in the fall of 1999, it had been four years since Marta was taken. In police lingo, it was a cold case, but it was made harder because the abduction took place in a foreign country, a country that subsequently disintegrated. All he knew was that Marta was originally from Ljubljana and her last name was Cecelja. Maybe her parents were still alive? Maybe she was looking for Dimitri?

Without a better plan, Angus contacted the UN refugee agency in London and Liverpool to see if Dimitri's name showed up on either list of refugees resettled in the UK. Angus figured that if anyone looked for Dimitri as a refugee in the UK, they might try the UN agencies there. The London office had his name in their archives but listed him as having settled in Liverpool. The Liverpool office had him listed only as "in transit." The clerk said he could have gone to anywhere in England, the Crown Dependencies, Scotland, Wales, even Ireland.

"And how long has he been on your list?"

"Our policy is to keep clients on the active list until they've been placed. We register their placement and keep it updated for a year. Then it goes into our archives."

"But you don't have his placement information at all, only that he was in transit from Liverpool. Why is that?"

"Someone dropped the ball is all I can say. We don't know where he ended up."

"Well, I can help you out on that. He was sent to the Isle of Man a few years ago and lives in Ramsey." After telling the clerk Dimitri's address at the boarding house on Waterloo Street, Angus said, "Unfortunately the phone at the boarding house is a pay phone for outgoing calls only."

"I can update the information. But if you already know where he is, why are you calling us?"

"His wife, if she's still alive, will be looking for him. And he's looking for her. So, if she contacts you guys, will she be able to get hold of this updated information?"

"We can only hope. She will if she contacts us in Liverpool directly, but I can't speak for our London office. They're awash with refugees and way behind in their record keeping."

"That'll have to do, I guess. It's a long shot, anyway. Mr. Sava is pretty sure his wife was killed when she was abducted by gunmen. But he doesn't know for sure."

*   *   *

A few months later, in Ljubljana, Marta was busy helping Amina and Adrijana get settled in the vacant apartment upstairs from her parents' apartment. Adrijana handed Marta a flyer she had picked up in the lounge of Marta's hospital and asked, "Is this the organization you contacted when you first started looking for Dimitri?"

Marta scanned the flyer. "I don't think so. I only recall calling the Red Cross. I didn't think of calling a UN agency. This one says 'UN High Commission on Refugees.' I didn't know about them. Shall we send them a letter? It can't hurt."

"Sure," Adrijana said. "I have some of Dimitri's personal papers with his identifying information that could be useful."

As Marta feared, when the UNHCR wrote back a month later, they had nothing. The letter said, "We have no record of anyone by that name, but we are forwarding your inquiry to our Liverpool, Edinburgh and Dublin branches. We are backlogged at the moment, as you might imagine, but if we come upon the name, we will certainly contact you. We will keep your name and address on file in case we locate your husband and child."

Nobody really expected any results, so five weeks later when the three of them went to the post office to pick up a registered letter from the UNHCRA, they were understandably excited.

Marta read the letter aloud. "Dear Mrs. Cecelja, this is in response to your inquiry about your husband, Dimitri Sava, and your son Dushan, refugees from the former Yugoslavia. Our records show that a placement was found for them in the city of Ramsey, Isle of Man. We are providing you with the address we have on file. It was updated by the police in that city during the past six months, so it is hopefully still current. It appears that Mr. Sava doesn't have a phone."

The three women erupted in happy screams before they even left the post office. "That's fantastic! I can't believe it!" Adrijana said.

"Where's the Isle of Man? I've never heard of it," said Amina.

Adrijana and Marta likewise didn't know where it was. "I assume it is in England, since this letter is from Liverpool. Wherever it is, I'm going there as soon as I can arrange a leave from my job," Marta gushed, her hands trembling as she held the letter.

"What do you mean 'you?' You're not leaving us behind," Adrijana said.

CHAPTER EIGHTEEN:
EAST MEETS WEST IN THE NEW MILLENNIUM

Even though Marta, Adrijana and Amina learned of Dimitri's whereabouts in early 2000, it was May of that year before Marta could arrange to get some time off to make the trip to the UK. She had received no reply to her letter to Dimitri at the address she was given, but was determined to go anyway. "The hospital is giving me a month," she said to Adrijana. "I think we can go as soon as you and Amina can get ready."

"Well, I'm retired," said Adrijana, "so I'm already ready. Amina told me she can go at the drop of a hat, since Séifu said he would cover for her at the community center."

The three women had experienced a fair amount of delay and bureaucratic complications before they were able to obtain travel documents for their upcoming trip to the Isle of Man. It was considerably easier for Marta than for the other two. Because she was a native of Slovenia, it was no big deal to obtain a passport. But Amina and Adrijana were both citizens of the Bosnian and Serbian provinces of the former Yugoslavia, and it took them almost two months to get their passports via the respective interest sections of the Austrian embassy in Ljubljana. Finally, in mid-summer 2000, they were ready to head to the airport.

Their plane touched down at Heathrow on July 1. Heathrow was a madhouse, of course. The crowds and confusing airport procedures were doubly unnerving to these three friends from the Balkans. They had never flown before. Not only was the flight itself a breathtaking experience, but their passports and identification were closely scrutinized by suspicious customs officials in one of the planet's busiest airports. It was an experience the women were only too glad to put behind them as they made their way to the nearest British Rail terminal. They were bound for Liverpool and then for the Isle of Man.

As they rode the ferry across the Irish Sea, Amina picked up a little tourist map and brochure for the Isle of Man, which included a street map of the town of Ramsey, their destination. A few moments after she returned to where the other women were sitting, she announced, "I think I've located Dimitri's street." Pointing to the map's extremely small print next to a crooked little line near a river, she said, "Waterloo Street, that's it."

Marta took the map and looked closely at the grid of streets and waterways. "It looks easy to find. His address is that large building next to the church. Is the ferry terminal near Waterloo Street? I don't see it."

"Not far, I see it here," Adrijana said, pointing to what appeared to be a port of some kind.

After disembarking at the ferry terminal, the three of them walked into town. Marta was eager to proceed immediately to the house, but the other two wanted to have a bite to eat first. An hour later, they were standing in front of the residence listed in the UN letter as Dimitri's. "It looks like a boarding house. It's huge," Adrijana said.

Marta rang the doorbell and they waited for what seemed like forever before someone opened the door. That someone was an elderly woman who, judging from the fact that she was holding a broom, appeared to work there. The woman scrutinized the three women carefully before asking, "What can I do for you ladies?" She looked and sounded pleasant enough. The three friends' initial nervousness evaporated at the warmth of her smile and the fact that she spoke with some type of East European accent. Marta, whose English was better than the others, replied, "Yes, good afternoon, ma'am. My name is Marta and these are my friends Adrijana and Amina. We were told that Mr. Dimitri Sava lives here. He is my husband. It is long story, but because of war in Yugoslavia we became separated back in 1995. He and our little boy escape the war, but I could not escape for several years. Just recently I learn that Dimitri living here at this address."

"Ah, yes. Dimitri. A fisherman and a very good chap. I do remember him. Always had a good word. Come in, come in. My name is Mrs. Shelton. I'm the manager." Motioning to the little office just inside the doorway and to the right of the rather large living room, she said, "Have a seat in my office. Let me put away this broom. When I come back I'll fill you in on Dimitri." Somehow,

Marta expected the woman's expression to be somewhat more like a smile instead of the frown she wore as she turned away from the ladies. Adrijana said to Marta, "From what she said, it sounds like Dimitri doesn't live here any more." Marta didn't reply.

While the three friends sat waiting for Mrs. Shelton's return, Marta couldn't help but notice that the expansive living room bore no evidence of a child's presence, such as toys left lying around. When Mrs. Shelton came back and sat at the desk, Marta asked, "Excuse, but doesn't Dimitri and our little boy still living here in your place?"

"No, they don't. But I'm afraid I have some bad news, ma'am. Just about a year ago, the boy was taken from Dimitri and has not been found. A terrible thing. Dimitri moved into a room here not long after that. He told me he couldn't stand staying in their little apartment any longer; too many nightmares. The person who took the boy was a woman Dimitri hired to be a babysitter while he and his fishing crew went to the North Sea. The police have been investigating but so far without any luck. Then, probably about a month ago, Dimitri moved to an apartment not far from here."

When Marta heard this, she teared up and was momentarily speechless. Adrijana and Amina began sobbing. Marta began sobbing as well, and then her sobs broke out into full-throated crying and moaning. The elderly woman quickly put her hand on Marta's elbow and said, "Why don't I pour you some tea and tell you what I know about the situation, which isn't much I'll warrant."

When Mrs. Shelton came back into the office from the kitchen, Marta and her friends had managed to compose themselves and sat mostly silent. Marta had lain her head back against the wall and covered her eyes with her right arm. Her breathing was labored. Mrs. Shelton spoke to her quietly, "Now, Marta, at least I can say that your husband is doing as well as can be expected. I can give you his address, but if I'm not mistaken he is off with his fishing crew on another trip. He told me, about a week ago, that he expected to be back in a week or 10 days. So, you'll have to wait another few days."

When Marta did not respond, Adrijana said, "Mrs. Shelton, I'm Dimitri's aunt. Amina here was worked for him and Marta. We are come a long way and we have so thanks to learn about Dimitri is safe. Is there anything details you can tell us how it happened?"

"I'm afraid I don't know too much more. But the person who

probably can is the police inspector in charge of the investigation, Angus Ailshie. I can tell you how to find him if you like. The office is not far from here, walking distance, actually. In the meantime, you'll be needing a place to stay while you wait for Dimitri to return, I expect. I have a nice bedroom that's currently unoccupied and I can rent it to you if you'd like to stay."

The women accepted the offer and deposited their luggage in the room. Mrs. Shelton moved in two rollaway beds. Even with three beds, the room had enough space to walk around in, but no place to sit. Marta said to Mrs. Shelton, "I will ask you to take one of the rollaway beds out when my husband returns; I will be moving in with him." She blushed as she said this, and Mrs. Shelton managed a smile, as did the other two women.

Besides the beds, there was an armoire for their clothes and a sink. The WC was down the hall. The residence had a comfortable living room with a TV, a coal fireplace, three worn, overstuffed chairs and three couches of approximately the same vintage as the chairs. Two men and a woman were sitting in the chairs reading magazines and chatting when the three friends entered. The residents nodded and smiled before resuming their conversation.

Marta walked over to a large side window and gazed at the yard. She could see a bit of river beyond some trees. Adrijana and Amina sat on the couch and waited for Marta to join them. Adrijana spoke first, "Well, we've still got another hour or so before Inspector Ailshie might be quitting work. Why don't we walk over and talk to him. If he's out, we can at least get to know the town a little in the meantime."

Without even sitting down, Marta motioned to the door and the three of them walked out onto the spacious front porch of the building. It was a fine July day, and the sea air was invigorating. "Reminds me a little of Belgrade," Amina said, "although the breeze is not quite the same as the breeze off the Sava River."

"Speaking of Sava," Adrijana said, "we can try to locate Dimitri Sava's apartment on our way to the police station. Mrs. Shelton says it's not far." The three women dawdled a bit on the porch, watching the townspeople strolling by enjoying the gorgeous late afternoon. Even Marta was starting to take in her surroundings.

CHAPTER NINETEEN:
SECOND REUNION

It was July 8 and Dimitri's fishing trip was a success. He had a week's furlough coming to him but he wasn't really looking forward to it. At least when he was out on the water, battling waves and large nets full of fighting, uncooperative fish, he could keep his depression and loneliness at bay. Dimitri was walking down Waterloo, across the street from his former boarding house, when he heard a shout followed by two more shouts. They were women's voices and they were shouting his name.

On the long veranda of the boarding house, three women were leaning over the railing waving to him and jumping up and down. One of the women turned and ran down the steps onto the sidewalk. Without stopping or looking for traffic, the woman ran across the street toward Dimitri. Then he recognized her.

"Dimitri, my darling, my love!" Marta practically knocked him over when she jumped into his arms. They embraced, holding each other, then kissed, then embraced some more, their hearts pounding.

The other two women arrived seconds later and grabbed onto the two embracing lovers. For a few moments, there was a noisy little dance right there on the sidewalk before the noise of sobbing and laughing evolved into words.

"Marta, I thought I would never see you again. You're here! How did you find me? What happened to you?" Dimitri wiped his eyes and continued. "Too many questions, I know. Let's go to my apartment and talk. Where are you staying?"

Marta answered without letting go of his hands, "We're staying in the same boarding house you used to stay in. We just arrived." Then her smile disappeared and the tears returned. "Dimitri, darling, Mrs. Shelton told us what happened to Dushan! I can't believe it. But, yes, let's talk about everything at your apartment." Before they turned to walk back, Dimitri hugged Adrijana and Amina. "Ladies, it is so good to see you again. What a story you must have! And I want to hear every word."

The foursome walked to the apartment speaking very little. Once in there, the stories they all had came flooding out. Dimitri was dumbfounded at Marta's description of her time as a working prisoner of his former employee, Goran. "I can't decide whether to be angry at him for keeping you prisoner, or happy that he protected you from what might have happened otherwise."

Dimitri eagerly listened to, and frequently interrupted, Adrijana and Amina as they related all that had befallen them during those bad times. Through an unspoken agreement, the four of them waited for Dimitri's story 'til the very end. When he unraveled that sad tale, the ladies were mostly silent but for their quiet sobbing. Late afternoon turned into late night before they agreed to meet again at breakfast. As Amina and Adrijana left his apartment, Dimitri said, "After breakfast I'll let the Inspector know of your arrival. He's a wonderful friend now, and I'm sure he'll be very happy to meet you all."

CHAPTER TWENTY:
THE BROTHERS' NEW LIFE, 2005-2006

Irene couldn't help but feel conflicting emotions as she listened to her son Dani's sobbing confession that he had no friends in school, which he hated. On the one hand, she was saddened by her son's anxiety over his school situation. On the other hand, she was proud of his friendship with his new stepbrother, who was not so new anymore; their friendship had matured into a deep bond over the past six years since Dushan came to live with them. *This is his saving grace*, she realized.

"Dani, I understand how you feel. A lot of kids your age can be very cruel. When I was in school back in England, it was even worse."

"I doubt it, mom. You don't know what it's like here in this stupid town, in this stupid school, with these stupid kids."

"But think for a moment—you have a couple of friends, don't you, friends who you can always trust?"

"My only friend is Dushan. But he's my brother, and he's not in my grade, and not in my classes at school. I never get to see my friends from our old neighborhood on the other side of town. And the kids in this neighborhood are snobs and hate us."

"But Dushan's your friend, right? Someone you love and who loves you, right?"

"Oh, mom, that's not the same thing! And plus, we can't even hang out together at school. He's younger, he's my brother, kids would tease him and me even more if we did. I hate these kids! I wish we never moved here. Why did we ever move to Victorville? What was wrong with San Francisco? And what was wrong with our old neighborhood in Victorville; that wasn't so bad, was it?"

"It's a long story. But for now, just focus on what's good in our lives. You have your family—me, your dad, and especially Dushan. Honestly, I've never seen two boys, or even brothers, as close as you and Dushan. And the fact that he's your adopted brother makes it even more amazing."

"Mom, I'm not really talking about Dushan, I'm telling you that this place stinks. So what if I have one good friend, my brother? Anyways, you're right, okay? We're close, no question. He and I became friends as soon as he moved in with us that summer before I turned six. I think it's not only because his own parents are gone somewhere, but because he felt sorry for us. Because Markos died only two months after Dushan came to live with us. Still, it would be nice if we had more friends in this neighborhood."

Irene sighed and looked out the window. After a minute or two, she decided to shift the subject away from Victorville and said, "Dani, we don't really know what happened to his parents. Maybe you and Dushan can find out some day after you grow up."

"Well I can tell you that Dushan believes his parents are alive and he'll see them again someday. He *knows* that, mom, and I believe it too! Sometimes his mom visits him in his dreams. He tells me all about it."

Those past six years since the Sandor family, with Dushan an official member, relocated to Victorville had not been easy. Shortly after Markos's death Burt was offered the new job he sought so intensely. They packed up and moved, arriving in their new city a week after school started for the boys. It was then that Burt chose to spring the news on the family that word had come from England: Dimitri's boat was officially judged to be missing, with all aboard presumed dead. It was devastating news for Dani and, Irene presumed, for Dushan as well. But it almost seemed to Irene that Dushan's reaction was just a little bit staged, for whose benefit she couldn't tell. Maybe his grief was suppressed, or mitigated by all that had happened in the past month—Markos's death, the move to Victorville, and a new school. To be sure, Dushan cried along with Dani. Although Irene cried as well, it was for a very different reason. Could Dushan tell what that reason was? Was the quality of her tears a clue to him that Burt was lying? Did he know Burt was lying anyway?

Irene also speculated that Dushan's less-than-genuine reaction to Burt's announcement had been because the boys' school term was already a week old when they enrolled, Dani in first grade and Dushan in kindergarten. Back then, six years ago, it was entirely possible that they were so preoccupied with adjusting to the new environment and the sadness of Markos's death that Burt's announcement of Dimitri's disappearance had less of an impact on them than it might have had.

Then there was the continuing, and worsening, friction between Burt and Irene. Irene had been kept in the dark concerning Burt's plan to change jobs and relocate the family if need be. The relocation to Victorville from San Francisco was, to say the least, a huge shock and disappointment to Irene. She had just been hired as a teacher's aide at the Presidio Day Care Center in San Francisco, walking distance from their house in the Marina District. She was devastated by Burt's announcement that the family would be pulling up stakes and moving to the less-than-lovely Southern California community of Victorville, not far from the even uglier city of San Bernardino.

At first, Dani and Dushan did not notice the increasing friction between their parents, although it did seem that Irene was being worn down by it. Their new elementary school had been challenging enough. Mercifully, though, their first year at school was a balm to their tortured souls because the kindergarten and first grade classes were combined due to low enrollment. That only cemented their friendship further. They became partners in this new endeavor, an adventure in a new way of life.

Their next few years of elementary school, even though the boys were now separated into different grades, saw their partnership become stronger and deeper. They made friends at school and in their neighborhood. But they found it harder and harder to ignore their parents' increasingly volatile arguments, especially when Burt occasionally hit Irene during his tirades. Irene would later tell them, "It's not his fault, boys. I've been pretty upset and I think I just push him too much. He doesn't mean to hurt me. He's frustrated at work and sometimes loses his temper." Neither boy believed her attempt to sanitize the situation. What's more, they noticed that Burt often blew up even when Irene hadn't done or said anything to provoke him.

Now that the boys were 10 and 11 years old, their opinions on their parents' dysfunction and their new neighborhood occupied more and more of their conscious lives. "I think," Dani said one evening as he and Dushan did homework in their room, "that mom is coming down with something, and dad gets mad at her even for that!"

Dushan put down his math book and looked at Dani. "I definitely agree with you. I'm worried about mom. And mad at dad. He yells at her for being lazy. But she sleeps a lot because she's tired, not because she's lazy."

Their worries about Irene's health made them have more and more difficulty sleeping. But soon, perhaps because of that, they began sharing dreams. They would appear in one another's dreams and compare notes after waking up. Sometimes they would "talk" about the dream while they were still inside the dream. As a result, the brothers' close bond became even closer. Their shared dreams became a regular occurrence and gave them much to talk about. When they awoke after having one of those shared dreams, they would almost simultaneously start laughing and talking about the dream. A few weeks after they began, Dani asked, "Dushan, do you dream in English or in your own language?"

Dushan put down his homework and looked at Dani. "I never really thought about it. What about you? Oh, right, you only have one language, English."

"Sure, but remember the first time when you and I had the same dream? We were talking to each other. We must have been talking in English because I don't speak Serbian."

"I don't really think we were talking. We were just thinking to each other or whatever. No speaking."

"But I woke up when you yelled 'stop' at me in the dream. What was I doing, do you remember?"

Dushan got up and picked up the Lego pirate ship. "In our dream you picked this up and told me you were going to float it in the bathtub. I told you to stop."

"See! That's what I mean. We were talking, not just thinking. Wow, I forgot about the pirate ship. It was so real."

"Real except that you didn't really pick it up—only in our dream. This thing hasn't moved from the bookcase since we put it together last year."

Dani put his hands behind his head and leaned back in his chair. "Once in awhile I dream that my mom and I are talking. Mostly she says things like 'don't be mad at Dad—he's afraid, that's all.' Do you still dream about your mom?"

"Yeah, but it's not like with you. I can't really talk to her, or I should say 'think' to her. And she mostly says she's okay and Dad's okay. When she asks me where I am, I start crying and can't answer. I wake up. I've told you this before."

"Yeah. I was just wondering if you still do it."

"I do, and it always reminds me that my Dad didn't die like Burt said he did."

Dani raised his eyebrows and said, "Oh, for sure. I don't believe him either. Nobody does. Carolyn didn't believe him either. Or at least she didn't when she was still living with us in San Francisco. Speaking of Carolyn, mom says she doesn't even call us anymore. Not that anyone cares about Carolyn, she's such a creep."

"Dani, I don't know what I'd do if I didn't have you and Irene. I have a feeling our family is in for some rough times. But I know, and I know you know, that we're partners."

Dushan set the pirate ship back on the shelf and stood at the window for a minute before sitting back down at the desk to finish his homework.

The boys found solace in their freedom to wander around the outskirts of Victorville, a freedom granted more because of their parents' inattention than any specific permission. Like most boys their age, they found adventure just about everywhere. And unlike most boys their age, they had no difficulty understanding girls. In fact, they understood that girls had friendships akin to their own—partnerships, in fact. Girls told each other their deepest secrets and worries and observations; so did Dushan and Dani. Girls would cry together when they felt like it; so did Dushan and Dani. Occasionally Dushan and Dani would hang out with pairs of girls. The resulting foursome would last weeks, their adventures interrupted only by the occasional confrontations with groups of boys to whom camaraderie with girls was not allowed.

Up until this year—Dani's first year in middle school and Dushan's last year in elementary school—school had been a source of wellbeing for the boys. But now, at the end of the school year, things changed drastically. Even though Burt had been passed over for a promotion, he nonetheless decided to move the family to a better neighborhood and buy a bigger house to compensate for the bruising his ego had taken at work. The excitement he experienced from spending so much money didn't last long and had no lasting effect on his frustrations. Nor did having a bigger house in a better neighborhood compensate the boys for having to change schools.

In September 2005 Dani entered seventh grade in the middle school serving their somewhat more upscale neighborhood. But despite the physical beauty of the neighborhood, the boys missed the familiar haunts of their old stomping ground. Dushan was in sixth grade, his first year in middle school. Both boys found themselves the object of a certain amount of suspicion in this small-minded community, which was worse here than in other parts of Victorville, even in so-called bad neighborhoods like where they used to live.

"If one more kid calls me 'spic' I swear I'm gonna kill him," Dushan said to Dani as they walked along the railroad tracks that cut through a corner of town.

Dani replied while trying not to step off the track rails. "They're a bunch of bozos. They just think you're a Mexican because you're darker than them. Besides, there's nothing wrong with being Mexican. In case you haven't noticed, there are tons of them here and they're not the trouble-makers."

"Dani, I wanted to ask you, have you noticed anything wrong with mom? She seems a lot more tired than usual. I'm worried about her."

"Yeah, I did notice that. Maybe it's dad; he's been a real asshole lately. She says it's his job; I say he's just a jerk. He's been picking on mom a lot lately, even more than usual, which is a lot."

"And he picks on you, too, Dani. I saw him grab you the other day and throw you up against the washing machine. What did you do to make him do that, anyway?"

"Forget about it. I just told him to leave mom alone and he lost it. Look, it was just a shove. It was nothing."

"I don't think it was nothing; you were crying afterwards. If I see him do that to you again, I'm not gonna just stand there."

"Please, Dushan, don't do anything. It's my problem. Besides, I don't intend to get in his face again. I'll be more careful."

The railroad tracks veered to the left and left the outskirts of the bad neighborhood, the one they used to live in, and followed a long curving route out of town. The boys stopped following the tracks and instead turned right back into town, on their way to a Taco Bell for a late afternoon snack. It was Saturday, and their parents were probably not home yet from their various errands. As the boys got closer to the Taco Bell, they saw some junior Sureño gangbanger wannabees that Dani used to know last year. Dani put his hand on Dushan's elbow and said, "Bad news, those guys, let's cross the street and get out of this neighborhood." Both brothers were old pros at avoiding trouble after living in Victorville for these past six years.

They continued walking as the sun set behind them. They walked up to their front door, which was open, and saw Irene lying on the floor with two grocery bags next to her, their contents spilling out. Dushan was the first to reach her. "Mom, what happened? You hit your head, you're bleeding."

"I don't know. I guess I fainted. Maybe I was too hot. These Indian summer days really get to me."

Dani and Dushan helped her into a sitting position and then held her as she stood shakily for a few seconds. They maneuvered her over to the overstuffed chair in the living room and eased her into it. As she caught her breath, Dani said, "Mom, something's going on with you, and it's not the heat. You've been getting weaker lately. We've both noticed. And it's not just that dad's picking on you. Something else is going on with your health. What is it?"

"Boys, I have to tell you something. I'm going to need help in the next few weeks or months because your father won't be very helpful at all. In many ways, he has never grown up and remains a deeply selfish and lonely man."

"What do you mean," Dushan asked. "What's wrong?"

Irene teared up and took several deep breaths. Looking from one boy to the other, she said, "I've been diagnosed with pancreatic cancer. I've been struggling with it for a few months now. But soon it'll be time for me to go into the hospital for more intensive treatment. I doubt I'll recover from it; the treatment will give me a few comfortable months and then who knows what will happen."

The boys began crying softly while they stroked her arms. "We'll do whatever you need us to do, mom," Dushan said in a choking voice. "Just don't give up hope."

"Dushan and Dani, my treasures. I can't tell you how much you both mean to me. I love you more than life itself, more than the world. My life has been so blessed with you boys." Irene reached for the tissue box on the end table but knocked it onto the floor. Dani picked it up and handed it to her. She dabbed her eyes and started to speak, but her words turned into sobs. To distract himself, Dushan picked up the bags of groceries and put them on the kitchen table.

Wiping his eyes on his sleeve, he walked back and sat next to Dani on the sofa.

When Irene managed to compose herself a bit, she continued. "I've been hiding something inside me, something dark, that has been eating into me. It's that something that maybe caused this cancer to come to life."

Dani and Dushan raised their heads and waited for Irene to continue.

"Dushan, Burt did a terrible thing when you first came to stay with us that summer before you were five. And I… I suspected it but I was not sure, and I didn't think I could do anything to stop him."

"What are you talking about, mom?" Dushan asked.

"Dushan, you were not given up for adoption by your father. And the whole story of your dad being lost at sea is a complete lie. I got the true story out of Carolyn a few months ago when I called her in San Francisco, at least as much of the truth as she is capable of telling. I recorded our conversation and have the cassette hidden away where your father will never find it."

Dani interrupted, "But mom, how could dad do something like that? What exactly happened?"

Dushan slid off the couch cushion and slumped over, his head and arms on his knees. He sobbed gently and said, "I just knew something like that was what happened. I knew it. I could tell from the way he talked about it. Go on."

Irene continued, "Burt and Carolyn arranged to steal you from your dad, Dushan. At least that's what Carolyn told me. But I don't think Burt really knew what she was planning to do; all he wanted was for her to adopt a boy the same age as Markos and bring him over to become part of our family. That's what he told me."

Irene paused, got up and walked into the kitchen to pour herself a glass of water. She walked back and sat down before continuing. "Carolyn told me she arranged to get hired by Dimitri as his babysitter while his fishing company sent him on a month-long fishing trip. When he left, Carolyn took you to Liverpool; you remember that boat ride, don't you Dushan? She met Burt there and the two of them brought you to San Francisco with them. After Markos died, just before we moved to Victorville, Burt announced to us all that your dad had been lost at sea. When I confronted him privately, he swore to me that it was the truth, that he had heard it on the BBC news the night before. I swear to you, Dushan, I had nothing to do with his scheme, and I only decided not to say anything because I had no way of challenging Burt's story, and there was no chance of changing the outcome. You were here. What was done was done. I thought maybe your dad really was lost at sea; I didn't know one way or the other. I fought with Burt over this on many occasions, and eventually he started hitting me whenever I brought it up. I finally gave up. I was afraid to tell anyone; I thought he would really hurt me. Maybe even kill me."

"But mom," Dani asked, "why would dad want to adopt another kid? We had Markos, even though he was really sick."

"It was always about the money. You never knew this, but your grandmother Margaret Sandor, over in Liverpool, was paying Burt a very generous allowance for Markos and you, and had promised to give him and you, Dani, a lot of money when you both turned 18. Burt didn't want to lose Markos's share of that money if he were to die, so Burt arranged with Carolyn to adopt a boy the same age as Markos and keep the whole scheme, including Markos's illness, a secret from your grandmother. He even kept the secret from your schools; he enrolled Dushan as Markos Dushan Sandor, and never said anything about Markos dying."

Dushan looked up with hopeful eyes. "So, I was right. My dad, my real dad, is alive! I sometimes dream that my mom and dad are talking to me, but I also worry that I'm only imagining things, that my dreams aren't real. "

"I really don't know, Dushan, if everything Carolyn told me is the truth or only part of the truth. But promise me, please, you won't confront Burt with this. There's no telling what he'll do. You don't know how violent he can get when he gets challenged. I would never forgive myself if he hurt either of you. If you want to pursue your own investigation, do it. But it might be an impossible task to find out what happened to Dimitri."

* * *

It was less than a week before Irene was admitted to the hospital. Her symptoms—abdominal pain, weight loss, nausea, diarrhea—had been rapidly getting worse. She could no longer even get out of bed or eat. During her first week in the hospital, the boys visited her each afternoon and evening, doing their homework next to her hospital bed. After that week, Irene was transferred to a ward where visits were restricted to adults. Dani and Dushan were beside themselves with grief, and had to fend for themselves at home when Burt spent evenings at the hospital.

It was all Dushan could do to restrain Dani from confronting Burt over Dushan's adoption, something Dani should have known would only provoke the man. Dushan, for some reason he couldn't quite understand, had little interest in such a confrontation. He only thought of the present—praying for Irene's cure—and the future. Beyond that what he wanted to do was find his parents—his real parents.

"You must feel something, Dushan. I mean Burt and Carolyn took you away from your father! Doesn't that make you angry? Or at least make you want to force Burt to admit it? We could even look for mom's cassette of Carolyn's confession on the phone and play it for Burt. What do you think?"

"I don't want to do any of that. Of course I feel angry. But more than that I feel sad and worried for my dad—Dimitri that is. I can't explain why I don't feel angrier. Maybe I'm stuffing that anger down deep inside of me. I guess I just don't want to dwell on something I can't do anything about. What I can do something about is try to find out where my mom and dad are. Remember when Mom said my dad might be alive? Do you know that the night she said that, I had a dream about both my parents, a dream that felt like more than a dream, like they were talking to me, looking for me. Remember how I used to tell you about my dreams of my mom talking to me? Well, this time it was both of them, and they were together! I don't know, Dani, I just wanna find them, and I think I can. Anyway, I definitely don't want to let Burt know about the cassette tape. He'd probably destroy it and beat the shit out of us for even having it."

"Well, I still feel like we should say something. Give him a chance to fess up. It'll do him good."

"Please, Dani. This is my problem. Let me handle it my way."

"Fine. And just what might that be? You gonna fly to England and look for people named Sava?"

"Not England, the Isle of Man. They're separate but connected, sort of like Puerto Rico and the United States. The Isle of Man is pretty small."

"But really, Dushan, you obviously can't go there. You're not even 11 yet. So you must be thinking of a phone call."

"For starters, I can search the Internet for fishing boats on the Isle of Man. I can post things on blogs there if there are any. One way or another, I'm gonna find out where my parents are. In the meantime, let's focus our prayers on Mom. I don't want her to die."

For the next month, Irene was in and out of the hospital. Her stamina seemed to increase, then hold steady, then plummet rapidly. She made another trip to the ER and intensive care. Then she was back home again and the cycle was repeated. The boys were consumed with the need to care for her and comfort her on those occasions when she was home.

Burt sensed that something had transpired between the boys and Irene. He was wary when they were around. They were sullen when he was present, and said very little to him. Dani seemed to be more tense around him than Dushan was. Dushan had an air of expectation, of longing for something that he wouldn't talk about. Of course, Burt rationalized, Dushan and Dani were stressed out over Irene's imminent demise. Perhaps that explained their reticence around him. But still, he was their father. Shouldn't they show a little affection once in a while?

The end finally came for Irene on November 4th after a month-long stay in the hospital's hospice program for terminal patients, exactly three days after Dani's 12th birthday and Dushan's 11th birthday. After talking softly to the boys during a visit, she closed her eyes as if to sleep. Maybe she was sleeping, but she didn't wake up. "We love you, Mom. We'll always love you," Dushan murmured as he and Dani laid their heads on her shoulders. Their tears rolled gently down their cheeks.

The boys took it better than Burt, surprisingly, who acted as if the rug had been pulled out from under him. He sobbed openly in the chair next to her bed. He stayed like that for several minutes and waved the boys off as they stood and suggested they leave. They left the room and walked the mile and a half home. Burt showed up an hour later, puffy eyed and silent. He went straight upstairs and left the boys to themselves for the rest of the afternoon and evening.

"You'd think he really loved her," Dani said to Dushan as they walked home from school about a week after Irene's passing. The two of them had observed their birthdays almost alone. Burt did nothing more than buy a cake and give them cash—"You're too old for toys, so here's some money. Spend it wisely," were all the words he could muster. Under the circumstances, the boys hardly registered the absence of any meaningful birthday celebration. Their emotional reaction to their mom's passing and simmering anger at Burt was almost all they could think about. Dani continued, "I mean, for the past two years he's done nothing but yell at her. When he bought our bigger house, I thought the reason was so he could have his own bedroom and his own 'office,' as he calls that little den."

Dushan walked quietly alongside Dani and pondered what he just said. "Maybe he used to love her more before we moved to Victorville. I get the feeling that now he just realizes she was the only person who made him feel real."

"You oughta be a psychiatrist, Dushan. You sure talk like one. How come you're so forgiving, after the way he treated Mom, not to mention what he did to you?"

"It's like I said to Mom when we first heard what Carolyn and Burt did. I don't see any advantage in dwelling on the past. I'm all about the future. The future is where I wanna be. In the meantime, it's the present I've gotta deal with, and you've gotta deal with it, too. Don't forget your promise to me. No provoking Dad. Don't mention anything about what he did with Carolyn. It'll be our secret. We'll figure out how to find where my real parents are. God, sometimes I have a hard time even remembering what they look like, and how they talked! But still, I know they're alive, and I'm gonna find them."

CHAPTER TWENTY-ONE:
THE LONG DECLINE, VICTORVILLE 2007-2009

With Irene's death, the brothers' middle school years passed with relatively little of the school-related anxiety most middle schoolers experience. A year passed and it was almost the end of their 2006-2007 school year—seventh grade for Dushan and eighth grade for Dani. At home, besides their schoolwork and Dushan's still unsuccessful attempts at locating his parents, they were preoccupied with trying to avoid Burt's explosive moods. The boys were bonded even more closely now, an alliance against the domestic bully who suspected them of treason but couldn't prove anything.

One Tuesday night, Dushan looked up from his English assignment and said to Dani, "Having to watch out for Burt kind of puts middle school in its place, don't you think, Dani?"

Dushan, ever the conscientious good student, was finishing up his seventh grade homework as Dani was trying to glue the landing gear onto the plastic model F-15 fighter he'd been working on for the past week. Without looking up, Dani said, "I think I'm about ready to call my model collection complete. I mean, I don't have any more room here, and I have an even dozen. So, basta!"

"Did you hear what I said, Dani? What's your take on Dad? And, by the way, don't you think you should be doing your homework?"

"I can finish my homework tomorrow morning in study hall. As for Burt, I can't be bothered with him. He has his own life and all its problems. We have our lives. Besides, I'm going into high school in three months; I'll have enough problems dealing with that, let me tell you."

"Yeah, you're right. I was just thinking, though, that in a strange way, Burt is some kind of anchor here at home. Just when I think I can't stomach another day of seventh grade in this sorry excuse for a town, I think of what Burt must be going through. Whatever he says to us, however he acts around us, I just feel like it makes me stronger. I think you feel the same way, don't you?"

"Yep. You nailed it once again, Dr. Dushansky, with another brilliant diagnosis. Now, can you let me concentrate on this F-15? I gotta put the last dab of glue on the landing gear without ruining the paint."

"You do that, Captain Danilo. We can't have a less-than-perfect jet plane sitting on our shelf."

Time passed quickly. The boys managed to get through the rest of the school year without a major incident involving Burt's explosive temper. A year later, in June 2008, Dani finished ninth grade surprisingly well, and Dushan's last year in middle school was even better. But as the 2008-2009 school year began, Dani's sophomore year in high school was proving to be a trying academic experience.

A trying experience of a different type happened in December 2008, the Friday before Christmas vacation. The boys had turned 14 and 15 the month before. Dani had been invited to spend the first week of that vacation with a friend's family in their cabin in the San Bernardino mountains. Knowing how close Dani and Dushan were, Dani's friend's family had invited Dushan to come with them, much to Dushan's relief.

As with Burt's unpredictable outbursts over the past few years since Irene passed away, the boys were surprised at his reaction to Dani's request. "You've got to be kiddin'! After fuckin' off all fall, lettin' your grades fall into the toilet, you expect to just take off on a little ski trip like you're some kind of privileged rich boy? You don't either of you know how to ski, anyway. And what about all the homework your teachers have piled on you for the vacation?"

"You're exaggerating, Dad. My grades are not that bad, and they'll get better. The homework is not that much, either. I can easily finish it when I get back. I'll have a whole week!"

"Absolutely not. I've been pretty lax on the discipline lately, but I'm gonna put my foot down. You'll spend the whole vacation hittin' the books, young man. Maybe your little brother can help you with the hard stuff."

Dani was red as a beet. Dushan cleared his throat and shook his head ever so slightly to warn him not to respond. Dushan spoke up, "Dad, I understand you're concerned about Dani's school work. But he's not doing that bad. We were planning on doing a homework marathon when we get back from the mountains. Plus, there'll be time at the cabin when we'll be stuck with nothing to do BUT homework. So, whaddya say? Can you give it a try? We've never had this chance before; we've never been on a ski trip." In saying this, Dushan tried one of his mental pushes he had been experimenting with at school with some of his more troublesome classmates. It didn't work; in fact, it felt like Burt slapped it away like he would a fly.

Burt leaned back in the recliner and looked out the window. In a low monotone he looked back at Dushan and said, "I'm done talkin'. Now leave me alone."

Dushan motioned to Dani to follow him upstairs. When they got to Dushan's room, Dani collapsed on the bed. "It's all I can do to keep from yelling at him, Dushan, or worse. I tell you, one of these days one of us is gonna get hurt."

"I know what you mean. But you've got to keep your cool. Let's see what he says tomorrow. Did you notice he was drinking? He'll be different in the morning."

But Burt wasn't feeling any different in the morning. He didn't even give the boys a chance to bring up the subject again. He left the house before 7 a.m. so he could avoid the subject. "They can get their own damn breakfast," he muttered as he started the car. He continued his soliloquy as he fastened his seatbelt, a well-worn rant he'd been reciting to himself for most of the past year. "I'm tired of their little games, their little secrets, their little alliance. What did I ever do to them to make them treat me this way, anyway?" Burt gripped the steering wheel and drove slowly through the early morning near-darkness to the desert highway leading to the airport.

As he pulled into the employee parking lot, the sight of the big military jets reminded him, once again, of exactly what it was that he did do to them, at least what he did to Dushan. "Ya basically fookin' stole the kid from his da', tha's wha' ya did, ya fookin' sod." Burt's unconscious slip into his "Liverpoodle-talk," as Dani used to call it when he was a wee lad of three, caught Burt by surprise.

Burt put the memory of his crime out of his mind. But the boys' secretiveness around him paled in comparison to the secretiveness in his work environment, especially his relationship to the new power structure in his particular department. In the aftermath of yesterday's conversation with his supervisor, the liaison with the Transportation Security Administration, Burt had a premonition that this morning he was going to find out more about this new power structure. Yesterday's conversation was just a couple of questions about Burt's start as a foreign grad student at Stanford and then becoming a US citizen so quickly without returning to the UK first. The conversation was pleasant enough, but Burt had a feeling his boss was fishing for something.

Before Burt reached the employee entrance off the parking lot, he saw a TSA vehicle parked in a reserved space. Burt had seen TSA vehicles before, but only the ones with the cop stuff: light bar, spotlight, siren. This one was longer and had nothing but a small TSA logo below the trunk to the right of the license place. *The car is almost a limo, for chrissake.*

Despite the chill in the early morning air, Burt was sweating as he walked to his office. He hung up his coat, set down his briefcase and sat at his desk. Before he could turn on his computer, there was a knock at his door. He opened the door to two tall gentlemen he had never seen before.

"Mr. Sandor, I'm Mort Kandinsky and this is my colleague Hal Johnson. We're with the TSA office out of LA and we'd like to talk to you. Do you have a few minutes?"

"Nice to meet you, gentlemen. Sure, I just got here and this is a good time to talk. Can I get you coffee or tea before we get started?"

Johnson said, "No, we've had our coffee already. But if you want to go get yours, we'll wait here."

"I'm okay; actually, I don't drink caffeine anymore, makes me jittery. What's on your mind?" Without knowing exactly why, Burt turned on what he privately called his persuasion mode.

The two men sat in the chairs on either side of the door. Kandinsky glanced at Johnson, turned back to Burt and spoke first. "Mr. Sandor, the TSA is reviewing its executive hiring procedures all the way back to when it was created almost eight years ago. We do that by methodically going through the personnel files to make sure that we covered all the bases in terms of background checks. After 9-11, as I'm sure you know, airports in the USA have come under heightened scrutiny, especially ones like this one, that are designated 'logistics airports' and granted foreign trade zone status."

At this point, Mr. Johnson continued the explanation. "In your case, Mr. Sandor, the agency has uncovered a number of irregularities in how you came to work for the SCLA. If you were to be considered for employment here today, your background would probably disqualify you. The question for the TSA is, as we are improving our security procedures, what is to be done with those airport executives such as yourself whose hiring would not qualify under the proposed new regulations."

Burt took advantage of Johnson's brief pause and before Kandinsky could take up the slack, he asked, "What kind of irregularities are you referring to? I went through an exhaustive hiring process, one that took several months and three or four interviews. There's nothing in my background that gave anyone pause."

Kandinsky smiled when he felt the push coming from Burt to back off. He looked directly at Burt and deflected the push back at him. "That's one of the problems, Mr. Sandor. No one involved in checking your credentials really looked very deeply into your background. By that we mean your family background, your immigration status, and in particular where your family came from prior to settling in the UK." Kandinsky adjusted himself in the chair and continued. "I found it interesting that one of the women who interviewed you admitted to me that she cut the interview short for some reason she couldn't put her finger on."

Burt began to worry at his inability to deflect Kandinsky's interest in his case. With a slight tone of exasperation, he replied, "My grandparents came over to England from Greece around 1914 or so. I put all that down in my application, and gave you their names."

"But you only gave us your maternal grandparents' names, their countries of origin, their daughter's name, Margaret Markos, and the names of your father and his brother. For some reason, and we'll find out why, no one ever asked you anything about those Sandor brothers, in particular who their parents were and where they came from."

Burt put everything he had into his next response. "That's because I don't know where they came from. The family lore is that my dad and uncle were raised in a foster home until they were teenagers. I know nothing about the foster home. I always assumed my dad and uncle were Liverpool blokes from the get-go. I mean, Sandor is an ancient English surname, maybe even Celtic, too. My dad, Bruce, died of lung cancer when I was a kid, and my Uncle Dennis was killed in a coal mine accident."

Johnson's reply, although it sounded like it came from under water, shook Burt's confidence. "No offense, but we believe your family lore is largely a myth, Mr. Sandor." Johnson leaned forward in his chair. "We've done some digging, and we believe it likely that the two brothers were the two sons of Bela Sandor, a corrupt Hungarian communist party official who emigrated to the UK in the 1920's after looting a bank in Budapest. The records we have show that Bruce and Dennis were born in the UK in the early 1940's and were UK citizens. But their mother died when the boys were youngsters. Some time after that, their father put the boys in a foster home, set up a generous trust for them in the Bank of Scotland, and disappeared. We don't know much more about their father after he left the UK. So the story you told us, which you apparently believe, that they worked in a coal mine, wasn't the whole story. They were very wealthy, indeed, as your mother can probably attest."

Kandinsky continued the tale. "We have documentation on a certain Bela Sandor who left the UK around the same time your father and uncle were placed in the foster home. Bela Sandor was later captured by the Soviets during the war. The Soviets made an attempt to ransom him to the Brits. He was apparently part of a military unit posing as a communist unit. The unit's members were either British double agents, as the reds claimed, or had defected to the Nazis. When the Brits wouldn't pay the ransom, Sandor was executed. That Sandor, Bela, must have had some sort of connection to the UK, but the Russians, or the British for that matter, won't let us see those particular documents yet. We're working on that."

Burt slumped back in his desk chair and fiddled with the Boeing 747 paperweight on his desk. "That's it? Speculation that my grandfather might have been a Hungarian communist or Nazi? I can assure you I knew nothing about him, like I told you. I put everything I knew about my family in my application for this position and for my security clearance. Besides, let's say he was this man Bela Sandor, how does that have anything to do with me?" Burt's confidence had all but evaporated, and along with it his knack for persuasion.

"Relax, Burt," Kandinsky said. "We're just conducting our investigation. No decisions have been made about any contingencies just yet. We'll keep you informed of our progress. But there is one other thing, two other things actually, that concern the agency. The first is not as important as the second. First, it would appear that the US immigration folks goofed up when they processed your application for residency after you finished grad school at Stanford. And because of that error, you were on a fast track to citizenship that never would have been granted otherwise. However, since it was, your status is okay for the time being, assuming everything else about your background checks out and you don't get into trouble with the law."

"Jeez, this just never ends. I had no idea. I did everything by the book, and became a resident and then citizen. I got a passport—in fact, we all got passports, since my wife Irene also became a US citizen at the same time—and we traveled to Canada to celebrate our new status. We brought our boys, Danilo and Markos, with us."

Kandinsky looked briefly over at Johnson, who handed him a manila folder. At that point, Burt knew what Kandinsky was going to bring up. Kandinsky said, "That brings us to the second thing, which we view as potentially more serious. Is this a copy of your passport?" Kandinsky asked, handing Burt a multipage photocopy.

Burt looked it over. "It appears to be, yes."

"Do you see the page where you entered Canada and returned, and your baby, Markos, is on your passport? Both the Canadian and US customs officials indicated on the passport, going and returning, that Markos was traveling with you, as well as Danilo. Now look a few pages later when you went to the UK in 1999. It seems you only stayed some 24 hours and traveled alone over but accompanied by Markos on the way back. How did that happen?"

Burt had been preparing his answer to this question for years, but his preparation didn't allay his realization that the answer wouldn't be good enough. "I traveled both ways with Markos. I wanted my mother and her family to finally meet him, so I decided to pay them a surprise visit. But when I arrived and called the house from the B&B in Liverpool, my cousin Carolyn told me that my mom and several other family members were very ill with the flu and were contagious. They were worried that the baby would catch it. We all thought it would be best if I postponed our visit. So, after visiting some cousins at the B&B, Markos and I flew back to the States the next day without visiting my mom. The passport control folks at SFO and Heathrow must have failed to indicate Markos was with me on the way over. I never noticed that. You know how when you're going through customs, especially with a sleepy, cranky three-year-old, you just want to get the whole thing over with."

Kandinsky exchanged a look with Johnson. Finally, Kandinsky said reassuringly, "Yes, I suppose it could have been something like that. Where is Markos now? He must be, what, 14 now?"

Burt sighed but tried to restrain his sense of relief. "Yes, he just had a birthday last month. He's a freshman here at Victor Valley High. He and his older brother are doing great. Dani is a sophomore. Markos is the intellectual in the family; Dani is more like me, a techie kind of guy who likes to play with planes."

"We'd like to take a look at Markos's school records, if you don't mind. We'll need you to sign this release and we'll be on our way."

Burt took the filled-out form and signed it. Then he said, "So where do we go from here? How long before I hear back from you? Now you've brought up the subject of my grandfather, I'm curious to find out if that fella in Hungary was him."

"Sure thing, Mr. Sandor. We'll be in touch."

Three months later, in March 2009, Burt got a phone call from the boys' high school asking him to consent to a TSA official's request for copies of the boys' school records. Since Burt's interview, he had been increasingly nervous and on edge at work. His supervisor had steadily decreased Burt's involvement in the more sensitive foreign-trade projects at the airport. As a result, when Burt got the phone call from the school, it made him even more irritable and distracted.

At home that evening, Burt paced around the living room, glancing out the window from time to time. Dushan was working on schoolwork in the living room. Dani hadn't arrived home yet. Dushan put down his algebra homework and asked, "Dad, what is it? Is something bugging you?"

"Yes, something is bugging me. Lots of things, actually. My twit of a boss is bugging me, the TSA is bugging me, and now your school records are bugging me."

"What do you mean, my school records? And what is the TSA anyway?"

"The TSA is the government agency that clears airport executives to work at airports like the one we've got here in Victorville, airports that service what are called 'foreign trade zones.' The TSA is going back over all their clearance procedures since 9-11 to make sure all the proper procedures were used. In my case, they say there are some gaps in my background check. So they want to take a look at my family history, including the school records for you and Dani."

"Well, don't let it get to you, dad. I'm sure it'll all work out."

Burt paused. "I think, Dushan, that it would be best if you and Dani said as little as possible to these guys if they decide they want to talk to you. What I mean is, just try to avoid talking about my family. You don't know much about my family anyway, so it probably won't be a problem. Just talk about school, how we moved here from San Francisco, what your hobbies are, that sort of thing. Please, please, don't say anything about you being adopted or about Markos, especially about Markos. They don't need to know that. It's none of their damned business. I just don't want them invading our privacy that way."

Burt went into the kitchen, and Dushan could hear him open the fridge and crack ice cubes into a glass. *Probably making himself a double Jack Daniels. That's some nasty stuff.* Dushan decided to finish his homework on the picnic table in the backyard rather than stick around for Burt's inevitable bad temper.

A little later, Dushan heard the screen door open and Dani came out to join him. "What's the deal with dad?" Dani asked. "He looks positively explosive. And getting drunk a little early for a week night, what's that all about?"

"He's worried again about work. He told me the feds are investigating him all over again. And they're checking out our school records. Get this, Burt tells me that if the feds start talking to us we're not supposed to tell them anything about his family or Markos or about what he calls my adoption."

"He's worried they'll find out that your being adopted is a crock. Or they'll find out about Carolyn or your real dad. Man, Dushansky, this whole thing stinks. I personally think the feds are onto something."

"Yeah, that's right. And something else, you know what my official name is in the school records? Markos Dushan Sandor. You remember that story Burt and Carolyn told us that my first name is Markos and my middle name is Dushan? It was all a lie, of course. And Burt is worried I'll blow it by telling the feds my real name is Dushan."

"Not to mention that there's no records of your adoption, Dr.

Dushansky. For that matter, what if they start digging into the San Francisco days and come up with something about Markos dying of cancer?"

"Nice literary reference to 'digging' and 'come up with,' Captain Dante. You'll make a fine punster someday. But I doubt they'll go that far into the past. I'll just tell the TSA goons my full name is Markos Dushan Sandor and I go by my middle name because it's so cool. Just like you go by Dani because Danilo is so lame."

Dushan ducked before Dani's attempt at a bitch-slap could even come close. "Cool it, Cap'n Dante," Dushan smirked. "The Doctor knows best. Now go take your medicine and get that English paper done. Let me know if you need help spelling anything, like 'D'Urbervilles,' for starters."

CHAPTER TWENTY-TWO:
BLOOD ON THE TRAIN, 2009-2012

ight months passed without further contact from the TSA. Dushan was having a decent 10th grade year academically, and by Christmas vacation 2009, he was optimistic that he and Dani would be able to ride out the remainder of their high school years in Victorville and move on to college without any more grief from Burt. Dani's junior year academic performance was not as good as Dushan's sophomore year, certainly not good enough to start thinking about college.

During the following year Burt became increasingly miserable and paranoid. He hadn't heard back from the TSA during the rest of 2009 and all of 2010, but that had not done anything to allay Burt's suspicions that he was a marked man at work. Fewer and fewer of his executive responsibilities had anything to do with the logistical aspects of the foreign-trade zone traffic he used to be at least partially responsible for. Nowadays, his work was increasingly bureaucratic, meaningless make-work. He suspected the airport brass were encouraging him to seek work elsewhere. *Since they couldn't find any skeletons in my closet, they're going to just try to get me to leave out of boredom.*

In early 2011, the higher-ups at the airport decided to up the ante, since Burt was not taking the hint. They put Burt on an unpaid, one-month furlough to allow the TSA, in the airport HR department's words, "to complete the investigation into the matter of your younger son." Burt's one-month furlough had been extended twice. In June 2011 Dani graduated from high school and that fall enrolled in classes at the local junior college, but his heart was not in it. Dushan would start his senior year in two weeks. The brothers sat in the bleachers at the college's first football game while Dani shared his anxiety with Dushan. "I'm no good as a student, I guess. I don't know what I'm gonna do with my life, Dushan. I sure don't want to stick around this town any longer than I have to. Maybe I'll get a job and an apartment. Yeah, you and me could get an apartment together and not have to face Burt every day. He's so pissed at being furloughed, he's taking it out on us. I can't stand it."

They arrived home from the football game just after Burt had finished his second double Daniels. He lay sprawled out on the sofa with a crumpled paper lying on his chest. "All right," Burt growled at the boys as he sat upright on the sofa, "which one of you shot off your mouth about stuff you shouldn't have oughta done?"

"What are you talking about, dad?" Dushan asked. "Is everything okay at work?"

"No, everything is NOT okay at work, if ye must know. Some git has got my number, it appears. And I know bloody well they couldn't do this to me without one of you two blokes bein' at the bottom of it. Come on now, fess up. A little slip of tongue, maybe? Whadja say to 'em, that's what I wanna know! Which one of you told the TSA blokes about Dushan's adoption?"

Dushan spoke first. "Dad, we never spoke to anyone about this. No one from TSA or anywhere else came to school to talk to us. If they got our school records, they never told us anything."

Burt was now fully off the sofa and weaving dangerously.

Dani stepped forward to offer his support, but Burt swatted away his hand, losing his balance and falling forward onto the floor. Dani gave him a hand up, but this time Burt swung on Dani and hit him in the nose with his closed fist. Blood shot out from Dani's nose. Burt swung at him again, hitting him in the shoulder and knocking him to the floor. Burt hovered over Dani, a small trickle of drool sliding down his chin, looking like a crazed boxer. Dani slid back up against the sofa. "Dad, what the hell are you doing? What did I do?" He started weeping and slowly stood up.

Burt began to swing on Dani again. Dani moved his left arm in defense. With his right arm he threw a perfect punch that smashed into Burt's left eye and cut his eyelid. Burt grabbed Dani's wrist and raised his other arm for another punch.

Without hesitating, Dushan grabbed Burt's raised arm and pulled it back behind Burt's back. Dushan reached around Burt's face and pulled his head back, screaming, "Don't do it, Burt. Stop."

Instead, Burt bit down hard on Dushan's hands covering Burt's mouth. Dushan screamed. Dani, free of Burt's hold, lunged at Burt and threw him to the ground, releasing Dushan from Burt's bite. Both boys repeatedly punched Burt, crying and screaming as they did so.

Burt stopped struggling and lay on the floor panting, his face bleeding and covered with cuts and bruises. Dushan screamed at him, "You stole me, Burt! You stole me from my dad, you bastard!" Dushan ran into the kitchen, grabbed a dishcloth, and began wiping the blood off his face, arms, and hand. Dani was walking in circles around Burt, screaming at him, "Mom told us all about it, dad, you asshole. She said you cooked up the whole scheme. You stole Dushan from his father, you bought him from Carolyn! You pig. I hate you!"

Burt bellowed, "That fuckin' bitch is a liar. I never did that, I swear."

Dushan threw down the dishcloth. "Who're you talkin' about, Burt? Who're you callin' a lyin' bitch, you asshole? Mom or your cousin Carolyn?"

"Who're you calling an asshole, you little Serbian twit? We adopted you from your dad. He didn't want you, d'ya hear? He didn't want you! Now, how's that for a dad, huh? A dad that didn't bloody well want ya."

Something clicked in Dushan's normally controlled, rational mind. Screaming and crying, he kicked Burt in the teeth, as if to make him swallow the words he just vomited out. "You're the fuckin' liar, Burt. I can't call you dad anymore, ya hear? You're not my dad, you never were!" Turning to Dani, crying just as hard as Dani, he said, "Let's get outta here, Dani. We don't need this pig."

The boys ran out of the house, leaving Burt gagging on the floor, choking on his teeth and blinded by blood flowing into his eyes from the cuts on his forehead and eyelids. They jumped into the car. Dani started it with the extra key he'd made some months earlier and drove into the night.

For a while, Dani piloted the Lexus SUV aimlessly through town, gradually wending his way toward the outskirts of the city. The boys' sobs were becoming less frequent and violent. Dani tried to wipe the tears out of his eyes, but instead he wiped blood into his eyes and was momentarily blinded. Panicking, he took both hands off the wheel and tried to clear his vision. "Grab the steering wheel, Dushan,

I can't see a damn thing."

Too late, Dushan grabbed the wheel just in time to see their slow-moving vehicle collide with a young oak tree growing at an almost horizontal slant off the embankment. Luckily the airbag didn't inflate, but the car was stuck a quarter of the way up the tree. Dani whimpered, "What the hell, Dushan, what did you do that for?"

"I wasn't the one driving, you were. By the time I grabbed the wheel, it was too late." The boys tried to catch their breaths. Dani started crying again. "You know, Dushan, this whole thing is just so fucked up! There's no way in hell I'm going back home. That pig. Did you see what he did to me?"

"Did to you? He did that and more to me. How do you think I feel being called a Serbian twit? He all but admitted he knows more about my so-called adoption than he lets on. He's a hopeless liar and a cheat, not to mention a thief. What the hell do we do now, Dani?"

"I say we split this town and head down to San Bernardino. There's a little bundle of cash in the trunk of this car; I saw dad putting it in the spare tire kit last week. Maybe he was saving a stash for a rainy day."

Dushan added, "I've got some money in the bank from my allowance and my job in the school cafeteria, almost a grand I guess."

They climbed out of the car and popped the trunk. They pulled the pouch out from under the spare and opened it up. "There must be at least a thousand here," Dushan exclaimed, pulling out the cash and thumbing through it. Handing it to Dani, he said, "San Bernardino, here we come. We can get jobs and an apartment. Maybe even move in with your buddy Jerome who works at the Costco there."

"One way or another, we're outta here. But the question remains, how do we get there without transportation? I'm pretty sure Burt has called the cops on us by now."

Dushan said, "Remember when we were little and used to explore the railroad tracks? We passed the tracks about a half a mile back. You didn't see them 'cause you were too busy driving this puppy into the tree."

Dani groaned, then laughed. "So, let's do it. The Union Pacific freight runs past here almost every half hour all evening and night. We used to dream of jumping on board and riding the rails like hobos, remember? Well, now's our chance. We got this cash and the money in your bank account. It'll work; Jerome will put us up. You can transfer to San Bernardino High, or even finish high school at a junior college."

The boys reached the tracks and positioned themselves on the small hillside beside the tracks, partially hidden by bushes. They didn't speak, each worried the other might change his mind about their plan, and afraid a police car would come screeching to a halt a few yards up the hill with lights flashing.

Finally, they saw the oncoming freight train. They got into a crouch and held onto the bushes to keep from sliding down the hill onto the tracks. The train began to pass them slowly, but not as slowly as they would have liked. "We're gonna have to move fast, Dushan; these cars are rolling at a pretty good clip. Do you think we can do it?"

"We'll give it the old college try, Cap'n. Here comes an empty car. When we see the leading edge of the open door, we gotta jump as high and far as we can, dude!"

Easier said than done, at least for Dushan. Dani, because he was quite a bit lighter, made it all the way into the open boxcar without a hitch. Dushan, although a year younger, was a little beefier. He made it halfway into the doorway, but his hands couldn't get a grip on anything. He let go and landed back on the hillside. Before he managed to stop his slide down the hill in the loose dirt, the boxcar with Dani inside had passed, his brother leaning out and yelling Dushan's name as he waved furiously.

"I'm here, Dani," Dushan yelled. He stood up on the slippery slope, holding onto a bush, and watched the freight train continue to roll past, his brother Dani inside one of the empty boxcars in the middle of the train. Dushan said to himself, "I'm here, Dani, and you're there. What's gonna happen to us now?"

Dushan brushed grass and dirt off his backside and brushed tears away from his eyes. The train looked like it was about to disappear into the night with Dushan's beloved older brother inside. As the end of the train approached, Dushan saw another empty boxcar and made one more attempt to jump into it. This time he made it a little further into the car, but was dangling from the open doorway and didn't seem to be able to pull himself in all the way. After a few minutes of struggle, he was so exhausted he let go and fell backwards onto the ground. He landed at the edge of the wooded field they had passed earlier before the car crashed into the oak tree.

Dushan limped away from the railroad right-of-way and after a few minutes collapsed inside the wooded area. He slept for several hours before waking to the pre-dawn light. Feeling dejected and hopeless, he decided to return home and take his chances with Burt. Maybe Dani would have given up as well and would soon return home. Dushan saw no other option. He began the walk home.

CHAPTER TWENTY-THREE:
NO BODY AND NOWHERE, 2011-2013

When Dushan walked back home from the railroad tracks he saw a police car and ambulance in front of the house. Inside, paramedics and police officers were talking to Burt. Burt began screaming at Dushan as soon as he saw him.

"That's the punk, officers. That's my stepson. He probably killed my son! Look at him, he's covered in Dani's blood and my blood!" Burt had just given a statement to the police officers accusing Dushan of assaulting him and Dani and elaborated on it now. "For years, my late wife and I tried to get this boy, our adopted son Dushan, to feel like one of the family. But he saw Dani as his enemy and rival. I guess Dani reacted by teasing Dushan for being adopted. Whatever the reason, Dushan never acted like he was part of the family. I came home from work last evening and found the boys fighting. I tried to intervene, but Dushan turned on me, knocked me down and kicked me in the mouth. I think I lost two teeth. Just before I passed out I saw Dushan hit Dani over the head with an andiron from the fireplace. When I came to, the boys were gone and so was the car."

Dushan was stunned into silence for a few seconds, then yelled. "That's a lie, dad! You were beating both of us. We fought back and then we took the car to the railroad tracks. Dani jumped into a boxcar but I didn't make it. That's all, that's all that happened! The whole thing is your damn fault!" One of the officers approached and placed him under arrest. "Don't say anything else, kid, you know the drill, it'll be used against you."

The police took Dushan to the youth lockup in Victorville and placed him in a holding cell with a dozen other youths ranging from 10 to 16 years old. Several of the older boys sported tattoos with what looked like gang insignia. They stared at Dushan, apparently amused and impressed by his ripped and bloody clothes. Dushan sat on the floor, shocked and frightened. When a guard opened the door and tossed sandwiches and juice containers to the boys, the tension in the cell dissipated. Dushan lost track of time. Every now and then, the cell door would open, a name would be called, and a youth would walk out, escorted by a guard. After what may have been 10 hours, a guard escorted Dushan to another cell with just one cellmate.

Dushan's roommate squinted, scanned Dushan from head to toe and asked, "So, little bro, whadja do? You got lots a blood on you and you're just plain tore up. Did the other guy get the worst of the fight? Dead?"

"I didn't do nothin', man. Got in a fight with my old man, that's all. He attacked me and my older brother and we fought back."

"Where's he now, your brother?"

"That's a good question; probably on his way by freight train to San Bernardino. Last night we tried jumping on a train rolling past Woodland Park at the edge of town. He made it, I didn't. So I came home and the old man starts accusing me of beating them up. All I did was kick him in the teeth after he punched me out."

The cellmate frowned and said, "Hmm, I'd say your brother is nowhere near San Bernardino. The southbound freights that go past Woodland Park only do it during the day. At night the only freights that pass that park are on their way to Nevada or Utah. Believe me; I made the mistake of jumping on one last year, but I got off before the train left the county."

"Oh shit! That's just great; I hope Dani figures it out soon. Man, this whole thing is screwed up."

At his court appearance the next morning, the judge appointed deputy public defender Rafael Trujillo to take Dushan's case. They had a quick conference in the holding area just outside the courtroom. "So, what's gonna happen, Mr. Trujillo?"

"I have a bad feeling about this. Did you hear when the judge read the charge? Murder. Apparently they haven't found your brother's body."

"That's crazy! He's not dead. He jumped a freight out of town the night we got into it with my dad."

"Listen, you have to understand some rules between you and me. I don't want to hear any confessions from you. The DA says you killed your brother, like your dad says. The DA is going all out on this case, which in my opinion is really a chicken shit case. They have no evidence to support a murder rap except all the blood."

"Sure there's blood, my blood along with everyone else's blood. It was a free-for-all, I'm telling you! Our dad started the whole thing. Dani and I fought back and ran away with the old man's car after he got knocked out. I told the cop all this."

"I believe you, kid. I'll do what I can. But I have to say I think the DA is going to ask the judge to transfer this case to adult court. I'll fight that, but if it goes that way we're in a whole different ball game."

"You gotta check the Union Pacific schedules. We thought we were jumping the southbound freight to San Bernardino, but I didn't make it into the boxcar. My cellmate told me last night that that train was headed to Utah or Nevada, not south to San Bernardino. Dani will either be on the train or will have jumped off as soon as he realized his mistake. I told all this to the cop who talked to me."

"Like I said, I'll do what I can. I'll stop by tomorrow morning and let you know what I find out."

Tomorrow came and went but no Mr. Trujillo. The same thing the next day, and the next. The weekend arrived and there was nothing to do but watch TV, read, lift weights and try not to get into a fight with any of the other guys in the common room of juvenile hall. From the looks of it, the Hall officers kept the Norteños and Sureños separated. Dushan stayed away from both groups; he'd had some experience telling them apart. Even though they couldn't wear their blue or red bandannas in the Hall, they still had their XIII and XIV tattoos, 13 for the Sureños and 14 for the Norteños.

Trujillo stopped by Monday morning. He told Dushan they were going to be in court at 1:30 that afternoon. There would be a motion by the DA to transfer the case to adult court, "based on new evidence."

"What new evidence?"

"That I don't know. We'll see. I'll be in court when you come in. Stay cool."

Dushan's case was first on the afternoon calendar. Before the judge called the case, the prosecutor approached Trujillo and handed him a report. Trujillo walked back to the defense table as he read the report. He sat next to Dushan. "It doesn't look good for you or your brother. The police apparently contacted the railroad company and asked them to check on the northbound freight that passed through Victorville about the time of night you say your brother jumped into a boxcar. This report says the Union Pacific found lots of blood in an empty boxcar on a siding outside Salt Lake City, Utah. That particular boxcar and the cars connected to it originated in San Bernardino and passed through Victorville about when you say your brother hopped on. A sample of the blood is being sent to our county crime lab for a comparison with the blood found in your house and the car. We should know the results in a couple of days. In the meantime, the DA is going to ask the court to continue the case till then."

"So, more delay, is that what you mean?"

"Yep. Get used to it."

*   *   *

When Trujillo returned a week later, he informed Dushan that the blood turned out to be Dani's, which did not surprise Dushan since he saw how bloody Dani was when he jumped into the boxcar. But what was surprising was that Dani was missing. *He would have turned up somewhere, he would have phoned or something!* Trujillo explained that the blood evidence, combined with Burt's account of the fight and his injuries, as well as the alleged rivalry between Dani and Dushan, had convinced the prosecution to seek to transfer the case from juvenile court to adult court on a murder charge.

Dushan practically shouted, "But I'm not even 17; how can they try me as an adult?" At that point, Dushan realized he didn't know the date. "What's today's date, anyway?"

Looking at his watch, Trujillo said, "September 6, 2011. As to your other question, in a murder case, especially one where the theory is that the defendant not only killed the victim but went to all the trouble to dispose of the body, the judge has discretion to send the case to adult court and have a jury decide it. The nature of the crime and the efforts to cover up the crime show how evil you were; that's what the prosecution will try to prove. I doubt it matters, but when will you be 17?"

"November 1st, not quite two months from now. But, really, Mr. Trujillo, how can I can be convicted of murder when there's no body?"

"It's not easy, but it has been done. The prosecution argues to the jury, 'Look at all the blood. Consider how the father was brutally injured and saw his stepson brutally attack the victim with a fireplace andiron. Consider that the defendant then stole the family car, which is full of the victim's blood. Consider the fact that the victim's blood was not only all over that car, but the living room, the defendant's clothes, and inside a boxcar found hundreds of miles away."

Dushan sat spellbound and dazed. Trujillo continued with his dramatic argument to the imaginary jury, "Now consider the defendant's statement to the police that he was with the victim when the victim went into the boxcar. I suggest to you, ladies and gentlemen of the jury, that the victim did not JUMP into that boxcar, he was THROWN into the boxcar, either while unconscious or dead. At this moment, his body is probably decomposing in some desert in Nevada or Utah, after being pitched out of the boxcar by hobos riding the rails."

Dushan felt like throwing up. "But Dani and I were close, closer than most brothers are. You can ask any of our schoolmates. Everyone knew that about us. Nobody who knew us would believe that Dani and me got into a fight. And lots of our family friends knew about our dad's temper."

Trujillo put his hand on Dushan's shoulder. "Look, I know how you feel. I believe you, Dushan. I believe you didn't kill anyone. And my defense investigator, who interviewed your father yesterday, tells me your old man is the biggest liar she has seen in quite some time. I doubt his story will convince a jury. But you never know, especially in this county, which is not exactly a liberal bastion. Let's hope your brother shows up soon. Meanwhile, I'm going to ask for more time to conduct my investigation and prepare for trial in the event the prosecution's transfer motion is granted."

A week passed, and Dushan's attorney was now taking a different tack. "I have some good news, Dushan. Maybe not as good as you would hope, but better than we can hope for. My opponent is a young, wet-behind-the-ears prosecutor fresh out of law school. 'Fresh meat,' we call them. He is willing to accept a deal I proposed. If you don't like the deal, we go to trial. But neither the prosecution nor I relish that prospect. There are too many unknown factors, and that makes both of us nervous. Here's the deal: you plead guilty in adult court to a charge of voluntary manslaughter, the judge sentences you to the middle term of six years in state prison, and you serve three with good behavior. With any luck, you'll go to a so-called minimum security joint and serve some pretty soft time."

"But I didn't do anything! I can't admit to killing my own brother. I love the guy, I grew up with him. What am I gonna say to the judge when he asks me if I did the crime?"

"You're going to let me answer the judge's question. He'll ask me something like, 'is there a factual basis?' I'll then stipulate there is. You won't be required to admit the truth of the charge. When I say there is a factual basis for the plea, that just means that there's enough evidence in the police reports to convict you."

Dushan let his head drop to the table and he started trembling. Trujillo rubbed him on the back and waited. After several minutes, Dushan raised his head and dried his eyes. His voice cracking, he turned to Trujillo and said, "Let me think about it. Do you need to go to court soon?"

"By the end of the week. I have to tell you, Dushan, this is as good as it gets. Otherwise, we're rolling the dice and the odds are worse here than a crapshoot in Vegas."

On Friday, Dushan appeared in adult court with Trujillo. He was resigned to taking what Trujillo called "a little three-year vacation doing soft time in some gentleman's prison." The deal was accepted by the prosecutor and the judge, and the parties agreed for Dushan to be sentenced at the same hearing. As expected, Dushan was sentenced to six years with an understanding he'd be eligible for parole in three. He was taken back to his cell and waited.

And waited, and waited, and waited. Two weeks passed before Dushan learned where he would be serving his sentence: Calipatria State Prison, near El Centro in Imperial Valley. "Where the hell is that, Mr. Trujillo? That sounds like an even worse place than this pathetic excuse for a jail."

"Don't knock this jail here, Dushan. This is a county jail; there's room to stretch out here. You have only one cellmate; you have a basketball court, you have trees in the courtyard. And you've been earning custody credit here, so your sentence has already begun. Calipatria is not so bad, though. I've got a few clients there; they have good jobs in the laundry, the library, the garden. Some are carpenters. One guy is a computer genius, so they gave him an IT job in the warden's office. Some deal, eh? You'll do fine."

A few days later, Dushan was transported to Calipatria. In early October 2011 he began his new life as inmate number C10101007, or "double-0-7," as his new cellmate called him. They hit it off right away, although Dushan at first thought he was a gangbanger. Their introduction took place right after Dushan had been processed and taken to a small cell with bunk beds, a sink, a small desk, and a toilet. When the guard left after handing Dushan a package of sheets, towel, washcloth, soap, toothbrush and a blanket, Dushan sat down on the bottom bunk and set the package on the desk. He lay back for a few moments to take stock of the day's events, in particular those questions in his reception interview asking about his skills. Remembering what his lawyer told him, Dushan told the clerk that he was a computer whiz, an avid reader, had experience teaching ESL to immigrants at a local Victorville church, and was good at cooking and ironing.

He must have dozed off for a few minutes because he woke up to the loud clanging of the cell door opening and slamming against the wall. A deep voice said, "Take it easy, Hector. Don't break the door just yet." In walked a large, heavily tattooed inmate escorted by an even larger prison guard. Before Dushan could raise himself off the bottom bunk, Hector said, "That's my bunk, cuz."

Dushan replied without skipping a beat, "Can't argue with that," and stood up.

"Damn right," muttered Hector with just a bare hint of a smile at Dushan. At this point, the guard stepped around Hector, faced him, and said, "Screw that, Hector, you get what's left. I told you that back in reception."

"That's okay, officer. Go on, Hector," said Dushan, "I don't care which bunk I have. I just got here, too, and was just taking 40."

Hector's smile widened. "I like your attitude, cuz. We're gonna get along fine, ain't we?"

Justice done, the prison guard exited the cell and carefully closed the cell door without slamming it. Looking through the barred opening on the door, the guard said, "That's how it's done, Hector, that's how you close the damn door."

Dushan at first wasn't sure whether Hector was a gang member since his tattoos weren't the usual Sureño or Norteño ones. *Whatever, it doesn't hurt to have a gangbanger for a cellie.* Dushan broached that very subject early on but Hector set him straight. "I guess it's the tats that make some dudes, like you for example, think I bang. But the real bangers here know that I'm not one of their enemies, and they leave me alone. I'm just big and bad, and they don't wanna find out how bad I am. 'Nuff said."

Hector's turn to ask questions. "I like your name, bro. 'Dushan', what kind of name is that? You look Chicano, but Sandor, I'm not sure."

"Nah, not Chicano, but you're not the first dude to think that. I'm Yugoslavian, actually Serbian, from Belgrade. But I was raised here in California by my stepparents."

"So, whadja do to get invited to this dump? I'm a car booster myself, third-time loser gets you some serious time. I got six years this time."

"I pled to voluntary manslaughter, got six years, will serve three. I didn't do nothin', you understand. It was one of those chicken-shit pleas where you don't admit nothin'. Didn't want to go down for murder." Dushan realized he had lapsed into some slang he'd probably picked up from cop shows on TV.

"I hear ya, bro. Smart deal. Who was the victim?"

"There wasn't no victim, no body. Me and my brother got in a fight with our old man, beat the crap out of him, and took off with the family car. We tried to jump a freight, but I fell out. When I came home, the old man accused me of killing my brother and the cops and DA bought it. My brother still hasn't showed up. I just hope he's okay, wherever he is."

"Wow, man, that's some heavy shit. Be brave, my cuz. We'll be partners here. Anybody get in your face, they'll have me, Hector Cruz, to deal with."

The next two months were tough on Dushan. When his 17th birthday came and went, he didn't mention it to anyone. He didn't sleep well and often had to stifle his sobs at night so Hector wouldn't think him a wuss. Fact was he was pretty depressed. He kept thinking how long three years would be, and how much longer it would be in the joint, sleeping in a small cell on a lumpy bunk bed in a noisy cell block. Many nights he heard angry shouts and muffled screams from other cells that he was pretty sure were the sounds of assaults or rapes.

When Dushan didn't get a computer or library job, as he had hoped, he was disappointed at first. But once he started his job in the prison cafeteria and bakery, he felt his mood improving. By January 2012, not only had he learned how to bake bread and cakes and pies, but he had become a decent cook. He also gained a little weight but, as Hector said, "That's no big deal, homie. Gives you more cred in the joint. You don't wanna be some skinny little dude everyone picks on."

Dushan settled into a routine that kept him busy and stopped him from obsessing too much about Dani. He worried, of course, but he had a feeling Dani was okay. His dreams tended to be vivid, and often involved scenes of Dani and him reuniting. Other scenes, though, didn't seem like dreams at all. They were strange scenes where Dani was surrounded by snow, where he was hunting rabbits and fishing in ice-covered ponds. Often Dushan yelled out to Dani but he didn't respond, except once when Dushan yelled at Dani and it seemed that Dani looked up. One dream in particular had recurred several times: Dani was putting wood on a fire in a stove and spoke into the fire, "Don't give up on me, Dushan, I'm not dead, I swear to you, I'm not dead. And I'll find you wherever you are." That dream woke Dushan up every time, just as he started to answer Dani.

Dushan was startled out of his routine one May evening as he sat in the prison library after a full day working in the bakery. He was catching up on his reading by perusing the three-day-old Sunday LA *Times*, when a small article on the local news page caught his eye. The title said, "Victorville Airport exec shoots two from TSA." Gripping the paper so hard he almost tore it, Dushan read:

"Friday morning at his home in Victorville, a middle manager at the Victorville airport shot two officials of the TSA, Mortimer Kandinsky and Harold Johnson. The shooter, Burt Sandor, then called the police. When police arrived, Sandor shot himself in the chest. According to his supervisor, Sandor had been involved in a dispute with the TSA for some months over his security clearance. Officials would not comment further on the dispute. Sandor and the two TSA officials were taken to the Victor Valley hospital, where Johnson was pronounced dead. Kandinsky suffered a superficial wound in the abdomen but is expected to be released from the hospital after the weekend. According to the attending emergency room physician, Sandor was still alive on arrival, but died early the next morning. The doctor said Sandor was delirious and raving about one of his sons, who had disappeared last year under mysterious circumstances."

Dushan could hardly breathe as he dropped the paper on the table. *That bastard, may he rest in peace!* Realizing that there may be follow-up news in today's paper, Dushan grabbed it. He was in luck. There was a longer article in the local section, with an extensive interview with the surviving TSA official, Kandinsky. Kandinsky told the reporter that he and Johnson went to the Sandor residence "to question Mr. Sandor about his attempt to pass off his stepson as the biological son who died back in 1999." According to Kandinsky, he and his colleague confronted Sandor with their discovery that his biological younger son, Markos Sandor, died in the fall of 1999.

"When we confronted Sandor with the possibility that he stole or purchased a 'replacement' son in mid-1999 and brought him to the States from England, Sandor claimed he had documents to prove that the boy he brought home with him from the UK was legally adopted. Johnson and I said we would really like to examine the documents. Sandor went to his bedroom and returned carrying a shoebox. He looked at us and said, 'This is all the proof you need.' He pulled a gun out of the shoebox and opened fire on us, hitting Johnson square in the heart. He shot me in the side; I fell off the chair and played dead. Then Sandor calmly walked out of the room and I heard him call the police."

Dushan dropped the newspaper and slumped back in his chair. His mind was racing as he tried to envision the scene, Burt's last hurrah. When the librarian announced closing time, Dushan returned to his cell. Hector was lying on the bottom bunk reading the latest *Mad* magazine. "Whassup, Dushan? You look like you fell off a freight train. Just joking, no offense."

"Hector, you won't believe what I just read. But lemme catch my breath and I'll tell you all about it."

Hector listened intently. "You ain't saying it, but I think you know you may have a problem, dude. You better hope the feds don't get wind of this story. But they probably will. I mean, Kandinsky is a fed and those guys all sleep together. I can tell you, once ICE gets wind of this—meaning you're an illegal alien, right?—they'll be on you like white on rice. I should know, half of my family are illegal and two of them are now back in good ole Oaxaca."

"What's ICE? Is that the same as the INS?"

"You got it. President Bush, bless his lizard-skin heart, he didn't think INS was tough enough so he decided to go postal on the illegals with a new bunch of cowboys he called ICE. Couldn't tell you what it stands for, though, but it's a cool-ass name."

Hector's hunch turned out to be prophetic. Less than two weeks later, Dushan was informed that due to his status as an illegal alien, he was going to be transferred to the federal deportation prison in Eloy, Arizona, pending completion of the paperwork needed to send him back to England. That August, an officer with the Immigration Control and Enforcement bureau (*so that's what ICE means*, Dushan realized) arrived at the prison right after dinner to transport Dushan to the alien detention facility in Eloy, Arizona, about 50 miles south of Phoenix. Dushan was placed in the back seat of the ICE police car. The driver told him it would be a long drive to Eloy.

CHAPTER TWENTY-FOUR:
A COOK GOES TO COLLEGE, 2012-2013

About 50 miles into the trip on east Interstate 8, the ICE driver exited the freeway at the "Foothills Blvd" marker, 15 miles east of Yuma, and drove along the south frontage road to look for a gas station. It was well after sunset and a fairly dark, moonless night in August 2012. At each intersection, the driver looked in both directions searching for a station. When the driver entered the Foothills Boulevard intersection, he looked first to the right. Before he could turn and look to his left, a top-down convertible sped across the frontage road from that direction without stopping or slowing down. The convertible swerved just before broadsiding the ICE car, causing both cars to roll over onto the shoulder.

Dushan screamed at the same time as the driver. A sickening thud and crunching noise stopped the driver's scream almost as soon as it began. Dushan was hanging upside down in the cage-like back seat, tangled up in his seatbelt harness. Both back doors had popped open from the impact.

Dushan released his seat belt and managed to extricate himself from the wrecked ICE vehicle. Checking to see if he had any injuries, he saw and felt none. He walked gingerly around the ICE car and grimaced as he looked at the mashed body of the driver. Dushan walked over to the convertible. The driver looked even worse off than the ICE driver, smashed beyond recognition. At that point, Dushan almost instinctively stopped looking at the wreck, looked inside his mind and called out Dani's name. Looking up at the sky, Dushan spoke the words, "I'm not dead, Danilo, not dead. Find me."

The passenger in the convertible, a young man, must have been thrown from the car and lay about 20 feet away on the asphalt shoulder of the road. Dushan examined his body, which appeared unscathed except for numerous scratches to his face and hands.

Remarkably, his clothing was not even torn, just a little dirty. Judging from the angle of his head in relation to his body, the young man appeared to have died from a broken neck. He looked to be about Dushan's age and bore a physical resemblance.

In a moment of inspiration, Dushan carried the young man's body to the ICE car and exchanged clothes with him. In the man's trousers were his wallet, cash and a set of keys. Dushan removed the watch and the man's pinky ring, and placed the body on the ground next to the back door of the ICE car. Dushan reached into the backseat where he had been sitting and inserted the tongue of his seatbelt back in its receptacle. Holding the receptacle as still as he could, he bent the seatbelt back and forth several times. Then he twisted it and yanked it back out as hard as he could so it would break loose from its receptacle.

Dushan walked back to the convertible and carefully scanned the back seat to make sure there was nothing else that might indicate someone recently occupied it. He examined the popped-open trunk. He removed a small wheeled suitcase bearing a luggage tag with the passenger's name, Douglas Armitage. He inspected the whole car once more to ensure there was nothing to suggest that the driver was accompanied by a passenger.

Standing next to the convertible's unbroken driver's-side mirror, Dushan examined the contents of the passenger's wallet. There was a fair amount of cash, at least $300, a social security card, and a Visa credit card, both in the name of Douglas Armitage. There was also a driver's license with a picture so badly taken that it could pass for that of Dushan, were it not for the fact that Douglas Armitage sported a buzz cut in the photo. Both Douglas's and Dushan's hair was a little longer than a buzz cut, and that worried Dushan. Addressing himself with his new name, he spoke to his reflection in the mirror, "Well, Douglas, I think you might have to pay a visit to a barbershop soon if you want to regain the well-groomed look in your license photo." At the disquieting thought of getting a buzz cut, Dushan wondered if he might be able to convince anyone that any dissimilarity between him and the license photo was due to the difference in hair length and style.

Inside an exterior pocket of the suitcase he found a manila folder containing Armitage's passport, an airline itinerary, and a printed e-ticket in Armitage's name for a flight from Tucson to New York the next morning. There were two letters in the folder. The first was from the Culinary Institute of America in Hyde Park, New York, offering Armitage admission on a full scholarship with a work-study job and dormitory housing included. The second was a letter of recommendation from a catering company in El Centro, California. The passport was not quite four years old and showed Armitage's age as 13 at the time it was issued. *Wow; no problem passing this off as my picture*, Dushan thought.

By this time it was getting late, a little past 9:00 p.m. according to Douglas's watch, and fully dark. Dushan walked back along the south frontage road to where it met the exit from Interstate 8. Not knowing whether hitchhiking was illegal on Arizona highways, he decided to risk an attempt to hitch a ride to Tucson. He walked out onto the shoulder of the highway and waited for a car to slow down and pull over.

He didn't have to wait long before he was picked up by a young man in a Marine Corps uniform. Dushan decided to practice acting out his new identity. He put on his best "I'm off to a new adventure" act and told the young Marine he was headed to the Tucson airport. He said he had a job offer back east. Dushan explained that at the last minute, his buddy flaked on him and said he could not give him a ride to the airport as promised. The Marine told Dushan he was stationed at the Marine Corps airbase outside Yuma and was on his way to visit his girlfriend in Tucson. The Corpsman was happy to give him a ride to the airport.

CHAPTER TWENTY-FIVE:
CAROLYN TAKES A CRUISE, 2012

"Oh shit, this nightmare will never end!" Carolyn moaned as she threw down the left-over copy of the Montreal Gazette in the little coffee shop where she was finishing her scone and tea. She couldn't believe what she had just read in the "news from the States" section. "Burt murdered someone, for God's sake! And killed himself in the bargain!" When she saw another customer staring at her, she got up and exited the little shop. It was a fine May day, but not fine enough to quell the rising sense of panic in Carolyn's chest. "Christ, the asshole must have told the feds my name. Oh my God, what now?"

Carolyn had long feared the international police agencies would sooner or later uncover her name. That was why she ended up in Montreal. She had been on the run for eight years, ever since she ran into her ex-husband Trevor Owens in San Francisco in June of 2004. That unpleasant encounter took place in her third year as a waitress at the Cliff House, making good money for an illegal alien. Trevor, who had taken his new wife and young son on holiday to the States, was of course just as surprised as she to be talking to an ex-spouse. He introduced his wife to Carolyn, and they briefly chatted. He apparently didn't want to extend the conversation any more than she did, so they cut it short. When he and his family were done eating, they took leave of Carolyn and left the restaurant without much more talk.

Not only did that meeting dredge up past hurts from their rocky marriage, but it left her with a sense of dread and foreboding. Trevor's wife had made a passing remark as they paid the check and got up to leave. She said that San Francisco was the first stop on their vacation and they would soon depart for Great Britain to see the sights and, as she put it, "maybe hook up with some of Trev's old mates on the Isle of Man" before heading home to Australia. "That's just great," Carolyn muttered as she walked home to her little apartment on Page Street near Golden Gate Park. "No doubt dear old 'Trev' will look up Derrick and share old times, especially those bad old times with me."

The reason this observation put the fear of God in Carolyn was the likelihood Derrick would let the Douglas police know that Carolyn Owens was living and working in San Francisco. What if Trevor told Derrick Carolyn's maiden name?

Soon after that encounter eight years ago, she decided she could not risk letting the police track her down. So she pulled up stakes and said good-bye to San Francisco and the USA. She was getting tired of working as a waitress anyway, hang the decent money she made. She still had a little more than $5,000 in her Hibernia account, which she promptly closed before leaving the City for British Columbia.

Looking back on her decision from the superior vantage point of hindsight, Carolyn cringed at her hasty decision to go to Canada. She hadn't realized that crossing the Canadian border she would have to show a passport. "That didn't used to be how it was," she muttered to herself as she dug out her UK passport. "It's all this 9-11 hysteria," a fellow bus passenger commented when he saw her consternation.

When the border agent handed back her passport, Carolyn realized her maiden name was now registered there. If, as she feared, Trevor had told Derrick and the Douglas police that the former Carolyn Markos and/or Owens was now in San Francisco, the Isle of Man police would for sure realize she was the same Carolyn Markos who left Liverpool in 1999. She couldn't stay in BC for long.

That August 2004 she bought a ticket in Vancouver on the Green Tortoise bus for a cross-Canada trip to Montreal. She chose a bus trip in the hope that she didn't need to use her real name, and she was right. Looking back on that trip she recalled with a certain fondness how that "hippie bus" had tickled her despite her worry over being found out. Lots of nice folks taking a somewhat adventurous alternative to the usual mode of cross-country travel. She and the other passengers stayed in international youth hostels along the route to eastern Canada, and the experience almost put the fear of discovery out of her mind—almost but not entirely.

Of course, she couldn't get a "real" job anywhere in Canada without using her UK passport and setting herself up to be tracked down by the international police 'bloodhounds'. For the first month in Quebec, she stayed in a youth hostel and carefully mapped out her options. The only jobs she could get would be those not requiring any kind of official ID, such as babysitting and housecleaning. In October 2004 she scored the first of several a full-time jobs as a nanny, caretaker and English tutor. She managed to eke out a living like that for almost eight years.

Now, May of 2012, when she read about Burt's murder/suicide, her last au pair job had ended and the economy was abysmal. Even though she was pinching pennies by living in a hostel again, her money was fast running out. She was approaching the end of her little nest egg. Jobs were simply nonexistent, especially for someone without papers and even more especially for someone whose papers were as incriminating as hers.

The couple she most recently had worked for must have sensed her desperation, and told her about jobs working on those freighter "cruises" that plied the Atlantic between eastern Canada and the countries of northern Europe. The couple would give her a reference if she wanted to apply. As Carolyn walked back to her room at the hostel, she realized how fortuitous that job recommendation could turn out to be. She decided she would apply and hope for an interview.

The particular ship that hired her was one that went from Quebec City to Ireland. She would be doing food prep and dish washing in the ship's cafeteria to pay for her passage.

Although the food was decent, plentiful and free, she found she wasn't able to eat much. The passage was rough, the sleeping quarters smelled of diesel and vomit, and she was seasick most days. Added to the physical discomfort was the fear that when she disembarked at Cork Harbour, her name on the UK passport might trigger her arrest.

She got lucky. She passed through customs without incident and managed to find a room in a private home before evening fell. It was November 2012 and Carolyn's first order of business was to figure out where to go next.

CHAPTER TWENTY-SIX:
A SEASON IN THE MOUNTAINS, 2011-2012

When Dani pulled himself into the empty boxcar without Dushan, he was beside himself with apprehension. Leaning out, he yelled and waved his arm at Dushan. He saw Dushan make another attempt at jumping into a boxcar further down the train, only to fall back onto the grassy slope. The train's speed had increased significantly at this point, and began traversing a long railroad bridge over a dry creek bed about 50 feet below. *Shit, there's no way I can jump out now!* As the train accelerated, Dani collapsed onto the floor of the boxcar and started crying. Finally, he was so worn out and depressed that he fell asleep on the filthy floor of the boxcar.

Dani awoke several times for the next few hours, but each time, the train was traveling so fast and through such inhospitable territory that Dani rejected out of hand the idea of jumping from the train. Dani's last bout of sleep lasted well into the next morning, and when he awoke he was aware that the train was moving very slowly. He got up and looked out the open door. The train was practically crawling up a winding hillside in some desolate mountains. His watch indicated he had been on the train for almost 14 hours.

As he turned around and began examining the inside of the boxcar, he heard a scrambling noise behind him at the open door. He turned back to investigate and saw two scruffy older men climbing into the boxcar. After they got their bearings, they looked at Dani and walked over to him. One of them said, "Hey, that's a nice-lookin' watch, boy. I need a watch and you won't where you're goin'."

Dani turned to walk away from the door, but the other man yanked him backwards onto the floor of the boxcar. The two men stood there grinning at him. "Like I said, George, gimme your watch. I wants it, I does, it's precious to me," the taller of the men said in his best Gollum imitation.

The shorter man added, "And while you're at it, son, we'll need your wallet and everything else you got. So get up and break yourself."

Dani realized he stood no chance of winning a fight with these two guys, who looked like everyone's stereotype of train-jumping hobos. So he handed over his watch and wallet to the taller man. Without a word, the shorter man stepped forward and squeezed Dani's pockets. When he determined they were empty, the man gave Dani a quick shove backwards. Dani reached for the edge of the boxcar door, but missed it completely. He fell backward out of the car, turning in midair just before he hit the ground.

Before he landed in the loose clay soil he put his hands out to launch himself into a roll. He rolled downhill for a good 20 feet before coming to a stop against a stunted pine tree. He looked up at the still-moving train to see the two men waving to him and laughing.

Dani stood and took hold of the tree to steady himself and to avoid rolling further down the hill. He was in the mountains somewhere, fairly high up judging from the stunted trees dotting the landscape. The air was brisk and snow was visible on the peaks nearby.

The first thing Dani had to do was find shelter. He was wearing only his torn and bloody denim shirt and jeans and a ragged pair of high-top Keds basketball shoes. *Lucky my shoes weren't new or I'd be barefoot.* He climbed carefully back up the slope and looked along the railroad tracks in both directions. Facing what he determined was north, he could see that the track crossed a dirt road half a mile or so ahead. He began walking along the track toward the road in hopes of seeing a sign. When he got there, he saw nothing indicating where the road might lead. The road seemed to peter out not more than 100 yards ahead. The railroad track split in two at that point. A track switch at the junction sported a weather-beaten sign saying "Mineral Mountains."

About 50 yards away from the junction Dani saw a mountain trail, possibly a hiking trail, winding off at an angle toward a sparsely forested area to his left. He could make out a sign posted on the trail, so he trotted up to it hoping to see some useful information. The sign had the graphic symbol of a cabin and the number 2 with an upward-pointing arrow next to it. Dani hoped that meant there was a cabin two miles further up the trail. *It's the only game in town, I guess.* Dani set out on the trail, nervously looking up at the snowy peaks from time to time.

The trail crossed a narrow but deep rocky stream that meandered near the trail for another mile before heading off down the slope. The stream sported several small waterfalls and pools. The trail soon began a fairly steep ascent, and Dani could see the snow on the nearby peaks and slopes more clearly now.

Dani reached the cabin as the sun was climbing toward noon, but the sky was becoming crowded with dark clouds. Outside the door on the covered porch was a large stack of firewood, a pair of snowshoes and a shovel. A sign painted on the door read, "Beaver County Cabins, Mineral Mountains." The cabin door had no lock and opened easily. On the wall just inside the door was one of those cutesy plaques with a portrait of everyone's grandma pointing her finger at you and saying, "Your mother doesn't work here. Clean up when you leave!"

Inside, Dani saw two cots with heavy, folded-up army blankets on top. On a hook on the wall opposite the door hung a heavy hooded man's jacket. On the floor under the jacket was a pair of mukluks in a shoebox and large padded gloves. Leaning against an adjacent wall were a fishing pole and tackle. Just inside the door Dani saw a pile of kindling, an axe, a six-inch high stack of yellowing newspapers, and two boxes of large wooden kitchen matches.

The cabin had no kitchen or plumbing, but there was a wood stove with a flat top that was obviously used in cooking. There were two cast-iron pots and a skillet hanging on a wall. A wooden produce box on the floor held a badly rusted hunting knife, a coil of rope, a ball of twine, and a 25-pound bag of yellow onions, many of which had started to sprout. A second produce box next to that contained several forks and spoons, two well-scratched ceramic dinner plates, and some chipped cups and glasses. Another 25-pound bag lay beside it, this one practically full of potatoes. On a simple wooden table near the door was a kerosene lantern and a gallon can half full of what smelled like kerosene. There was a chair next to the table. *Wow; someone is looking out for me!*

Dani sat on the edge of a cot, overcome by mixed emotions. On the one hand, he was stranded in a desolate, mountainous no-man's land with no idea where he was. On the other hand, he was alive, and had shelter and the means to feed himself for the time being. Dani was tempted to just lie back on the cot and take a nap, but realized he had to find food before it got dark or, worse yet, started raining or snowing. He decided to take the fishing gear to the stream and see if he could invite a fish or two to dinner.

That evening, Dani cooked a dinner of trout and potatoes on the wood stove. He lay down on the cot and pulled the heavy woolen blanket over him as the sky opened up. The sound of rain and wind put him to sleep. The next morning the ground was wet and icy, with touches of snow on the tops of the trees and the roof of the cabin. *It's only early October and it's already this cold. Christ, there's no way I'm gonna try to find my way outta here in this weather!*

Dani's routine for the next two weeks or so consisted of exploring the area for indications of his location, fishing the pools of the stream, and collecting firewood. He also noted the presence of rabbits and squirrels, which gave him the idea of trying his hand at making a trap to vary his diet. If he didn't soon figure out a way to become a hunter, he foresaw the possibility of starving if his fishing holes became ice-bound. He saw nothing in the way of edible greens, which in any event would soon disappear with the onset of winter. On a hunch, he emptied the two wooden produce boxes, put several shovelfuls of dirt in them, sliced the sprouting onions into quarters and planted them in the boxes. He placed the little nursery on the floor next to the window. *Maybe I can grow some onion greens.*

Dani's explorations of the surrounding area soon became very circumscribed as the trail and landscape became more and more snow-covered. As winter settled in, Dani's little cabin was surrounded by a snowy wonderland. He was still able to ice-fish the little ponds, but his diet now was supplemented by the occasional rabbit that he managed to snare with a twine-and-twig trap he made based on a video he once saw on a nature survival program. He dreamt of Dushan often and spoke to him while dreaming and while awake. Dushan never replied, which worried Dani.

One afternoon as Dani returned to the cabin from a successful fishing and hunting foray, he encountered a man sitting on the front porch of the cabin with a pair of skis lying on the ground. The man appeared to be injured and was attempting to remove one of his boots. Dani gave a cheerful "hello" as he approached the cabin so as not to startle the man. The man looked up with a surprised expression. But his concerned frown quickly became a smile in obvious relief to see another human being.

"Let me help you with that," Dani said, setting down the rabbit and two trout he was carrying as well as his fishing and trapping paraphernalia. "That's gotta hurt. What happened to you?"

"I fell coming out of a turn just up the hill there. I was lucky to be able to limp down here from where I fell."

"Where exactly is 'here,' if you don't mind my asking? The sign on the trail near the railroad tracks said 'Mineral Mountains.' Where is that?"

"Utah, a couple hours south of Salt Lake. How did you get here?"

"I got pushed out of a train down there and made my way to this cabin. It's a long story. But first let me get these boots off you."

The man's right ankle began to swell noticeably as soon as Dani got the boot off, making Dani think the ankle was either broken or sprained. Dani pointed to the man's backpack and asked, "Anything in there that might help us fix you up? By the way, I'm Danilo Sandor, Dani for short."

"I'm Claude Prejean. Just up here on a short ski weekend, not so short now, I am afraid. Yes, my backpack has a small first aid kit."

Dani tended to the ankle, which on further examination turned out to be a pretty bad sprain, but might also be broken. "But even if it's only a sprain, I'd say you're effectively grounded at the cabin for at least another week, unless you have people who'll come looking for you. When we get you inside the cabin, you can tell me a little about this place."

Dani helped Claude hobble into the cabin. He put another log in the stove, took off his jacket and boots, and sat down at the edge of the cot. Claude sat on the chair next to the table.

Claude looked around and smiled. "Mon Dieu. You must have been surprised and relieved to see this cabin so well equipped after your hike from the train tracks."

Claude stretched out his legs and arms in the direction of the fire. Glancing around the room, he asked, "Where did you get the fishing tackle? Did you bring it with you?"

"No, it was here. I had nothing when I arrived. I don't even know what month it is, or even if it's still 2011."

"It's early January, 2012, and the height of the ski season here, although you will be hard-pressed to see any skiers in this remote location. As I said, we're in the Mineral Mountains of Utah. I am living in nearby Milford. I am a geologist for an international mining company. A little over a year ago, a combination of economic and technological factors forced my company to furlough most of the employees until things improved. I was more fortunate than many other employees, and was assigned other duties until things improved. Still, there hasn't been much for me to do, so I took some time off. I told the office I'd be on an extended winter camping trip, maybe a couple of months. I packed my car full of provisions, intending to bring them down here in my backpack one ski run at a time. No chance of getting any of that stuff now."

When Claude paused to rub his swollen ankle, Dani asked, "So, you decided to make this cabin your camp?"

"Yes, this and several others a few miles away. I like to ski and this particular area is usually pretty deserted. There are a few dilapidated cabins situated here and there along these trails. Most have some sort of provisions for short-term comfort, but this one is the best by far and is not dilapidated at all. It's my favorite. I came here several times during the last winter season."

Looking at Dani as he hung up his jacket and put Claude's boots against the wall, Claude continued, "At the end of my ski trip last January, I left a spare jacket, mukluks and gloves here for the next occupant, who turned out to be you. I don't know who left the fishing tackle or veggies."

"And I thank you and the gods for everything. Are you from the area? You sound like you have an accent. French?"

"French Canadian; Quebec. After graduating McGill University I was a newly minted mining engineer and worked on various projects in the far north of Canada. Now I'm here for another year or two."

Before Dani could interrupt, Claude continued, clearly still relieved at having been given shelter. "I parked my car at the top of the mountain and skied down, only I was interrupted by my fall. Unfortunately, I don't know how soon anyone will notice my car parked there, or even if it's still visible. In this weather, the car is probably buried in snow by now."

Dani looked at the snowshoes and turned back to Claude. "I don't ski, but maybe I could get to your car on snowshoes."

Claude shook his head. "That would be suicide. You have no idea of the lay of the land, or where the car is. Even if you knew where to go, getting there and back on snowshoes would be impossible. Forget about it. Now it's your turn to tell your story. How did you get here?"

"Like I said, I was thrown out of a train not far from here. What led up to that is a long, sad story, which I'll fill you in on after we get you settled in. I've been here since October. I've been learning how to survive until I can hike out when spring comes."

By the first week of February, it was even more evident that it would be premature to attempt to leave the mountain and get back to Claude's car. Dani looked out the cabin's only window at the growing snowdrifts all around. "I think this winter weather and your slow-healing ankle are conspiring to keep us cabin bound for the time being. How long and how heavy does it usually snow in these mountains?"

"It's hard to tell. It might last until May, at least that was the case last year." When Dani turned away from the window and put another log in the stove, Claude asked, "So, is it time for you to finish your story about why you were thrown off the train? Were you just riding the rails for excitement, or what?"

"Definitely not. More like confusion and fear. Me and my brother had a huge fight with our dad and decided to leave home. We took the old man's car but crashed it and had no other way to get out of town than hopping a freight train."

"Where's home?"

"Near San Bernardino. In fact, that's where we thought we were headed, but chose the wrong train. I managed to jump into an empty boxcar but my brother didn't make it all the way in and fell back out. I slept for a long time in that boxcar, only to be robbed and thrown out by two assholes. First thing I've got to do when I get back to civilization is to try to find out what happened to my brother."

For the next several months, Dani put the snowshoes to good use as he improved his proficiency in trapping rabbits. By the end of May, it had pretty much stopped snowing, and the two of them were hopeful the trail would soon be clear enough for them to leave and make it up the mountain.

The good weather continued for another week. The hillside was now free enough of snow and mud to allow them to leave the cabin. They made their way slowly up the mountain, Claude holding onto Dani as they walked. Avoiding all the steeper ascents, they basically crisscrossed the various slopes Claude had skied down several months earlier. Pointing to a clearing about 100 yards farther up, Claude said, "There is the trailhead. I hope my car is still there and the battery isn't dead."

They were in luck on the first count, but not so lucky on the second. The car was sitting in a patch of sun with patches of melting snow all around. Claude opened the driver-side door and sat in the driver's seat. "Here goes. Keep your fingers crossed." He put the key in the ignition and turned it. Nothing but a half-hearted groan from the engine, which barely turned over once. "Now what," Dani said. "I don't suppose Triple A would come up into these mountains."

Claude climbed out of the car and looked around. "I should have known the battery would be dead. This clunker is not exactly on its last legs, but it's not new, either."

"I have a suggestion. A buddy of mine has an older stick-shift Toyota Corolla that he's constantly having to work on to keep it running. He and I have pushed the thing more than once to get it started after the battery needed charging. Your's is a Corolla, too. Is it a stick or automatic?"

"It's a stick. Assuming the only thing keeping it from starting is the dead battery, we could push start it. That is, if you could do the pushing. I'm for sure not going to be able to help push."

Looking at the lay of the land, Dani said, "I won't have to push it far; the car is parked on a fairly decent slope. Once I get it rolling, gravity will take care of the rest. All you'll have to do is to pop the clutch when I yell."

Sure enough, Dani was able to get the car rolling at a fair clip before he yelled for Claude to pop the clutch. Bingo. The engine caught almost immediately. Dani shouted to him, "Keep the engine revved up; don't let it die." He ran up to the driver-side door and said to Claude, "Let it run at a fast idle for a minute or two, just to make sure the gas is coming from the tank and not just from the fuel line. How are you fixed for gas, by the way?"

"Practically a full tank." Dani walked over to other side of the car and got in the front seat. After another minute, he gave Claude the go-ahead sign, and they took off to Milford.

CHAPTER TWENTY-SEVEN:
A DETECTIVE IS BORN, 2012-2013

During the ride to Milford, Dani saw antelope, deer, turkey, pheasant, wild horses and burros, as well as what looked like ruins of old wild-west towns. Seeing Dani's look of amazement at the ruins, Claude said, "Yes, there are several ghost towns in this area, as well as abandoned mines. My company is involved in a joint venture hoping to reopen an abandoned copper mine near the town. But in addition to the economic downturn, the local partner has proven to be incompetent, so it will be some time before the mine will be operational. It's a shame, really, because this area is quickly becoming recognized for its obvious recreational opportunities—hunting, hiking, skiing, to name a few."

Dani pulled his gaze away from the scenery. "What a great place to live. It's on a major railroad line, and I saw from your map that it's near an Interstate highway and only about 200 miles south of Salt Lake City. I could see living here. That is, if it weren't for the unfinished business I have to attend to."

"What are you going to do now? Where will you go?"

"Well, those are very good questions. I'm completely broke, since those guys in the boxcar stole my wallet and cash. I had about a thousand dollars. I don't even have my ID; my driver's license was in the wallet. Do you suppose there are any job openings in Milford?"

"Could be. I recall seeing a help wanted sign in the local petrol station. But come to think of it, there might be a job for you working with a crew that disassembles and cleans the various pieces of mining equipment. Would that interest you? I can also let you stay in the little in-law unit attached to my house in town. That way you can save a little money for your next move."

"That would be great. I just want to earn a little money to be able to try my luck back home. I need to confront my dad about what he did to us. Most of all, I need to reconnect with my brother, Dushan."

By the end of summer, Dani's desire to locate his beloved brother was overpowering. He began making plans to return home and face whatever would happen. He didn't mind giving up his budding career as a mining machine mechanic. Dani decided he would buy a bus ticket from Milford to Victorville, but Claude had a better idea. Knowing that Dani had travelled to the Mineral Mountains courtesy of the Union Pacific Railroad, Claude arranged for Dani to accompany a train crew back to Victorville.

"I have to say, Dani, this has been one of the most memorable experiences of my life. I am forever in your debt. Here is my card. If I can ever repay you for what you did for me, don't hesitate to call or write me. My email is on the card as well."

"Sure thing. But really, the debt is all on me. You really saved my life by showing up at the cabin, and then bringing me into town and giving me a place to stay. I definitely will be calling or writing you when I get my life back on track."

The train ride back to Victorville was, to say the least, quite different from the ride to Milford. The crew was a quirky bunch of old-timers, alternately fascinated by and outraged at Dani's story about being robbed and thrown out of the boxcar by hobos. One of the cars on this particular southbound train from Salt Lake City was a refurbished dining car on its way to the train museum in San Bernardino, and Dani did not suffer from want of food. Dani marveled at the scenery he missed coming from the opposite direction.

When Dani arrived in his hometown some 14 hours later, he had a little over $400 in his pocket and new clothes given to him by the mining crew. But he was afraid to just walk up to his father's house and say "hi." So he decided to go to his former classmate Rick Orozco's house to find out what he could about the situation.

Rick wasn't home. There was a housekeeper there whom Dani had never seen before. She told Dani that Rick worked at the local Subway. As Dani walked the half mile to the place, he tried to get his thoughts in order. Most of all, he was worried about the situation at his own home. Would Dushan be there? Would Burt have called the cops on them?

Rick was outside the Subway having a smoke in the parking lot by the dumpsters. When he saw Dani walking up to him, he threw his cigarette on the ground and gave him a hug. "Man, where've you been all this time? You're supposed to be dead."

"Whaddya mean, dead?"

"The story ran in the local paper for weeks. Your dad was beat up something terrible. So was Dushan. Your old man accused him of murdering you. You were nowhere to be found. The clincher was when the investigators found your blood in a boxcar in Salt Lake City. The police bought the murder story and the DA charged him with murder in adult court. I heard he copped a plea and is serving time down in Calipatria."

"Shit. As you can see, I'm far from dead. But I'm afraid to go home. What's Burt gonna do when I walk in the door? I tell ya, Rick, we had a hell of fight. Me and Dushan really worked the bastard over. But it was his fault, really. He started hitting us first. God, this really sucks! Do you think he'd be at work now, or at home?"

Rick pulled out another cigarette, lit it, and slowly filled Dani in on what had happened to Burt in the intervening months. "It was pretty sensational news, dude. Your whole family went ballistic, seemingly."

Dani slapped his forehead and moaned. "I can't believe that! I knew he was always complaining about the feds bugging him at work, but I never expected this. I just don't know what to say. It all sounds like a sick joke."

"No joke; I would not joke about something like that, Dani. I know how you and Dushan were tight; you were best friends, inseparable. I'm sorry to have to be the one to tell you this, dude."

Dani contacted the police and the district attorney's office to see what he could do to set the record straight about his "murder." The authorities, after some understandable skepticism, and subjecting Dani to multiple sets of fingerprints and interviews with people who knew him, corroborated his story. Dushan's former attorney, Rafael Trujillo, was overjoyed to see Dani. "Wow, you look just like your little brother described you, except he's not so little. That prison food is pretty fattening, and your little brother is a big guy to start with."

Trujillo and the police helped Dani obtain the cooperation of the district attorney's office, and within a week, a motion was filed and granted in superior court declaring Dushan's conviction null and void "*ab initio.*" "That means from the get-go," Trujillo explained. "It's like the conviction never happened. Unfortunately, Dushan will never get back the year he spent in the joint. He'll just have to chalk it up as a learning experience."

Dani's hopes for a quick and joyful resolution to this royally screwed-up situation were quickly dashed. When Dani contacted the Calipatria State Prison, they told him that Dushan had been ordered deported as an illegal alien. An assistant warden continued, "And I'm sorry to tell you this, but your brother was killed en route to the ICE detention facility in Eloy, Arizona. There was a horrific accident when another car slammed into the ICE vehicle, killing all three: both drivers and your brother."

When Dani heard that, he went into a familiar zone for a few seconds. A picture reappeared in his mind, a picture he saw in a dream not long ago of two cars approaching each other in slow motion. He saw crushed cars, crushed and bleeding people. And he saw Dushan, alive and standing looking at the wreckage. Then Dushan turned and looked directly at Dani. The picture disappeared at that point, and Dani exited his zone, thanked the prison official, and hung up the phone. Because of the vision, or whatever it was, the assistant warden's report didn't ring true to Dani. Not just because of the vision that washed over him. He also felt in the very depths of his being that Dushan was still alive. They had been such close blood brothers for so long that Dani felt his presence on a daily basis. Dani passed along the disturbing news to Dushan's former lawyer, Trujillo. "Let me know what I can do to help you out, my man. I really liked the guy, he was a prince." Dani thanked him, but still didn't accept that Dushan was dead. He resolved to investigate the circumstances of the accident and find Dushan.

Before beginning his investigation, Dani applied for a duplicate driver's license and immersed himself in the much less depressing task of dealing with his inheritance. When Burt killed himself, he did not leave a will, only a letter revealing that Dushan was an illegal alien and describing how it all happened. The house, Burt's bank account, the Lexus SUV and the rest of his belongings now belonged to Dani, and Dushan, too, if he was still alive.

Dani was so overwhelmed by this turn of events he had to talk to someone, someone with a connection to Dushan. He called Trujillo. They met for lunch. "I'm paying, Mr. Trujillo. You see, I've come into a little loot."

"What, you broke open your piggy bank and took out all $3.42?"

"How does this sound? My old man's house, car, and bank

accounts are all mine now. Well, mine and Dushan's." At the thought of inheriting Burt's bank account, Dani teared up when he realized he would also inherit the cash in Dushan's bank account if Dushan had in fact been killed.

"I see you still can't face reality, Dani. Understood. But in the meantime, from a legal point of view, the inheritance is all yours. I understand you want to do some sleuthing, and I think that's a great idea. Closure and all that. I repeat what I said before. I'll help you out any way I can. Call me anytime."

Dani sold the house by the end of December 2012. Together with the rest of the cash in Burt's estate, and the $875 in Dushan's bank account, he found himself very well off. At least well enough off to take Burt's Lexus and embark on what might turn out to be a fruitless fishing expedition.

Because the fatal accident involved a former inmate, the prison had a copy of the accident investigation. As the deceased's only surviving kin, Dani was allowed to review the report and learn such details as where the accident occurred as well as the identity, address and phone number of the driver of the civilian car. The driver, a Mr. Darrell Scales, was married and had lived in Tucson.

First stop: Tucson! Dani drove to Tucson and telephoned Mrs. Scales. After explaining who he was—that it was his brother who was killed in the ICE vehicle—the widow agreed to let Dani stop by and talk about the accident.

"My husband was the founder and CEO of a small recreational equipment company here in Tucson. He was attending an industry conference in Yuma. When the conference ended, Darrell phoned to tell me he was about to leave for home. He said he was giving one of the conference catering employees a ride to his home in Yuma first. We knew the young employee casually from other events and have always found him to be a friendly and very capable young man."

"Do you happen to remember the young man's name? The accident report says only three persons were killed, your husband, the ICE driver and my brother."

"The young man's name is Douglas Armitage. I'm very relieved that my husband dropped him off in Yuma first, otherwise there would have been four casualties instead of three."

"What's the name of the young man's catering company, if you don't mind my asking?"

"It has a very bland name, sort of generic. Let me see, oh yes, the name is 'Conference Catering'."

Dani's next trip was to Yuma to see if he could get more information about Douglas Armitage from his catering company. The owner of the business expressed his condolences to Dani about the deaths of Dushan and the business client. "I haven't had the heart to tell young Douglas about the accident. He would be devastated. He knew Mr. Scales, had done catering for that conference before."

"You mean Douglas doesn't know yet? Doesn't he still work for you?"

"No, he's moving up in this business. Getting an education. He'll be getting a college degree in culinary arts and professional training as a chef. Douglas had singlehandedly organized the catering at this last conference, and his expertise will be missed in the business."

Dani's scalp began to tingle. "Do you recall where he'll be studying?"

"Sure I do, gave him the best recommendation I could. He's been given a full ride at the Culinary Institute of America in upstate New York, Hyde Park I believe. His parents had passed away some years before, and he was struggling financially. The opportunity to get a college degree and professional training there will be a godsend."

CHAPTER TWENTY-EIGHT:
A SLEUTH COMES TO DINNER, 2013

D eeply immersed in his new career as a forensic investigator into the alleged death of his brother, Dani now felt that he finally would be able to resolve the question in his mind about whether it was Douglas or Dushan who was still alive and studying at the Culinary Institute. Dani hoped beyond hope that the accident did not happen the way it was described in the police reports. Though it made him sad to think so, Dani hoped that the third person killed in the accident was Douglas and not Dushan. *It's more than just a hope, I know it is. I know my brother is still alive. I feel his presence every day!*

Dani had no trouble selling the Lexus. He took a midnight flight from Tucson to JFK. It was a one-stop flight, and arrived in New York a little after 8 a.m. From the airport he took a shuttle to Manhattan. Not knowing where to get out, Dani had the driver let him out at the Port Authority.

As he stood on the icy sidewalk trying to decipher the tourist map of Manhattan, Dani muttered to himself, "So far so good; not bad for a suburban kid who hasn't been on a plane since he was a baby. Now I just need to figure out how to get to Hyde Park."

"That's easy, my friend." An elderly gentleman standing next to him tipped his bowler hat and pointed to a subway sign up the block. With an upper-class British accent, the man said, "You take the subway north to Tarrytown. There, you must rent a car, I'm afraid, and take a one-hour drive to Hyde Park." Looking Dani up and down, the man added, "I'm guessing you are headed for the CIA. Are you hoping to become the world's next James Beard?"

"Who's James Beard? You mean James Bond? He didn't work for the CIA, too, did he? I thought he was a Brit. No, I'm just going to visit my brother at the Culinary Institute. Thanks for the tip about the transportation."

The gentleman chuckled and answered, "My pleasure. Glad to be of service. By the way, here's another couple of tips: people call the Culinary Institute by its nickname, the CIA. And James Beard is a food writer and chef, not a spy. Good day and good luck, young man!"

The Metro ride from Grand Central to Tarrytown took not quite 45 minutes. It was 11 a.m. when Dani picked up the rental car. The agent suggested he might enjoy visiting the Sleepy Hollow cemetery and museum if he had a little time. Dani had read the Headless Horseman book back in middle school and decided he had some time before he had to look for a motel in Hyde Park.

It was late afternoon when Dani checked into a motel. Feeling restless and a little wired from not having slept on the plane and drinking too much coffee at the museum cafe, Dani decided to take a drive to the campus of the CIA. It was an impressive college campus in its own right; its undulating grounds lay on the banks of the Hudson River. The only visible features revealing its culinary arts curriculum were the five world-class restaurants. Dani had dinner at an over-the-top classical French restaurant and strolled around the campus for an hour or so. Because of the late hour, and out of nervousness over the prospect of finally perhaps getting to the bottom of this mystery, Dani retired to his motel to try to get a good night's sleep.

The next day, Dani showed up at the campus registrar's office as soon as it opened, introduced himself as Dani Sandor, a friend of Douglas Armitage's former employer, and asked if he might obtain Armitage's class or work schedule or his phone number. The clerk gave him the phone number, but since the spring term had not yet begun, couldn't give out the class or work schedules. Dani realized it would be better to phone him anyway. Even if he knew where Douglas worked or where his dorm room was, and it was really Douglas and not Dushan, how would Dani recognize him? Dani made the phone call at 9:15, left a message, and went to have breakfast.

Dushan checked his little dorm mailbox and saw a written message from the registrar's office. The message was that someone claiming to be a friend of Douglas Armitage's employer had arrived and would like to visit him. This news triggered Dushan's ever-present worry of being discovered, since from time to time he received emails and phone messages from friends of Armitage's. Dushan never answered the phone. He always let it go to voicemail and used it as a secretary. He never responded to email or requests to join Facebook. Nor had he even recorded an outgoing voicemail message in his own voice, for fear that a friend or relative of Douglas's might call and hear a strange voice claiming to be Douglas. During the winter break, Dushan only left campus once, afraid of being caught if he pushed his luck a second time. That one time was an enjoyable trip into Manhattan where he managed to attend a wonderful jazz-and-poetry recital. But the whole time he looked over his shoulder and couldn't fully enjoy the experience.

Dushan would normally have enjoyed, even thrived at, being a student at CIA, especially after his recent experience learning to cook and bake in prison. He even found enjoyable the busboy job he was given as a work-study student. He was grateful for the chance to study and learn more sophisticated chef skills, not to mention to be taking college classes in other subjects.

But he knew deep down that all of this might probably come to naught. He was living a lie. A college degree in the name of Douglas Armitage would only help him as long as he remained Douglas Armitage. But, realistically, how long could he maintain that false identity? The worry of discovery gnawed at him. He had trouble sleeping, nightmares of Douglas's ghost confronting him, police arresting him, deporting him. But his biggest, deepest, source of depression was about Dani. Why hadn't Dani, if he survived the train ride, contacted him? Dushan knew in his heart that there was no "if" about Dani surviving—he had survived. Not only had Dushan felt his presence almost every night, there was that dream he had where Dani was telling him he was alive. But then Dushan remembered that Dani couldn't possibly know where Dushan was. All Dani would know, assuming he returned home or contacted someone from home, was that Dushan was reported killed in the auto accident en route to being deported. *I only hope I got through to him after the crash!*

At the end of Dushan's work shift later that day, he learned from his dorm roommate that he had a voicemail on their shared phone. Dushan listened to it and was startled. The voice sounded incredibly like Dani's. And then—Dushan's heart skipped a beat—the caller identified himself as Dani Sandor, "a friend of your employer at Conference Catering."

195

Dushan called back. In between sobs and laughter, Dushan said, "Dani, I can't believe it. You're alive. I don't know what to say. All these months I didn't know where you were."

Dani likewise couldn't hold back the sobs and giggles. "Dushan, I'm the one who should be saying 'you're alive.' You have apparently risen from the dead. And taken a new identity."

"Dani, before we go any further, let's meet and talk over old times face to face." Dushan glanced over at his roommate, who was studiously trying to look like he was not eavesdropping. "Are you on campus right now? I got a note in my mailbox earlier saying you were in town."

"Yes, I'm on campus. How about I take you out to dinner? Which of your fabulous restaurants is your favorite? I'm sorry to say I wasn't impressed with the French one."

"Let's do Italian. I'll be there in half an hour."

When Dani walked into the restaurant, Dushan was waiting for him at one of the tables near the door. They hugged, tears in their eyes. It was a minute or so before either of them could speak. Dushan spoke first. "Dani, you can't imagine how worried I was about you. Dad made up this story that I murdered you. Even though I knew he was lying, after a few months in prison I started thinking maybe you were dead. Where were you? I saw you once in my mind, sitting in a cabin staring at me. You told me you were safe, but I wasn't sure it wasn't just wishful thinking on my part."

"It was me, and I was in a cabin, just like you saw. And I saw you in one of my dreams a while back. You were standing next to a couple of wrecked cars; you looked at me."

They caught up on past events. Each of them was amazed at the other's story, stories that they could never have predicted. "So, you're quite the accomplished fisherman and hunter, now, my friend. Big game. Squirrel, rabbit, what's next, bear?"

"I'm embarrassed to say my usual fare was undersized trout and crawdads. But from the looks of you, being a cook agrees with you. Putting on a little weight, my brother?"

"They feed us well here, I have to admit. But the extra weight is what I acquired in the joint, as my cellmate called the prison. Lots of carbs, very fattening."

After an hour of sharing experiences they began evaluating their next step. They agreed that Dushan was in a precarious position. Any day now, someone from the prison or ICE, or more likely someone from Douglas Armitage's past, might show up.

Pondering those possibilities, Dushan tried to reassure Dani and himself. "I can hope beyond hope that no one will look for Dushan Sandor here. I covered my tracks pretty well after the accident."

Dani understood immediately that Dushan was trying to convince himself, and not very successfully. Dani, like Dushan, was not at all reassured. "Well, what if a further investigation into the wreck reveals what really happened? Photos of the dead bodies might show the prison authorities that it was not Dushan who was killed, that he was not in the wreckage at all. At that point, it would be logical to run fingerprints on the body, and check up on what led the driver of the convertible to be in that particular intersection."

"I've had nightmares about that, Dani. If they get hold of the driver's widow, they'll discover a possible inconsistency. The widow will tell an investigator what her husband told her—that he was giving Douglas Armitage a ride to his home in Yuma. I have no idea whether Douglas lived alone or with roommates. If he had roommates, what if they expected him home before going to the airport? And how was Douglas supposed to get to the airport from home? Had he reserved a shuttle pick-up? Had he asked a friend for a lift? That's the story I told the Marine who picked me up on the Interstate, that my buddy failed to show and I had to hitch a ride."

Finally, they agreed that the wisest course would be to leave the CIA—and the USA—as soon as possible. Dushan realized a college degree was just not in the cards, especially if it meant having to live a lie for the rest of his life. He would leave the CIA before spring term registration was completed in mid-January 2013.

Dushan already had a US passport under Douglas Armitage's name—plus he had the driver's license. When his dorm mate was gone for the day, Dushan cleaned out his desk and packed his clothes into the rolling suitcase Dani bought him. He looked at the various tickets and handbills of events he attended last term. He couldn't decide which of them he'd keep as mementos. Finally, he chucked all of them except the program for a poetry reading he attended in New York City last fall, entitled "Requiem Before the Times of Peace." The only reason Dushan decided to keep it was an insert by poet Nancy Hoffman explaining that the last stanza of the poem was dedicated to the cellist who shone the spotlight on a particularly horrific mass murder in Sarajevo in 1992. Dushan remembered his dad's stories of his mom coming from that place.

Dani drove them back to Tarrytown and turned in the rental car. They walked to the Tarrytown Metro-North station and took the train to Greenwich Village, not far from the downtown passport office. Dani had no trouble applying for his own passport, but when they learned it would take at least three days, even for an expedited passport, they had no choice but to stay in Manhattan until it was ready. Dushan had heard of a cool little boutique hotel in the Village, the Larchmont, and they booked a room.

After three days, just as Dani was beginning to worry that maybe the record of his death was causing problems at the passport office, he got an email telling him he could pick it up.

Dani looked up from the laptop in a Lower East Side café, where they had just visited the Tenement Museum. "Hey, it's time to roll, my brother. My get-out-of-jail card is ready. Let's go pick it up and stop by an American Airlines office and get tickets to London."

Dushan drained the dregs of his latte and replied, "Sounds like a plan, Stan. American Airlines has a ticket office midtown."

Dani chuckled, "Listen to you, talking about 'midtown' like you grew up in New York."

"I told you, I did spend a little time here over the break. It's fun trying to impersonate a New Yorker."

There was no wait at the passport office, and the walk from there to the American Airlines office took less than half an hour. Dani purchased two one-way coach tickets to London with the Visa credit card he had obtained before he left home. They took a taxi back to the Larchmont and let the hotel know they would check out in the morning. The clerk kindly let Dani use the phone to call his bank to inform them of his intention to take a vacation in England and other unknown countries. The brothers were ready to fly.

CHAPTER TWENTY-NINE:
ACROSS THE POND, 2013

Since the brothers had to leave the USA anyway, they decided to fly to the UK so they could search for Dimitri on the Isle of Man. After leaving Heathrow in their rental car, with Dani trying to remember to stay on the left side of the road, they drove to Liverpool and from there to the dock of the ferry to the Isle of Man. Dani was fortunate the weather in England was fairly mild for a January. "So, Dr. Dushansky, look in your crystal ball and tell me where we're going once we get to the island. We'll look up my relatives in Liverpool after we're done in the Isle of Man. Or is it **on** the Isle of Man?"

"According to what Carolyn says on the tape, the name of the town is Ramsey. I remember almost nothing about it or the rest of the Isle of Man, except vague memories of my daycare and playing with ducks on the bank of a river or bay. And me and my dad going to some kind of parties or something. I have dreams about it once in awhile."

The ferry ride over the Irish Sea was pretty rough. When Dani drove off the ferry and into Ramsey, Dushan was amazed at how much the town resembled his dreams. "God, this river, and the benches on the banks; I used to play near the banks while my dad read the paper!"

They stopped in a pub and ordered pints. They asked the proprietor if he'd heard of a Dimitri Sava. No luck. Same in two other pubs. "I think we'd better check in with the police before we get drunk," Dani said as they walked back to the car. They pulled over at a restaurant and entered to have lunch. As they were ordering, Dushan asked the waitress where the nearest police station was. She smiled and said, "Over on other side of River Selby, on corner of Christian Street and Taubman Street, just past East Swing Bridge, a block behind Parliament Street."

As they consumed their fish and chips, Dushan asked, "Where do you place the accent, Cap'n Dante? I'm going out on a limb here and say the Middle East."

"I'd have to say French, Dushansky. Her accent reminds me of Claude Prejean's, the guy I helped survive the winter in Utah. By the way, before we left Hyde Park, I took the liberty of emailing him to let him know I found you. I'm sure he'll be blown away. I hope he replies. Remind me to check email on the laptop when we have some down time."

When they arrived at the police station, Dushan introduced himself and explained why they were there. The officer at the desk raised his eyebrows and said, "Well, that's nothing short of amazing! I do remember Inspector Ailshie's efforts to find out what happened to you. His only failed investigation, he used to say."

Dushan had a look of wonderment on his face. "Thanks. Can we talk to him? By the way, this is my brother, Dani."

"Your brother? I don't recall anything ever said about two boys abducted."

"He wasn't. He's my American stepbrother. It's a long, sad story."

"And I'm sure the inspector will love hearing it anyway. He retired a few years ago but he still pokes his nose in here from time to time. I'll ring him and tell him about you."

The brothers didn't have to wait long. At the sound of gravel crunching outside, they stood and looked out the window. Dani exclaimed at the sight of the car pulling up. "Will ya look at that! That car must be an antique. What make is it?"

Dushan replied, "Got me. You're supposed to be the car buff. You've got almost as many model cars as airplanes and ships."

They turned back to the officer's desk when they heard him laughing. "That will be the inspector. He's a bit of a fan of old French cars. That's a Peugeot. It is indeed an antique. I think it's over 60 years old. He has a Citroen as well that's even older."

Inspector Ailshie interrupted their conversation as he opened the door and walked in. "Well, well. This is a day I shall never forget. I only wish I were still working so I could personally close this particular missing-persons file."

Ailshie shook both boys' hands and asked, "Now, the sergeant here told me a stepbrother was here, too. Who is who?"

Dushan smiled and said, "I'm Dushan Sava. This is Dani Sandor.

We grew up together in California." Dushan paused and looked briefly at Dani before turning back to the inspector. "I guess it still feels strange to call myself Sava when I've been a Sandor for as far back as I can remember."

"Very honored to meet you both. So, you're California lads. I'm sure there's a very interesting story there. But it can wait. There's someone on the island who wants to meet you very much. Shall we go there now, or do you have more pressing business?"

The boys practically answered in unison, "No, nothing we'd like to do more."

Taking leave of the desk sergeant, the threesome left the station and piled into Ailshie's car. Marveling at the incongruity of the car's immaculately restored interior and the old-fashioned radio, manual windows and a gearshift mounted on the steering column, Dani asked, "What year is your Peugeot?"

The inspector smiled and raised his eyebrows. "I'm impressed that you recognized the car. It's a 1959 Peugeot 403. They stopped making this model almost 50 years ago. I bought her in the early 80's and let me tell you, she was in pretty sad shape. I'm happy to say she's responded well to my loving care. Have you boys ever heard of the American detective TV show Columbo? Peter Falk was the star. His character, Frank Columbo, drove this very car. Not this particular one, of course, but one just like it."

Dani answered, "Yeah, I used to catch Dushan watching the show on late-night TV when he was supposed to be studying. I have to say, we loved the show. Columbo was a pretty cool dude, sort of like you, Inspector." Laughter all around.

Dushan couldn't hold his impatience in any longer. "Look, Inspector, this is a very odd conversation we're having. Talking about antique cars when Dani and I are extremely anxious about meeting my dad. But I am glad we've met up with you. I do hope you'll stick around when we get wherever we're going so you can fill us in on how everything happened."

"Your dad? No, that's not where we're going. But I'll explain when we get there."

Just then, they pulled into the parking lot of a charming older Victorian-style building. The sign planted in the yard in front of the building said "Ramsey Baha'i Centre." Ailshie parked, shut the motor and said, "Here we are, gentlemen. Someone you used to know is inside, Dushan."

No sooner had they entered through the open front door than an effusive, beautiful, middle-aged woman walked quickly up to them. Throwing her arms around Dushan and kissing him on both cheeks, she said, "Oh, my God, dear lost Dushan! I'm Jaleh, who you used to call Jolly! Your father, we all thought you were gone forever! You must tell me all about it. Let's go in my office and have some tea and talk. Good morning, my dear Angus. Thank you so much for this!" Turning to Dani, she asked, "And who are you, young man?"

Dani said, "I'm Dani Sandor, Dushan's brother." Jaleh paused briefly and looked closely at Dani. "Dushan's brother, yes, Angus told me your brother was with you. Interesting. You must tell me more." The group moved into the office, and the inspector and the brothers sat at one end of a long conference table while Jaleh busied herself in the kitchen putting the teakettle on and getting out a plate of cookies. When she returned, she asked Dani, "Okay, Dani, let's hear the story of how you came to be Dushan's brother. I knew Dushan from the age of two or so up to when he disappeared the summer before he turned five. He had no brother."

Dani said, "Before I do, let me make sure I understand you. You knew Dushan and his dad when they both were refugees?"

"Yes, indeed. I got to be good friends with Dimitri. And this boy here, who is not so little any more, absolutely loved coming here and playing with the other children."

Dani said, "I'll yield the floor to him for awhile. He's practically jumping up and down." Dushan turned to Jaleh and said, "I do remember snatches of those days. This place made me and my dad happy. But I could tell that he was pretty sad most of the time. He often told me stories of my mom, which I guess helped me have 'memories' of her. He used to constantly tell me how beautiful she was, and I would describe her to him as I saw her in my dreams." Dushan paused and took a breath before continuing. "I hate to sound impatient, but I really, really want to see my dad. Is he going to be coming here? Have you contacted him?"

Jaleh said, "Not yet. I'll explain, but first let me start the tea brewing." She got up and attended to the whistling teakettle. A couple of minutes later she returned to the table. With a twinkle in her eye, she said, "Your mother is still very beautiful, or was the last time I saw her."

Dushan's jaw dropped. "What? You mean she's alive? I knew it! You know her? How?"

"Our intrepid Ramsey policeman here, Inspector Angus Ailshie, made sure you and your father were properly registered with the UN refugee agencies in London and Liverpool. That way, if your mom was still alive, she would be able to track you both down. Eventually, she did just that, at least as far as your dad is concerned. She and two friends came here looking for Dimitri and you. You had been stolen by then, so it was something of a bittersweet reunion."

Before Dushan could reply, Dani said to Jaleh, "This is amazing. When was that?"

"It was the summer of 2000, I believe. Yes, isn't that right, Angus?" Angus nodded, and Jaleh continued. "I remember Inspector Ailshie had joined our little Bahá'í community as we were celebrating one of our Bahá'í holy days, July 9 it was, here at the Centre. When the program ended and the Feast began, Dimitri came in escorting three lovely ladies.

"Your mom, Dushan, had brought your dad's aunt Adrijana and your former nursemaid, Amina. Everyone had a joyous reunion, as you might expect. As joyous as could be under the circumstances. We helped your mom and dad find a bigger apartment not far from here."

Dani asked, "But are they still here? Tell us more."

"Amina and Adrijana returned to their home within a week or so. They lived in Ljubljana, Slovenia, same as your mom. Amina had to get back to her husband and daughter. Adrijana had to get back to care for an ailing family member. Marta, who had taken an open-ended leave of absence from her nursing job, decided to remain here. She and Dimitri stayed on the island another three years and Marta gave birth to two lovely twin daughters. They gave the girls interesting names for a Slavic couple from Yugoslavia: Aisha and Shimza. We, Angus, my husband Thomas and I, didn't have to wait to hear why Marta chose those particular names. Marta was only too pleased to explain. 'I chose "Aisha" for one girl because it is the name of the daughter of my best friend back home, Amina. I named "Shimza" after my dad's mother.'"

Pouring the tea, Jaleh added, "I have to say I think it's wonderful that this Slovenian woman chose a Muslim and a Rom name for her daughters. But of course, Dimitri told me all about her being in the vanguard of the failed effort to promote ethnic harmony in Yugoslavia, so I wasn't surprised."

Dani and Dushan sat spellbound. Angus sipped his tea and watched the young men with fascination. Jaleh continued, "When Marta learned that her grandparents' increasingly poor health was becoming precarious, she and the family moved back to Ljubljana. I get an email from Marta every now and then. Dimitri's not much of a computer person, and I suspect he's a little embarrassed that his written English is not perfect. The two girls email me now also. They're 12 years old and loyal Facebook friends of mine."

Dushan didn't know whether to feel disappointed that he was once again separated from his parents, or overjoyed that he had found them. Probably he felt both emotions, *like alternating current*, he thought.

Dani turned to Dushan and said with a sly grin, "Okay, I see a plan taking shape in that little brain of yours, Dushansky."

Jaleh's eyes widened and she smiled at Dani's words. "I can see you two are good friends, Dani. I know there is a story there and I am dying to here it."

"A very long story. We're stepbrothers. This cassette," Dani pulled out the tape Irene made of Carolyn's confession, "tells how it began. We're hoping to turn it over to the police here, which I guess will be Inspector Ailshie." Turning to Angus, Dani said, "We can all listen to it. After that, we can fill you all in with the rest of the story. Better than fiction."

Jaleh said, "I guess I only know the very beginning of your story, how Dushan was stolen by a babysitter named Carolyn something. Angus was very disappointed he was never able to find out anything about the kidnapping. It was his only unsolved case, he would tell me over and over."

Dushan took the cassette from Dani and said, "This is Carolyn telling her story on the phone to my mom, Irene. Actually my stepmom, Dani's mom." Dushan stopped for a moment to wipe his eyes, then continued, "Sheesh, Dani, help me out here. I'm choking up."

Dani picked up the story. "Carolyn stole Dushan from his dad, as you know. She met my dad, Burt Sandor, in Liverpool, and they took Dushan to Burt's home, my home, in San Francisco. I was almost six when I met Dushan, a year older than him. The story gets stranger, sadder, scarier, more exciting, and then happier, from there."

Dani was holding back tears as he put his arms around Dushan and gave him a hug.

Jaleh sat back. She had been sitting so hunched over on the edge of her chair that she had to sit up straight and stretch her back. She looked at the brothers with tears in her own eyes.

After a moment to allow her throat to loosen, Jaleh said to them, "I see good news is on the way, though. Angus is retired now and has lots more time to visit me here."

Angus smiled sheepishly and joined in the conversation for the first time. "I moved to Liverpool last year but can't seem to leave the Isle of Man behind. Yes, I think we'll be most interested to hear Carolyn's voice on that cassette. I've been on the hunt for her for many a long year, and we still haven't got hold of her."

CHAPTER THIRTY:
THIRD REUNION

The next evening Jaleh and her husband Thomas Kilpatrick threw a small dinner party at their home for the brothers and Angus. The party lasted well past midnight. Angus and the Kilpatricks insisted on hearing all the details of Dani and Dushan's ordeals. The group couldn't decide which of their experiences was the scarier. As Angus put it, "I've no doubt that being a prison inmate in a region infested by gangs is pretty near the top of the list of frightening experiences. But being thrown out of a moving train at the beginning of winter in the mountains is perhaps even worse."

Thomas asked the next question, "Perhaps this is obvious, but it hasn't occurred to anyone to ask yet. Leave it to the lawyer to ask it! Dushan, I congratulate you on your escape from deportation. What you did was simply amazing. But how did you manage to come over here? Surely you didn't use your real name, or rather, your adopted name, Dushan Sandor?"

Dushan and Dani had not broached that subject up to this moment, but Dushan decided that, Angus's presence notwithstanding, truth was the best response. "No, that would not have worked. I had no identity, really, not in a legal sense. Sandor was a name my stepdad, Burt Sandor, gave me. He never went through the adoption process as far as I know." Turning to Dani, Dushan asked, "You never turned up any papers to that effect, did you Dani, when you were taking care of family business last summer?"

"Nothing on that, but lots of other interesting stuff. The local police had locked up the house after going through it, looking for 'evidence' I suppose. When I showed up and got everything straightened about my 'murder,' they gave me Burt's keys and removed all the yellow crime scene tape. In their search of the house, they also were looking for next-of-kin documents. They told me they didn't find anything. But they obviously didn't look very hard. I found a couple boxes of papers in the garage behind two shelves full of jam and fruit preserves that mom had made over the years. The cops may not have even looked behind the dozens of jars on the shelves, but even if they did, the boxes could have fooled them. The cardboard boxes were the cartons that the Ball mason jars originally came in; the cops might have thought the cartons were full of jars."

Smiling at Dushan, Dani continued, "Inside one box was a copy of dad's nice letter to the immigration folks outing you as an illegal alien, a little folder of stuff relating to your 'murder' of me, and documents pertaining to my parents' citizenship applications and the names and addresses of their families in England.

"In the other box I found a bunch of family photos and Mom's old job application. She was trying to get a job as a daycare teacher before dad made us all move away from San Francisco. Underneath her application and resume was this cassette, a recording of Carolyn confessing to my mom on the phone. I guess dad kept that box of papers as a keepsake without ever taking them out and going through them. I doubt he ever looked underneath the photos and mom's job file; he certainly would have destroyed the cassette had he seen it. The police never looked back behind the preserves."

Dani paused and said to Dushan, "Back to you, bro."

Dushan resumed his explanation. "Anyway, not only was I, as Dushan Sandor, not a legal adoptee in the USA, but I had no idea whether I, as Dushan Sava, ever had any legal status in the UK or the Isle of Man. Obviously, I had nothing that might show such status. Certainly I didn't have any such documentation when I was in New York trying to figure out how to get out of the country. So I took the only way out I could think. I travelled on the passport of Douglas Armitage, the kid who died in the auto accident in Arizona."

Angus set down his coffee cup and looked at Jaleh and her husband. Then he turned to Dushan and said, "Now, that's very interesting, young man. I don't mean in a law-enforcement sense. Even though I've spent my entire adult life in law enforcement, I've never been a fan of the send 'em back where they came from mentality. Your secret is safe with me, certainly."

Dani responded, "I could fill you in on all I know about Douglas if you like. I think I learned more about him than Dushan did. Dushan just borrowed Douglas's identity without knowing much about him. I actually followed up on several bits of information and talked to his employer and a woman who knew him."

"Did the lad have a family in California or Arizona?"

"Apparently he was a single child. His employer told me that both of his parents were deceased. Neither he nor the widow of the driver of the car he was killed in knew anything else about him. It's possible, I guess, that he had cousins or some such. I never went further than the widow and the employer once I found out where he was headed. Dushan, did you ever hear from anyone claiming to know Douglas, or be related to him?"

Dushan replied, "I had several voicemails and notes in my mailbox from folks wanting to talk to me. But I never responded. Obviously, I was not up to speed in my Armitage family lore, and I didn't think I could convince any of his friends or family of my claim to be Douglas Armitage."

Finally, the brothers were ready to call it a night. Dani said to the group, "We're going to head back over to Liverpool tomorrow and see if we can connect with my dad's family there. My grandma Margaret Sandor is still alive, I believe. Her address was in my dad's papers. After that, we'll make our way to Slovenia and connect with Marta and Dimitri and their new family."

Angus said, "Jaleh and I have their contact information. You won't have any problem getting hold of them. Actually, do you want me to call or email Dimitri and Marta and let them know you're on your way?"

Dushan paused, thought for a second and said, "Why don't you tell them a couple of their old friends from Ramsey are headed their way on holiday and would like to call on them? Keep it mysterious. We'll surprise them in about a week or so."

Before the get-together broke up, Angus asked if he could accompany the brothers back to Liverpool. They readily agreed, and arranged to meet at the ferry terminal at 7:45 the next morning.

*　　　　*　　　　*

When the ferry docked at Liverpool, the boys followed Angus's car in their rental car. After they dropped off his car at his apartment, Angus guided them on a brief tour of the city. They stopped for lunch at a waterfront café, and Angus said, "I'd like to talk to your grandmother about Carolyn, if you don't mind. I understand they're related, and Margaret might know where Carolyn is." Late in the afternoon, the party arrived on the doorstep of Mrs. Margaret Sandor, Dani's grandmother.

CHAPTER THIRTY-ONE:
CLOSURE IN LIVERPOOL

An elderly woman answered the door chime. Dani stepped closer to the middle of the open doorway and asked, "Hello. Are you Margaret Sandor?"

"No, I'm her housekeeper. Who may I ask are you?" The woman looked around at the three men standing at the door.

"My name is Danilo Sandor, this is Dushan Sava, my stepbrother. And this gentleman is Angus Ailshie, a friend of ours."

The housekeeper registered surprise at the name Sandor and dropped her hand from the doorknob. "Well, I'm sure Mrs. Sandor will be glad to meet you. Come in, come in! My name is Mrs. Perkins, by the way. Follow me."

When Margaret entered the sitting room and introductions took place, she got right to the point. "My, my. Danilo Sandor. Burt's boy! You know, the last time I saw you was just before your parents took you to America. You were just a baby. I don't think I know your companions here."

Dani answered. "This is Angus Ailshie, retired inspector with the Ramsey police, over on the Isle of Man. He now lives here in Liverpool and is a new friend of ours. And this guy is my stepbrother, Dushan Sava."

Margaret adjusted her glasses as she peered at Dushan. "And how did you become Danilo's stepbrother? I don't believe Burt told me anything about that."

Angus saw that Dani and Dushan were too choked up to respond, so he took the cue. "It's a long, sad story, Mrs. Sandor. A story I had but little part in, but perhaps I can start at the beginning and the lads can finish."

For the next hour, Angus, Dani and Dushan took turns relating the events of the past 14 years. They had been worried at what Margaret's reaction would be, and they weren't surprised. Several times they stopped as she wept and sighed. Finally, Margaret responded to what she had heard so far.

"Well, well, that's a very strange and sad story to be sure. To be sure. I don't know quite how to feel. But when you've reached my age, especially if you've grown up in a family as strange and mysterious as mine, it takes a lot to shock you."

Margaret took her glasses off and rubbed her eyes. "I hadn't heard anything about Burt's death. He did tell me about Irene's passing, though. But this bit about Markos dying, why it's nothing short of scandalous. I should have pressed Burt more often for family news. Perhaps he thought I didn't care about his life in California. I don't know, I just don't know what to say."

Dani leaned forward. "Margaret, may I call you grandma? My dad was a very troubled man. Not because of anything you did, or for that matter anything anyone else in the family did. He took a high-pressure job working with a lot of United States government bureaucrats and airport executives. He often complained that those people thought nothing of ruining other people's lives in order to advance their own careers. When he got in trouble with one of the most paranoid government agencies, the Transportation Security Authority, over irregularities in his family background, he was devastated, although I don't think he was entirely surprised."

Margaret frowned and her eyes opened wide. "I think you're referring to his grandfather, the one who disappeared and was reportedly killed by the Soviets as a spy. More likely he was killed because he had stolen millions of pounds from a Hungarian bank. My late husband, Burt's father, told me a little of that story. He had to, since he had an awful lot of money to account for. He swore me to secrecy, and neither of us ever told Burt a word of that story."

Dani said, "Yes, Burt had a copy of the TSA document summarizing the results of their research. I've read it. Fascinating reading, and certainly must have been shocking to dad. But in addition to that skeleton in his closet, which the TSA couldn't really blame dad for, there was the matter of dad's attempt to pass off Dushan as Markos after Markos died. I think when the TSA officers confronted dad with that, he just went off the deep end. He probably saw not only the end of his career but criminal charges as well."

Nobody talked for the next several minutes. Finally, Margaret took a sip of water and turned to Dushan. "So, young man, here you are in the flesh, the grown up Markos Burt used to write such glowing reports about. I do wish I had been able to overcome my fear of flying when Markos was a toddler. If I had been a regular visitor to San Francisco, I would certainly have known of his illness and perhaps this whole affair could never have taken place."

Dushan smiled and responded, "Well, as awful as it was for those years, things have turned out very well. With the help of Inspector Ailshie and my brother and our new friend Jaleh Kilpatrick, I have learned that not only is my mother alive but she has reunited with my father, raised a new family, and now they live in Slovenia, her home country."

"That's wonderful, my boy! What a capital ending to such a convoluted tale. And congratulations to you, Inspector. I can't imagine how you managed to locate the woman, but you did, that's the main thing."

"Thank you, Ma'am. It was actually Dimitri Sava himself who provided most of the clues to Marta's whereabouts. Now that that's taken care of, there's just one more unresolved part of this story. We never knew what became of Carolyn Owens. I have a cassette tape of her confessing her crime to Irene shortly before Irene's death. But the confession says nothing about her whereabouts at the time. During my investigation, I had looked all over creation for her, but only under her married name Owens. Apparently, Burt never revealed Carolyn's maiden name to the TSA agents. I was told Carolyn Owens had family here in Liverpool but without knowing her maiden name there was no way to find her. I only learned her maiden name from the lads here yesterday. By the time I had retired from the department, I had not found any record of her ex-husband ever returning to the Isle of Man from wherever he was in Australia. The Customs office in the UK had no record of a Carolyn Owens leaving near the time that your son left with Dushan."

Margaret's expression fluctuated back and forth between a smile and a frown. "Carolyn Owens is my niece. Perhaps she left the country using her maiden name, Markos. You won't have to look far for her, Inspector. She has returned to Liverpool. She has very little contact with me, but I do happen to know how to find her. We can arrange a little rendezvous, as I'm sure you will want to do."

"That would be wonderful, ma'am. I'll arrange the rendezvous with my friends in the Liverpool police department and let them take it from there."

Glancing over at Dushan and Dani, Margaret turned back to Angus and said, "Now, Inspector, I must ask you to stay a little while longer while I discuss a very important matter with my grandson and my brand-new step-grandson." Returning her gaze to Dani and Dushan, Margaret continued, "As you no doubt have learned, Dani, from having had to deal with Burt's financial matters after his death, I had set up a Sandor Family Trust for the benefit of you and Markos. Never knowing that Markos had in fact died in 1999, my monthly contributions to the Trust in both your names never ceased. I'm sure Burt wasn't overly generous with the money on your behalf, Dani and Dushan."

Dani interrupted, "No he wasn't, grandma. I've looked over his bank records, and it's astounding how little he actually spent other than the money he spent on the family's basic needs. He wasn't materialistic in the sense of buying jewelry, watches, expensive clothes, or even cars. We never owned more than one car at a time, and we didn't go on vacations. Even after buying two houses in less than 10 years, there was quite a bit of money still in the account. Dushan and I are looking forward to enjoying a somewhat more comfortable lifestyle than we had in the past."

"That's fine, very good. But what I have in mind now is to ask that you and Dushan accept an additional gift from me. I can't tell you how good it makes me feel to meet you, Dushan, and to see how well you and Dani have turned out!"

The brothers smiled sheepishly and waited for Margaret to continue. "I have no other close family, so I will deposit another substantial sum in your account in the next few days. I no longer need anything. I'm very comfortable, and the money I've inherited from my late husband, your grandfather, will long outlast me. What's more, I'll make an addendum to my will to ensure that the estate goes to you both, share and share alike. Your story is a wonderful testament to love, and I want to be part of that story."

CHAPTER THIRTY-TWO:
ALPINE REUNION

The brothers and Angus said goodbye to Mrs. Sandor in the early evening, declining her invitation to stay for supper. Dani and Dushan promised to stop back by soon and often. Dushan told her he might settle in Ljubljana with his family once he got his personal status situation taken care of. Looking at Angus with a nervous smile, he said, "Maybe I'll be able to establish my very first legal identity in Slovenia! It looks like the last flight Douglas Armitage will take will be from Heathrow to Ljubljana." Angus smiled, winked and said nothing.

Dani told Margaret he couldn't predict what his immediate plans would be after they took their trip to meet Dushan's family in Ljubljana. But he was sure his plans included a return trip, or many return trips, to Liverpool to get to know her and his Sandor relatives. Angus, for his part, was very pleased at the turn of events and especially pleased to finally be able to bring Carolyn Owens to justice.

Dani and Dushan drove Angus back to his apartment and made the drive from Liverpool to Heathrow airport. They dropped off the rental car and booked a flight to Ljubljana, which wouldn't leave for several hours and involved a connection in Milan. Dani checked his Gmail account he had opened on Dushan's CIA computer at Hyde Park to see if Claude Prejean had replied yet. He had, but Dani waited to read it later when he was less distracted. Dushan established a Gmail account under the name Douglas Armitage and emailed Marta and Dimitri. He told them he and Dani were friends of Angus's on holiday. They arranged with Marta to stop by for a visit the following evening.

When they arrived in snowy Ljubljana at 10:00 a.m. on January 19, they had half a day to kill. Not knowing where they would stay that evening, they took a taxi into the old city and booked a room at a charming old hotel right on the river. Dani opened up his laptop and decided to read Prejean's email. Dushan was startled to hear Dani's exclamation as he jumped up from the sofa in their room. "I can't believe this! The dude's in Trieste; he's working on some geological survey and will be there for another six months at least."

"How funny; he has no idea how close he is to you! He probably thinks you're still in San Bernardino or some such. We definitely will have to pay him a visit. Tell him where you are and find out what his plans are."

After lunch, the brothers spent an hour or so walking up and down the river in the old part of the city. Their hotel was just a short walk from the Dragon Bridge, which was very close to the house Marta and Dimitri bought so they could be near Marta's grandparents.

Despite the morning snow flurries, by early afternoon it was sunny when the boys arrived at the Sava home. In front of the house was a high wall and gate, which had no lock. Dushan opened the gate and the boys walked through the compound's small garden that looked as though it could extend around the house. Standing on the front porch, Dushan knocked on the door. Marta answered the knock. "Hello, Mrs. Sava. My name is Douglas Armitage and this is my stepbrother Danilo. We exchanged emails." Dushan looked around and said, "You have a beautiful house!"

"Hello, Douglas; thank you. Hello Danilo. So, I understand you are friends of Angus's. How is Angus doing? I really miss him." Marta ushered the brothers into the living room and, still speaking English, called for her husband to come to the room.

Dimitri entered drying his hands. Marta said to him, "Dimitri, Angus's friends from the UK, Douglas and Danilo, have arrived."

Pausing as if to awaken his dormant but now-passable English, Dimitri addressed the young men. "Hello. We're very glad to meet you. Our girls will be here shortly. They had a sleep-over with some friends and are probably just getting up."

Marta turned to Dani and asked, "Where did you get your name, Danilo? It sounds Slavic."

"It is either Celtic or Hungarian. My surname is Sandor, which is both Hungarian and Celtic."

Dimitri asked Dushan, "So, Douglas, you are friend of Angus or related to him? I used to know him well, and he never spoke of relatives in Britain, except for his dad who I hope is still well and living in Liverpool."

Dushan replied, "Well, I used to be American. To tell you the truth, I don't have any idea who might be related to Douglas Armitage."

Marta and Dimitri chuckled politely at Dushan's reference to himself in the third person. Marta asked, "So how do you know Angus? And why do you say you used to be American? I would have thought everyone wanted to be American these days."

Dushan and Dani exchanged glances. Dani said to Dushan, "I think it's time to let the cat out of the bag, Dushan."

Dimitri and Marta immediately sat up straight in their chairs when Dani said "Dushan." Dimitri said, "Now that is very interesting name also, even more interesting than Danilo. Our son's name was Dushan, or is if he's still alive."

Dani answered, "Oh, I assure you he is still alive. He's my stepbrother and is sitting right here with us. May I introduce Dushan Sava, alias Dushan Sandor, alias Douglas Armitage."

The room erupted in exclamations from Marta and Dimitri and laughter from Dani and Dushan. Hugs all around, and more hugs all around. Lots of tears. Dimitri held Dushan by the shoulders, "My champion is not so little anymore! Marta, will you look at this boy!"

Marta grabbed Dushan from Dimitri. "Let me have him; you had him four years longer than I did!" She gave Dushan another hug and held onto him for at least a minute. Dushan could feel her tears dropping on his neck and was sure his own tears were doing the same on his mother's neck.

Dushan stepped back for a moment, looked at his parents and said, "Now, about this stepbrother business. Let my stepbrother tell you a story, at least part of a story. I'll interrupt when it's my turn or when necessary to correct him."

As they did with Margaret, the boys spent a good hour filling in Dushan's parents on the story. As they were getting to the part when they parted company with Angus, the two Sava girls walked into the living room. At the sound of English being spoken, especially by their father, whose English they did not remember being that good, they stopped and looked at the two young men speaking to the girls' parents.

The boys turned and looked at them as Marta made the introductions. "Aisha and Shimza, meet Dushan and Danilo. Girls, these two young men are stepbrothers from America. Except that one of them was born in Belgrade and is your own long-lost brother." After the four young people shook hands, Dani said to them with a smile, "This young man right here, who has apparently lost the ability to speak, is my stepbrother and best friend. Dushan, say something to your sisters."

Dushan burst out laughing, as did the girls and everyone else. The girls were amazed to hear that the story they'd heard all their lives, of a long-lost brother, was now having a happy ending right before their eyes. Dushan asked them, "We definitely must have a long chat, Shimza and Aisha. First, though, the most important question: which of you is the older one? Am I speaking too fast?"

Laughter from both girls. Then, with the barest of a frown, Aisha said in perfect, if accented, English, "Shimza is, by two minutes! But I'm the better student."

Shimza took up the challenge. "No way. You're just better in English class. You call yourself a poet. But you couldn't solve a math problem to save your life!"

Marta laughed, "Okay, okay, we can move onto more important subjects during dinner." Turning to Dushan and Dani, she asked, "You are staying for dinner, I hope."

Dani answered, "Yes, indeed, thanks. We don't have any plans after this. We don't even know where we're going."

Dimitri responded, "Well, if I can say something, you both welcome to stay here in Ljubljana for long as you like. Dushan, I am hoping you will stay here but I don't know what are your plans. And Danilo, please to stay as long as you want. Marta's parents have vacant duplex unit, and you stepbrothers can stay there if you like."

The dinner conversation went well. Dimitri's English rapidly improved, mostly out of a desire to save face in front of his daughters. The girls hadn't heard the brothers' stories so they were repeated, this time not leaving out a thing. Dushan was in the middle of describing his time at the Culinary Institute, when Aisha asked, "Did you get to go to New York City? I'm dying to go there. One of these days, papa has promised us."

Dushan replied, "Only once. It's a pretty easy trip, though. Bus then subway. I should have gone more, but I was pretty paranoid, as you might imagine. The time I went I attended a combined jazz concert and poetry reading at a Catholic cathedral. Aisha, you being a poet you would have loved that concert." Dushan's eyes lit up with excitement, and he turned to Marta, "Mom, you would have found this one poem fascinating, since you spent time in Sarajevo. The poet in the program, Nancy Hoffman, read her poem "Requiem Before the Times of Peace." I have the whole poem with me; I brought it all the way from New York. I couldn't bear to throw it away; it made me think of you. If you don't mind, I would like to read what Hoffman calls the last movement."

The group, in particular Marta, waited in near silence while Dushan opened his backpack and pulled out a program for the performance, which had a single page inside. He opened the program up and before he began reading he told the group, "Here's what the poet said about the last movement: *The final movement memorializes the heroic gesture of the cellist, Vedran Smailovic, who played for 22 days at the killing site of 22 civilians in Sarajevo; his name is silently embedded in the first letter of each line of the poem on which the movement is based.*

Then Dushan pulled out the insert and read the final movement:

V. Not All

Vestiges of innocence are irrelevant.
Each disaster swallows innocence whole.
Despair retreats from power for one reason,
Reason enough, a reason, the sole reason,
Announcing that, as human reason fails,
Not all succumb to madness. Not all.

Singular in face of evil, rising up,
Magnificent, murmuring "no," the smallest voice,
Alone, without resources, innocent of safety,
Innocent of gain: an instrument saying "no."
Lost, not every voice is lost, not all!
O voice, vigilant, merciful and clear,
Victorious over fear, break over
Indecent silence. Not all be silent.
*Cataclysm, violence, malignity. Not all.**

*You can listen to the poet read this portion of the poem at:
www.stolenidentitynovel.com/poem

Aisha and Shimza spoke almost simultaneously, "That's beautiful!" Marta's eyes were wide; she put her hands on her head and said, "I can't believe it! I had no idea anyone ever wrote anything about that bombing. I was there! I saw the whole thing! That's what made me finally leave that place, it was so horrible that bombing. Oh my God!"

"What year was that?" Dushan asked.

"It was probably in the spring of 1992, as best as I recall. I think it was a little over a year before I met your father in Belgrade. Oh, my God! This is just amazing! Thank you, Dushan, thank you. Now, girls, we are definitely going to visit New York and try to meet that poet."

After Marta spoke to the girls, Dushan asked, "Mom, when you introduced Shimza to us, I had the same reaction I had when Jaleh Kilpatrick told us how Shimza came by her name. I have to say that the name resonates with me very strongly. It's almost as if I already knew the name, or knew someone by that name. Do you know why that might be? I don't usually get such feelings unless there's something to them."

"Shimza is your great-grandmother, Dushan. I grew up with her until she moved away to Bulgaria when I was a teenager. Now she lives in Istanbul, and is about 93 or 94; I've lost track of her birthdays. So, apparently, has she. In our phone conversations, she claims to be the picture of health. I believe it.

"It's funny you should mention her." Marta glanced at Dimitri, who was all ears and seemed eager to add something to the conversation. "Less than a year before you were born, Grandma Shimza showed up at our honeymoon hotel in southern Serbia. We all had a great evening catching up on the events of our separate lives."

Dimitri couldn't stand remaining silent any longer. "Dushan, your great-grandmother shocked both of us very much. She told us we would have boy baby and he would experience what she called… what is the word, Marta?"

"Disruption, turbulence. She said you would live through turbulence that would disrupt your life; our lives too, for that matter. But that it would come to an end. It's strange, but her words kept coming back to me all throughout those years of our separation. Whenever I thought about that disastrous turn of events, I remembered her words for it, 'turbulence,' 'disruption,' and knew once again that it would turn out okay." Marta paused and took Dushan's hands before resuming. "Not only did her words always bring me back from the brink, but I had many communications with you, my son. Do you recall any of those?"

"I think so, in many of my dreams. But I wasn't able to dream-talk to you, which is what Dani and I occasionally did."

Marta smiled, "Well, even though you didn't 'dream-talk,' as you say, you certainly conveyed your presence to me. I saw vague pictures sometimes, but no words. I never knew, with any certainty, that we were actually communicating or it was just my wishful thinking. Whatever it was, it soothed me."

"I knew you were with me the whole time, mom, the whole time. And dad, too, despite Burt's lie that dad had been lost at sea. I always knew things would turn out okay. And they have; more than okay."

* * *

The brothers spent the next week exploring the beautiful old city in Ljubljana. The following week they took the bus to Lake Bled and spent the day hiking around the lake. Finally, it was decision time. "Dushan," Dani said as they sat in a Ljubljana café at midnight. "Have you decided what you're going to do?"

"I think," Dushan said, looking over at his brother, "I think I want to stay here and get to know my family. I need to study the language so I will be able to talk to them and other people in their native tongue. I need to get an education, although I don't know what in. One thing for sure is I have to figure out what to do about my identity, my true identity. Probably have to go to Belgrade and get my birth certificate. Then a passport, my own passport in my own name. Even though I probably won't ever be able to re-enter the States because I travelled on a false passport, there are plenty of other places in the world. What about you? What are your plans?"

"Well, now that we're pretty well off, we don't have to make any final decisions. It's not like once we split up we'll never see each other again. I think for the time being I want to see some of Europe, maybe go to Trieste and hook up with Claude Prejean. Then I think I'll return to Liverpool and spend some time with my grandma before her health gets too much worse. After that, who knows? For sure I'll come back here and see some of the Balkans. Maybe I'll enroll in language school, or try to get a college degree somewhere."

"Well, Cap'n Dante, you know you always have a place to sleep if you come back here."

"What do you mean if? I'm definitely coming back. Many times, Dushansky, many times. And I'm taking you with me the next time I leave this place."

ABOUT THE AUTHOR

I was an Army brat (Japan, Monterey, Austria, Germany) until we moved to Pittsburg, CA, in 1956, when I was nine.

I was a voracious reader, and in junior high I published two science fiction stories in my school's creative writing magazine. After a long hiatus, I began writing again in my senior year of college at UC Berkeley. I joined a group of acquaintances in 1969 who started a poetry magazine we called The Open Cell. We contributed the content, did the layout, printed it at Waller Press in the Haight Ashbury district, and sold it on the streets of Berkeley and San Francisco. That experience rekindled my love of writing. I transferred from Berkeley (where I was a comparative literature major) to SF State as a creative writing major and wrote poetry and a few stories.

Upon graduation in 1972 my first wife and I joined the Peace Corps and worked as ESL teachers in Ethiopia for two years.

Grad school followed, twice, and I obtained a Master in Communication at University of Washington and a Master in Librarianship at UC Berkeley. My writing during those years became decidedly academic and non-creative.

After nine years as a librarian (including two as head librarian at Robert College of Istanbul), followed by a divorce, I decided librarians got no respect, so I went to law school where I wrote a law review article discussing a controversial Ninth Circuit Court of Appeals decision. I became an attorney, remarried, worked for 23 years at the California Attorney General's Office, Criminal Division, and wrote hundreds of appellate briefs.

During my years as a "brief-writing hack," I dabbled in creative writing. I published two poems in a Baháí magazine called World Order, published a poem in a small magazine put out by a colleague in my writing group at the Mechanics Institute Library in San Francisco, and a memoir of my peace corps experience was included in "Eritrea Remembered," published in 2011 on Amazon. I began but couldn't finish a mystery/suspense novel in the mid-90s called L'Ombra, about a mysterious group of savants bent on world domination.

In 2012 I wrote a novella called My Brother's Keeper, published on Amazon.

I'm retired, married, and have two grown sons and a granddaughter who is a senior in high school. I keep my state bar license active and have a (volunteer) case involving veteran's benefits.

March 2015

THE BIRTH OF THE NOVEL

This novel began with a simple piece of information. My wife, an immigration lawyer, was describing a recent conversation she had with a law firm that had taken a deportation case on a "pro bono" basis. It seems a young man serving a prison term for murder learned that he was being "outed" by his stepfather as being an illegal alien, rather than an adoptee as the young man had believed all his life. His dying father, apparently angry with his son, informed the prison that he had purchased the boy as a child from the child's babysitter, who had stolen him from his parents in England. As a result, the prison asked the immigration authorities to ship the young man back to England so the prison wouldn't have to pay for his continued incarceration in prison. Trouble was, England didn't want him, so he was stranded in the immigration prison in Arizona. The law firm volunteers asked my wife for advice on what to do.

I never learned how that real story turned out, but the idea of a child stolen by a babysitter and sold to an American family intrigued me. So I launched this novel. That was late summer of 2011. I had just signed up for classes at the Fromm Institute in San Francisco, a continuing education school for "mature adults" wishing to take classes in a wide variety of subjects. One of the classes was a creative writing seminar. I eagerly completed all of the class exercises and wrote draft after draft of what eventually became this novel. I signed up for another seminar the next term and continued the process. At the same time, I joined a writing group at my library, the Mechanics Institute, a 100-year-old private library in San Francisco. My group of 8 fellow writers gave me valuable feedback, and I was on my way.

When I had finished the first draft, I gave it to my long-time friend Linda Leeb, and my wife Nora Privitera, to read and critique. An extensive rewrite followed, and then I gave it to another good friend, Barbara Alderson, to read and critique. Another substantial rewrite ensued. I edited it some more after Nora took another look at my draft, and then I sent it off to Kathleen Gage for her editorial insights. Finally, I asked my friend Yofe Johnson to give Chapter Nine a thorough editing, because I felt the dialogue between the little five-year-old boys didn't ring true or age-appropriate. Yofe teaches yoga to young kids and is a particularly keen listener to the kids' conversations with each other.

In its early incarnation, the novel did not begin in Sarajevo, as it does now. When members of my writing group insisted on knowing the backstory of Marta's abduction and Dimitri and Dushan's becoming refugees, I obliged. In writing that backstory I remembered my friend N. M. Hoffman's poem describing, in part, the bombing of a bakery in Sarajevo. I decided to open the novel with that bombing, and later included that part of the poem as something Dushan heard Hoffman perform in New York.

41716317R00132

Made in the USA
Charleston, SC
05 May 2015